Too Naughty

Book Five

Too Naughty

Book Five

BRENDA HAMPTON

REPRINT EDITION October 2006
REPRINT EDITION December 2009
Published by: Voices Books & Publishing
P.O. Box 3007
Bridgeton, MO 63044
www.voicesbooks.homestead.com

Printed in the United States of America

This book is a work of fiction. Names, characters, places and incidents are products of the author's imagination or are used fictitiously. Any resemblance to actual events or locales of persons living or dead, is entirely coincidental.

Library of Congress Catalog Card No.: On File

ISBN-10: 0-9789292-4-1
ISBN-13: 978-0-9789292-4-4

Too Naughty

He's Whippin' up Somethin' Naughty

FELICIA
1

It was getting late, so I grabbed my briefcase to go. I turned down the lights in Davenports and headed towards the elevator. When it opened, I hit the L button to take me downstairs to the lobby. The elevator slowed, and as it was getting ready to make a stop, I looked down and searched for my keys in my purse. When the elevator stopped, the doors slowly separated. My eyes stared down at the expensive deep burgundy leather shoes, and then made contact with the navy blue pants that belonged to a Brooks Brothers suit. Next, I saw the diamond Rolex, and the lightly tanned sweaty hands were balled into fists. The bulge in his pants was there and the smell of Issey Miyake filled the air. I lifted my head and my eyes were locked with his cattish grey watery eyes that were red as fire. I tried to get away from him, but to no avail. All I witnessed was his fist go up and my entire face was numb. Following, I saw nothing but darkness.

I struggled to open my eyes. When I did, I realized I could only see out of one of them. There was a bright light shining in my face and a hand swayed in front of my eyes. I heard a voice that repeated the same questions over and over: Felicia, can you see me? Can you hear me? I slowly nodded and the white man, whom I assumed was a doctor, held up a tiny light, looking into my right eye.

For the moment, all I could feel was pain. My head was banging and my face was awfully stiff. Without even looking in a mirror, I could see the swelling in my face through my good eye. As for my lips, I wasn't sure. I tried to feel them, but they were numb. When I reached my hand up to touch them, the doctor took my hand and placed it by my side.

"We've given you something for the pain. You might feel a bit of numbness in your mouth because we had to remove a cracked tooth. If it gets too painful, I want you to let me know, okay?"

I nodded again.

"In the meantime, the police would like to speak with you about what happened. Are you prepared to speak with them, or would you like to wait until later?"

It took me a moment to respond, but when I was able to, I strained to get out the word, "later."

"Is there anyone you'd like for me to contact?"

I nodded. The doctor picked up a pen, a piece of paper and handed it to me. I wrote down Stephon's name and number.

"Okay. My assistant, Madeline, will contact Stephon for you. Try and get some rest and I'll tell the police to come back later."

The doctor squeezed my hand and walked out of the room. My eyes shifted around, and as I tried to open my closed eye, the pain became unbearable. Tears fell from the corner of my eyes, so I tightened them, hoping the pain would go away. No doubt, Jaylin had messed me up, and I guessed he was irate because Nokea had seen the CD.

The touch of someone's cold hands awakened me. When I looked up, I saw a blurred vision of Stephon looking down at me. He smiled and kissed the back of my hand.

"Wake up," he said, moving my long braids away from my face. "You've been sleeping for a very long time."

The pain I felt earlier had somewhat diminished, so I turned my head to the side and smiled back at Stephon. "How long have you been here?" I mumbled.

"Long enough. I got a call from your doctor. He told me that you'd been assaulted by someone. As soon as he told me where you were, I came quickly. Do you remember who...?"

I patted a spot on the bed next to me and Stephon took a seat. "I vaguely remember what happened, but I do know who did this to me. The last person I saw was Jaylin. He had a look that could kill, and all I remember was the sight of his fist as it landed on my face. The next thing I knew, I opened my eyes—well, the one I can see out of, and I was here."

Stephon pulled his head back and frowned. "So, Jaylin was the one who did this to you?"

I nodded.

"I can't believe that motherfu—

Stephon was interrupted by the police, as they came through the door.

"Ms. Davenport, do you have time to answer some questions for us?"

"Yes, I do."

One of the officers looked at Stephon. "Sir, would you mind leaving the room so that we can speak to Ms. Davenport alone?"

"I would like for him to stay," I spoke abruptly. "That's if it's not a problem."

Both officers looked at each other, and then started with the questions.

"Do you know the man who attacked you?"

"Yes. I know him very well. He was an ex-boyfriend of mine."

"Do you know why he attacked you?"

Stephon interrupted. "The reason why doesn't even matter! You can see with your own eyes what he did to her."

The officer placed his hand on Stephon's chest. "Sir, calm down, please. If you weren't there to witness what happened, I need you to be very quiet."

"I...I really don't know why he attacked me. After our break-up, things between us kind of went downhill. I thought he'd moved on with his life, but I guess I was wrong."

"Was he abusive to you during your relationship with him?"

"Very. Mentally and physically."

"Have you ever filed for a restraining order against him or had him arrested before?"

My eyes watered as I spoke. "No, but I should have. I was afraid of him. Afraid that he'd do exactly what he did to me today."

The officer who took notes closed his pad. He placed it in his back pocket and looked at me. "We have Mr. Jaylin Rogers in custody for assault and for carrying a loaded weapon. If the prosecutor decides to take the case, he might decide to try him for attempted murder. The cameras on the elevator caught the entire incident on tape, and as soon as Mr. Rogers left the building, he was apprehended. If you decide to press charges, in my opinion, you have a solid case. I advise you to immediately contact your attorney because this guy is anxious to leave St. Louis. From what I gathered, he has a darn good attorney, and on Monday, Mr. Rogers goes before the judge. Your alleged abuser lives in another city, so the judge will determine if he is a flight risk or not. Make sure you and your attorney are present, specifically to stop this maniac from getting away with what he did."

"Oh, trust me, he's not getting away with anything. If I'm not well by Monday, I assure you my attorney will be there on my behalf."

Both officers handed me a card and told me if I needed to obtain a police report, it would be ready later on today. After that, they left. I looked at Stephon and he looked at me.

"Revenge is so bitter sweet, my sista," he said. "It's time to shake, rattle and roll against this arrogant motherfucker and make him pay for what he's done to you and me."

"I agree, Stephon. And he will not only pay with his life, but also, with his money. Retirement at age 36 doesn't sound bad at all."

Stephon gave me a sliding high-five and we were pleased about what was about to happen.

JAYLIN
2

I was mad as hell! I specifically went to St. Louis to kill Felicia's ass for the hurt she'd cost my family. She was lucky that all she caught was a major beat down from me. Every blow that I gave her was worth it to me, and if it wasn't for this elderly white woman who entered the elevator and screamed, Felicia very well might be dead. As soon as I left the building, the police were scattered outside waiting for me. You would have thought that I robbed a bank or murdered a police officer the way they aggressively wrestled me to the ground and cuffed me. I didn't resist not one bit because I knew there would be consequences the moment I decided to make my way back to St. Louis. The only thing I didn't know was that I'd be stuck in this hell hole of a jail cell for hours.

When I called my attorney, Frick, he had the nerve to remind me that he was Felicia's attorney, too. Now, I'd been the one who introduced them, and it was because of me that he became her attorney. Basically, I told him that if he didn't get his ass to this jailhouse to get me, I'd make sure he was out of business for good. He hesitated, but then said he was on his way. That was many hours ago, so I spent those hours thinking about my wife, Nokea, and my kids. The last person I wanted to call was her. When I left, she knew how angry I was. She begged me not to go and told me it would all work itself out. Of course, I didn't listen. The only thing on my mind was killing Felicia for causing Nokea to lose our baby. Nokea didn't deserve any of this, and whenever anyone hurt her, they hurt me. Felicia had no idea that the tape she mailed of Scorpio teasing the shit out of Shane and me, took Nokea's and my child away from us. Not only that, but the hurt I saw in Nokea's eyes when the doctor told her she might not be able to have anymore kids from the bad fall she'd taken, it was a look I'd never forget. All I wanted to do was protect her. And through my own mistakes in our marriage, I failed. A huge part of me was angry at myself for bringing this bullshit to my home. It very well could've been prevented, but because of Felicia's stupidity, I wasn't sure if Nokea would ever truly forgive me.

I stood with my hands in my pockets and lightly tapped the back of my head against the wall with my eyes closed. My torn suit jacket was folded across my arm and my white wrinkled shirt with missing buttons revealed my chest. All of my expensive jewelry had been placed in a plastic bag and the officer took it, along with my wedding ring. I opened my eyes and looked at my ring finger. I rubbed my finger around the tanned line from my wedding band, thinking deeply of Nokea. I wanted to go home so badly. I wanted to hold her in my arms and I wished like hell that none of this had happened. I thought of my kids and my throat started to ache. I knew they were missing me, just as much as I missed them.

My eyelids felt heavy, so I closed my eyes to fight my emotions. Shortly after, the brotha who was in the same holding cell with me cleared his throat.

"What are you in for?" he asked in a feminine tone.

I ignored him, keeping my eyes closed.

He cleared his throat again. "Pretty Boy, did you hear me? I asked what you were in here for."

I slowly opened my red and sore eyes and stared at him. Then, I spoke calmly. "None of your motherfuckin' business. Now, don't say shit else to me."

The faggot fool started fanning himself. "Whew, it's getting awfully hot in here. I just asked you a simple question. You don't have to get all ugly about it, wit yo fine self."

I eased myself away from the wall and slowly walked in his direction. I tossed my Brooks Brother's jacket over my shoulder and placed my hands back inside of my pockets. As I neared him, he smiled. I stood a few feet away from him, sniffing myself.

"Do you smell that?" I asked.

He took a few sniffs and put his hand on his hip. "Smell what? I don't smell anything, but I sure as hell see something I can work with. Besides, what is it that I'm supposed to be smelling?"

I sniffed myself again, leaned my face close to his, and spoke sternly. "Pussy. If you get a tad bit closer to me, you might get a whiff of some good ass pussy I had last night. I wear it quite often because I crave for the fragrance. More than anything, the scent is to remind assholes like you not to approach me in such an offensive way. Now, I'm gon' go back over there and mind my own business. If you don't want to get fucked up in here, I suggest you not say shit else to me, alright?"

The brotha folded his arms and tooted his lips. No sooner had I turned and walked away, he opened his mouth.

"Wooo-whew! That backside sholl look good to me!"

I tried, but I couldn't control my anger. Before I knew it, I had him by his collar and had pulled him up from the bed.

"Did you hear what the fuck I said? I will kill you, fool!"

Just then, three officers came rushing into the holding cell. They couldn't wait to rough me up again, and one of them slammed me hard against the wall. He held his black stick close to my face and yelled, "You'd better calm your ass down, Boy!"

I breathed heavily. "You'd better get that stick away from my fucking face. And as for being your Boy, if you touch me again, I'm gon' show you what getting your ass kicked from a man feels like."

He continued to hold the stick close to my face and smiled. When I heard a whistle, and turned my head to the side, it was Frick. He calmly strutted in, dressed to impress with a leather briefcase by his side. His salt & pepper gray hair was neatly combed back and his black framed glasses covered his olive green eyes. He walked right into the cell and stood next to the officer who held the stick next to my face.

"I promise you that the NAACP would be here in an instant." He grabbed the officer's shoulder and squeezed it. "Mr. Rogers and I know of many important people, in very high places. Trust me, you don't want this situation to get ugly. Put the stick down and allow my client and me to leave peacefully. His bond has been paid, so if there's nothing further, we'd like to go."

The officer lowered the stick and mumbled something underneath his breath as he exited. It sounded like he called me a nigga. It was confirmed when Frick rolled his eyes, and the faggot fool covered his mouth.

"Nigga?" I said, as Frick already had his hand on my chest to hold me back. "You son of a bitch! I should kick your racist ass for disrespecting me! You are lucky that we are on your turf and not mine!"

The officer turned around. "Is that a threat?"

"It sounded like one to me," the faggot brother weighed in.

Frick stood face-to-face with me and pointed his finger. "Jaylin, don't say anything else to incriminate yourself. There's a better way of handling this, but I need you to keep your mouth shut. He's working you, man, don't you get it? All he wants to do is pick a fight with you, and believe me when I tell you that in this fucking place, he's going to win. Now, get your jacket off the floor and let's go."

I knew what Frick said was right, but as usual, my anger got the best of me. I snatched my jacket from the floor and followed behind Frick as he left the cell. As soon as the officer closed the bars, the faggot rushed up to them.

"Goodbye, handsome. I ain't never seen a light-skinned man as fine as you, and I regret not being able to twirl my fingers through your trimmed curly hair. Wait until I tell the boys what I done missed out on! Damn!"

I turned, but again, Frick told me to ignore him. I was able to maintain my composure, until I asked for my bag of jewelry and everybody seemed to be suffering from amnesia.

"Are you sure you gave it to them?" Frick asked.

I didn't respond, but gave Frick a devious stare. All jokes aside, somebody was about to get fucked up. I wasn't sure if it was going to be Frick for not believing me, or the officers who for damn sure knew where my jewelry was. Aside from my expensive Rolex, my diamond and gold cuff links, and my gold roped bracelet, the simple gold band Nokea gave to me on our wedding day was priceless.

I looked at Frick with hostility in my eyes and rubbed my goatee. "Within 30 seconds, I'm about to catch a major case. Please, call my wife and tell her that I love her and my kids."

Frick looked away and slammed his briefcase hard on the officer's desk. He opened it, pulled out his cell phone and placed it on his ear. He frowned at the officers who seriously thought the shit was funny.

"Fellas, I really tried to work with you on this one. Calling my client a nigger is one thing, but property theft is another. I seriously hope you all have other employment opportunities." Frick held the phone to his ear. "Uh, Mandy, get me to the Mayor's office. Tell him I'm on hold and that I need to speak with him pronto." He paused and then yelled. "Yes! Right now!"

Within seconds, the mystery bag somehow showed up. Frick snatched it off the officer's desk and handed it to me. "Does your wife have any idea how insane you are?" he asked. He then closed his phone, turned to the officers and gritted his teeth.

"Please, stop the nonsense. It's cops like you all who give good cops a bad name. If you can't handle your fucking job on a professional level, then give it to somebody else who can."

Frick grabbed his briefcase, and on that note, I smirked and followed behind him. When we got outside, it was a bit chilly so I slid back into my torn jacket.

"We need some one-on-one time, Jaylin. Not tonight because it's rather late. Anytime tomorrow will work better for me."

"Tomorrow is fine with me. Besides, I need to go somewhere and clear my head for the night."

"Can I drop you off somewhere?"

"Naw, my rental car is not too far from here. I can walk."

"Okay, but be careful. I wouldn't want any of these men to get after you," he joked, referring to the faggot in jail.

I could barely laugh because there was still so much anger inside of me. "I know you said that we'll talk tomorrow, but my case with Felicia doesn't look too good, does it?"

"Jaylin, I'm not prepared to talk about it just yet. I need to make some phone calls tonight and see what options I have. She's been calling me all day, and I know she's going to want me to represent her. Thing is, the police have a tape that makes you guilty as hell. I'm not sure what I can do to get you out of this mess, but I will put forth my best effort."

"Hey, do whatever. You got hella connections and I know you'll do whatever it takes."

"Yeah, like I did inside. The dial tone on my phone was so loud that I thought the fools heard it. It's not like I couldn't have called the mayor, but I'm sure he was probably at home resting."

We both laughed, and after a few more minutes of small talk, Frick jetted and so did I.

SCORPIO
3

Shane was so worried about Jaylin and so was I. I really didn't know what was going on, but when Shane told me that Jaylin was coming back to St. Louis, I knew it was serious. Shane also said that Jaylin was upset with Felicia, but a part of me knew he was upset with me, too, for seducing him and Shane that day. Hell, I didn't know Felicia had cameras in Davenports, and I damn sure didn't think she'd send a CD to Nokea. How stupid was that? But, I would have loved to be a fly on the wall when she saw her loving husband lust for me once again. And the kiss...I bet it tore her apart! Nokea needed to know, like everyone else, that Jaylin and I will always have a connection. Maybe it was just sexual, who knows? All I know was, for now, Shane had my heart, and maybe, just maybe, he'd do what it took to keep it. In the meantime, I had every intention of watching my back, because an angry Jaylin always meant trouble for me.

As usual, Jay's was packed to capacity. My stylists, Bernie and Jamaica had customers lined up and waiting. Since Deidra always seemed to have the least customers, I sat in her chair and waited for her next customer to come. I looked at my watch.

"Deidra, Traci should have been here by now, right?" I asked.

"She's always late. If she was going to be this late, I could have scheduled somebody else in her place."

Jamaica laughed. "Deidra, please. Traci ain't gon' show up. The last time she was here, you fucked that poor woman's hair up! Had her looking like an old man with a tangled and tinted weave."

Everybody laughed.

"Screw you, Jamaica," Deidra said. "Traci already looks like a man, and if anything, my style enhanced her looks."

"I doubt it," Jamaica said. "Everybody who sits in that chair gets up with a frown on their faces. That's with the exception of Scorpio. She over there fantasizing about something, and if I look up one more time and see that smirk on your face, I'm gon' be forced to smack you. Ain't nobody got no business grinning as much as you. If he was that good to you, then you need to tell us about it."

"I'm not telling you nosy hoochies nothing. Y'all talk too much and I have learned to keep my business to myself."

Jamaica cut her eyes at Bernie. "You mean Bernie talks too much. She's the one who told us about Shane sucking you dry in a limousine. Said he—

Bernie quickly cut her off. "Jamaica, your mouth is gon' get you a stiletto up your butt. You might have gotten rid of that thuggish Gangsta-Boo who used to knock you upside your head, but don't think I won't pick up where he left off."

"Whatever, but when all is said and done, didn't you tell everybody about Shane and his freak? Don't be mad at me if the *National Enquirer* wants to use your mouth to spread the word, instead of letting the news be known through a newspaper."

"Freak?" I said, folding my arms in front of me. "And, just who are you calling a freak?"

Jamaica placed her hand over her mouth. "Oooo, Miss Boss Lady, did I accidentally call you a freak? I'm sorry. I meant to call you a," she paused and stood with her hand on her hip, as if she was in deep thought. "Damn, what did I mean to call you?"

I stood up, smiling as I walked over to her. "Think real hard. And before you answer, remember, it's gon' be a sad day when all of your customers come in here and don't find you here."

"That's right, Scorpio!" Bernie jokingly yelled. "Check that hussy and throw that B out of here for disrespecting you!"

I turned to Bernie and pointed my finger. "She ain't the only one I need to throw out of here. Both of y'all need to be thrown out of here, and y'all are so lucky that I got much love for y'all."

"Awwww," Jamaica whined and held out her arms. "We didn't know you loved us, Boo. Come give me a hug."

I cut my eyes at Jamaica. "You are ridiculously silly."

She dropped her arms. "And, you are still a freak. Now, gon' back to your office and do some work. I'm trying to finish my customer's hair and you out here interrupting me."

"Please," Jamaica's customer said. "In less than an hour, I'm supposed to be getting ready for my date. I wish you'd hurry up and stop playing around so much."

"Oh, no, you ain't rushing me to go on a date that will end up being a waste of time. I will toss your butt out of this chair and scream for the next person waiting. Be patient, alright? Just like Deidra being patient for Traci, who obviously isn't going to show."

Deidra, Gena and Jamaica started going at it again, so I chuckled and walked back to my office. All in good fun, Jay's had a way of relaxing me and I truly enjoyed my career.

When I got back to my office, my desk was rather junky so I sat at my desk, sorting through papers. Almost immediately, my mind got preoccupied with the thoughts of Shane, and then Jaylin...Jaylin, and then Shane. I wondered if Shane had gotten in touch with Jaylin yet. Curious, I called Shane.

"Hi," I said.

"Aw, hey, what's up?"

"Sounds like you were waiting on another call. Didn't you see my number on the caller ID?"

"No. The number came up unknown. I thought you were Jaylin. I still haven't heard from him and I'm a bit worried."

"Well, if I know Jaylin like I think I do, he's probably somewhere rethinking his visit to St. Louis. Maybe he didn't come after all."

"No doubt, he's here. I went to Davenports and the police told me he'd been arrested."

"Arrested? For what?"

"I don't know the details." Shane paused. "Listen, let me call you back. Better yet, why don't you come over tonight?"

"Shane, I've been spending a lot of time at your place. I do need to go home sometimes, you know?"

"Yeah, I know. But, when you're away, I be missing you. I can't help it if you spoiled me. Besides, I want to go somewhere and chill tonight. Have a few drinks and get a bite to eat."

"That sounds like a plan. I'll see you later."

By 9:00 p.m., Jay's was almost cleared out. Yasing was up front wrapping up her last pedicure, while Bernie, Jamaica and I sat in the Jacuzzi room connected to my office, drinking wine.

"This is so relaxing," Bernie admitted with her head dropped back on an adjustable lighted pillow.

"Are you talking about the wine or the jets massaging our bodies?" Jamaica asked. "The water feels good, but this wine taste horrible. Scorpio, where did you get this shit from?"

"Girl, please. You don't know good wine when you taste it," I said, sipping from the glass. The wine left a sweet taste in my mouth and made me slightly tipsy.

Bernie opened her eyes and dabbed her face with a white towel. "I have to agree with Jamaica, Scorpio. That wine is not hitting. After a day like today, don't you have something strong for us to drink?"

I laughed and got out of the Hot Tub so I could get Jamaica and Bernie something strong to drink. Before going to my liquor cabinet, I dried off with a towel. I wore my hot pink bikini and pulled my wet hair back into a ponytail. Afterwards, I covered myself with a cotton robe and made my way up front. Yasing's customer had left and she was cleaning up her work station.

"We're in the back Yasing. Would you like to join us?"

"Oh, no. Yen waiting for me, so I gotta go."

"Okay. I'll see you tomorrow and be careful on your way home." She nodded and I went over to my liquor cabinet. My eyes searched the numerous bottles of alcohol. The Alize and Hpnotiq looked doable, so I reached for both bottles. Just for the hell of it, I grabbed three strawberry coolers. Yasing was still cleaning up and before I headed back to the Hot Tub, I asked her to lock the door on her way out. She said that she would.

Bernie and Jamaica were cracking up.

"What in the hell is so funny?" I asked, taking off my robe and returning to the Hot Tub. I gave both of them a wine cooler.

"Girl, I can't stop laughing about Traci not showing up," Jamaica said. "Deidra was mad as hell, but she seriously needs to rethink her career."

"I agree," Bernie added. "She my girl, but Deidra can not do no damn hair. Scorpio, when are you going to be honest with her? You know her customers be leaving here jacked up."

"First of all, y'all need to stop talking about Deidra and she ain't even here to defend herself. Secondly, I don't care if Deidra can do hair or not. As long as she pays for her rental space, her inability to do hair is no concern of mine."

Bernie poured the Alize in a glass and sipped from it. "Better. Oh, so much better than that cheap wine. But, how can you say that Deidra's problem isn't yours? Don't you realize that how she performs is a reflection on Jay's?"

"I agree," Jamaica said guzzling the Hpnotiq from the bottle. "I'm not requesting that you let her go, but send her butt back to hair school or something."

She and Bernie laughed again.

I ignored the both of them and downed the wine cooler. "You two are entitled to your opinions, but Deidra ain't going no where. So, drop the subject and we need to hurry up with the drinking so I can get to my man—

I paused and looked at Jamaica and Bernie, as their eyes were locked on the glass behind me.

"Don't move," Jamaica whispered underneath her breath. She rubbed her long braids back with her hand.

"What—

"I said, don't move. Whatever you do, do not turn around."

I sat still and nervously looked at Bernie. She had a blank expression on her face, and her eyes remained focused on the glass mirror. "Bernie, what's...who's out there?"

"Uhm, one fine ass man. I...I think it's Jaylin," she whispered.

I snapped my head to the side and could see him from the side of my eye. I took a hard swallow and put my glass on top of the Hot Tub. He walked into the steam filled room and stood with his suit jacket in his hand. His wrinkled white shirt hung out of his pants, and several buttons were undone. I couldn't help but notice his fiery red glassy eyes, and didn't know if he was tired and or drunk. Either way, I had to admit that Bernie was right—he was one fine motherfucka! Jamaica must have felt the same, and even though we were all speechless, Jamaica soon spoke up.

"May I, myself, help you in any way, shape, form, position or whatever it is you'd like for me to do?" she asked.

Jaylin didn't say a word. He stared at me and I could see the frustrations on his face.

I quickly spoke up. "Bernie and Jamaica, please give me a minute or two alone with Jaylin. It's obvious that he has something on his mind."

Bernie and Jamaica started out of the Hot Tub.

"No need to leave, Ladies," he said. "We can all listen to what I came to say, alright?"

As Jaylin started to undo the remaining buttons on his shirt, Bernie and Jamaica eyeballed me and eased back into the water. All three of us watched as he removed his shirt and tossed it over to a chair. He stepped out of his shoes, and once he reached for the button on his pants, I stood up.

"Jaylin, I don't know why you're here, but whatever you...

Jamaica pulled on my arm. "Girl, would you sit down and listen to what the man has to say? You gon' ruin it for all of us."

"Smart woman," Jaylin said, continuing to lower his pants. And once they hit the floor, he stood naked in front of us. His tanned body was flawless. The ridges on his six pack were tight, the muscles in his arms and legs were bulging, and his dick! Have mercy on me...I hadn't seen or felt his dick in quite some time. The thickness and length made my mouth water and seeing it brought back good memories.

Jamaica picked up the bottle of Hpnotiq, gulping it down faster. When Jaylin walked around the Hot Tub and sat between she and Bernie, Jamaica was all smiles.

"I am sorry," she said, placing her hand on her chest. "But, I have never, ever, ever had a man this fine and with a...a thing like that sit next to me. Is it real? It couldn't be."

"Ask Scorpio. She knows better than anyone," Jaylin bragged. He faced me, and Jamaica and Bernie had moved in closer to him.

"Why everybody so quiet?" he asked. "Before I got here, I'm sure you ladies were full of gossip."

Nobody said a word, until his left arm rested on Jamaica's shoulders and he lifted his right arm. He turned to Bernie.

"Do you mind if I use your shoulders to rest my arm?" he asked.

I couldn't believe that Bernie scooted even closer to him and gave him permission to rest his arm on her shoulders. He smiled and looked over at me.

"Now, I'm comfortable. How about you Scorpio? Are you comfortable?"

I shrugged my shoulder. "I guess, but what is this about Jaylin? Why are you here?"

"Truthfully, I came here to curse you the fuck out for what you did to me at Davenports. You knew that I was a married man, Scorpio, but you continue to play your games and fuck with my head. Once again, your games have not only cost me a bunch of hurt, but you've hurt my wife, too. Don't you have any regrets, and when you get around to it, I need an apology."

"No, I don't have any regrets and you won't get an apology from me. As a matter of fact, you're the one who should have regrets. You walked out on me, remember? Yes, I made some mistakes, but you made plenty of them. Don't be upset with me for pursuing what was initially mine. You made me many promises, and since *you* broke them, you can't blame me for what I did."

"Uh, maybe we should go," Bernie suggested. "I think Jaylin and Scorpio need some privacy." She looked over at Jamaica.

"And, I think I'd like to stay and listen. Besides, Jaylin don't want me to go anywhere, do you?" Jamaica asked.

"Please, feel free to stay," he said.

Doing the appropriate thing, Bernie got out of the Hot Tub. Jaylin checked out her well fitted body and she covered herself with a towel. On her way out, Jaylin asked her to cut off the lights. She put us in the dark and left.

I was getting irritated with Jamaica. Now wasn't the time for her to be bullshitting. "Jamaica, again, would you mind leaving me and Jaylin alone? Please."

"Yes, I do mind. Jaylin hasn't asked me...

"That's right baby," he teased. "Stay right here. And, while you're at it, why don't you move a little closer to me."

I felt the water shift around. Soon after, Jamaica laughed and Jaylin snickered. There was silence, and since I couldn't really see what was going on in the water, I quickly sat up.

"Since she won't leave, whatever else you came to say to me, say it to her. I'm out of here." I stood up.

"Girl, sit down. Even though I don't want to leave, I'm not about to hook myself like you've apparently done." I felt the water move around and could hear Jamaica whisper. When I heard lips smack, I got upset.

"I know you didn't just kiss him, did you?"

Jamaica stepped out of the Hot Tub. "Calm down, would you? If you must know, I kissed his cheek. He ain't your man, so why are you so worried about it."

Jaylin agreed, and soon after, there was a loud thud in the room. By her loud voice, I knew that Jamaica had slipped on the wet floor.

"Ohhh," she whined out loudly. "I've fallen and I can't get up! I think I hurt myself."

I rushed out of the Hot Tub and turned on the lights. Jamaica was already in Jaylin's care. He picked her up, holding her in his arms.

"Ohhh, I think it's my back. Would you mind carrying me to Scorpio's sofa so I can lye down?"

By the smirk on Jamaica's face, I could tell she was full of shit. I could have killed her, but I let her continue on with her charade. I opened the door and Jaylin carried her over to the sofa. I couldn't help but take a look at his naked, all-so-beautiful, muscular ass. He laid Jamaica on the couch, and as he leaned over her, she touched his chest.

"Thanks, sweetie. My ankle feels a whole lot better."

I couldn't help but to bust her out. "You mean your back, right? I thought it was your back, or is your ankle hurting, too?"

"B...both," she said, reaching for her ankle and rubbing it.

I took a deep breath and could have choked Jamaica. She was taking all of the attention away from me and I truly wanted to know what else Jaylin had to say. I pranced back into the Jacuzzi room, and just as much as I admired Jaylin's body, mad at me or not, I was sure he got a pleasure out of looking at mine. After all, it was and would forever be his weakness.

I bent over to let the water out of the Hot Tub. As the water slowly went down, I removed my bikini and reached for my cotton robe. Before I could cover myself, Jaylin came in and closed the door behind him. His eyes searched my naked body, and my eyes returned the favor. Once I allowed him to get a good look, I put on the robe but left the front of it open.

"You see, this is what I'm talking about," he said. "You put forth every effort to temp me, and you just don't give up, do you?"

I pulled my head back in disbelief. "Excuse me, but you're the one who came in here and got naked. And, for what? I didn't quite understand your purpose, and the only person who seemed enthused by your presence was Jamaica."

"Oh, I doubt that. You are one fake-ass individual, Scorpio. I was about to play your game with you tonight, and run back and tell Shane the details, however, I changed my mind. For the record, yes, your body is all that. Your pussy is spectacular, and I do occasionally think about all the fucking we'd done in the past. But, the past is the past. Let it rest and stop trying to get me to betray my wife. It ain't happening, baby, and the sooner you realize it, the better off you'll be."

I crossed my arms in front of me. "Are you finished?"

"Yes," he said, and then reached for his clothes on the floor. As he was bent over, I took a few steps forward and put my pussy directly in front of him.

"Since you're down that low, stay there. You can call me fake all you want to, but you're a fake-ass individual, too." I slid my index finger between my coochie lips and separated them. I was sure he'd gotten a good look at my hardened and juicy wet clit. "If what you see didn't belong to Shane, I'd surely give you a taste. And, you can say that you don't want me anymore all you want to, but I...we know better. Now, I'm sorry that you and your wife are going through troubled times, but placing the blame on other people isn't going to solve your problems. Admit that you fucked up, and why? Because you couldn't control your feelings for me." I removed my finger from inside of me and placed it on Jaylin's lip. He quickly stood up and snatched my finger. He tightly squeezed it, and while adding pressure, he stared me in the eyes.

"I really despise you, Scorpio. Just stay the hell away from me, alright?" He let go of my finger and slightly shoved me backwards. He hurried into his pants, tossed his jacket and shirt over his shoulder and reached for the knob on the door.

"You despise me because you can't stand the way I make you feel. If it doesn't work out between Shane and me, you can always have me again."

Jaylin turned and gave me a serious and stern look. "Don't make me disrespect you. All I ever wanted from you was your pussy. Our past so call love for each other was based on a fantasy. So you'd better hope that shit work out between you and Shane because there's no way in hell I'd allow you to come back to me. I'm already accounted for and forever will be."

"What a joke. And, are you saying you never loved me? Is that what you're saying?"

"What I'm saying is...I don't love you now, and I will never love you in the future."

On that note, he walked out. He said goodbye to Jamaica and she hated to see him go.

"Bye, sweetie. You come back real soon and see me, okay?"

Jaylin nodded, and once I heard the front door close, I turned to her and snapped.

"What in the hell is your problem? It was the wrong time and place for you to be acting a fool," I said.

She hopped up from the sofa, waving me off. "Girl, shut up. You need to thank me for saving your behind tonight. If I wasn't here, you would have eaten that man alive. You were hungry for him and I don't think he would have let you starve either."

"Hungry my butt, Jamaica, you really showed your ass. The falling incident was down right stupid. You looked like a fool."

"Fool or not, Miss Thang, my foolishness put me into the arms of your so desperately wanted lover. I got a chance to feel his goods, I kissed his lips and touched his nicely cut chest. I got further than you did and it seems to me that you're just jealous."

"Jealous, no. But, you better not had put your lips on him or touched his dick. I hope you didn't go that far, Jamaica. If anything, you know how I feel—how I've felt about him."

"Feel, felt, whatever," she laughed. "He's gone and I, indeed, had myself a darn good time."

I threw my hand back, and turned off the lights, leaving Jamaica laughing with herself in the dark. I wanted to call Shane to tell him Jaylin had stopped by, but I decided against it. Instead, I put on my clothes and headed to Shane's place to tell him.

SHANE
4

Yesterday, when Jaylin called and said he was already in St. Louis, I knew something bad was going to happen. By the time I got dressed and made it to Davenports, I saw Felicia being taken away in an ambulance. If you asked me, she looked pretty darn beat up. And, even though I hated to admit it, she got exactly what she deserved. I stayed around for awhile and talked to one of the officers who had been on the scene. He told me about Jaylin being arrested and advised me to go home and wait for his call. That's exactly what I did, but a whole day had gone by and I still hadn't heard from him. I was more than worried, but I didn't want to call his home and alarm Nokea. I wasn't sure if she knew what had went down or not, so I stayed by the phone and waited for anybody...somebody to call.

As I lay in bed gazing at the television, Scorpio was in bed with me. Her head rested on my chest and she massaged it with her hand.

"I know you're concerned about Jaylin, but would you like to go and get something to eat? You haven't eaten anything all day and starving yourself ain't helping this growling stomach of yours one bit. Besides, you promised me that we'd go somewhere tonight."

"We'll go get something in a lil while. I know I promised you earlier that we would go to The Jazz Corner, but baby, I'm really worried about my friend."

"I'm worried too, but Jaylin should have never come back to St. Louis and jumped on Felicia. I guarantee you that crazy skeeza is probably playing an innocent victim's role. I'm afraid he might have gotten himself into some trouble he might not be able to get out of."

"And I'm afraid to say I might have to agree with you." I kissed Scorpio's forehead and she snuggled up closer to me.

We held each other for at least a half an hour, and then, the doorbell rang. I looked at my watch and it was almost 11:00 p.m. Scorpio quickly sat up and I hopped out of bed. I hurried down the hallway with a bare chest and a pair of faded jeans that were unzipped. When I reached the door, I looked through the peephole and saw Jaylin outside. I pulled the door open and he stepped inside.

"Are you busy?" he asked.

"Naw, man. I've been waiting to hear from you. Why didn't you call me?" I asked, closing the door behind him. We stepped down into the sunken living room and Jaylin took a seat on the couch. I sat on the arm of a chair that was across from him.

"I didn't call because they only allowed me one phone call. Of course, I had to call Frick."

"What took so damn long? Normally, Frick have a brotha in and out."

"Yeah, well, he did get me the fuck out of there. I've been drinking and sleeping in my car and shit. This mess got me all fucked up and I don't know if I'm coming or going. I also think Frick is tripping because he's Felicia's attorney, too. I'm not sure how all of this shit gon' work out, but if need be, I might have to call another attorney, Jonathan, to take care of this mess for me."

"I don't think you'll have to do that. Frick has been your attorney for a very long time, and I'm positive he'll dump Felicia and her case in a heartbeat. Besides, when it comes to him, money talks and bullshit walks."

"Yeah, we'll see. I'm supposed to meet with him sometime tomorrow. For now, though, I need a couple shots of Remy, some aspirin, a phone and a bed. Do you think you can help a brotha out?"

I stood up and slammed my hand against Jaylin's. "Consider it done. The Remy and phone can be found at the wet bar to your left, I'll go get your aspirin, and the bed in my guestroom awaits you."

Jaylin nodded and scooted back on the couch. He leaned his head back and closed his eyes. I walked back to my bedroom and saw that Scorpio had gotten out of bed. When I looked in my bathroom, she stood naked by the jack and jill sinks, splashing water on her face. I opened the closet next to her and reached for the Tylenol.

"Are you alright?" I asked, as I watched her dab her face with a towel.

She combed her long hair back with her fingers and smiled. "I'm fine. Why did you ask?"

"Because you look a little flushed, that's all."

She sighed. "Honestly, I'm not too thrilled about seeing Jaylin. I know that a part of him is upset with me for what happened at Davenports, and if I wouldn't have ever put you and him into such a compromising position, then maybe none of this would be going on."

I moved Scorpio between my legs and wrapped my arms around her. "The last thing I need is for you to blame yourself for this mess. All of us could have done things differently and there's no one in particular to blame. Okay?"

She nodded and I lifted her lowered chin. I gave her a peck on the lips and told her to get dressed so we could go.

"Oh, so I see those hunger pains are calling."

"No doubt. Music, food and something to drink sounds awfully good right about now."

"I concur," she said, and then headed over to the shower.

When I got back into the living room, Jaylin had dosed off. I tapped his shoulder and he slowly sat up.

"Man, if you're that tired, why don't you get comfortable and go lay down in the guestroom?"

He held out his hand for the aspirin and I gave them to him. "Thanks," he said, as he shot the aspirin to the back of his throat. Seeing that he hadn't made himself a drink, I walked over to the wet bar and poured it for him. I handed the glass to him and the Remy was gone within seconds. Jaylin cleared his throat, "Please break me off another shot. I feel as if I need to be completely put out of my misery."

I poured him another drink. "Have you called Nokea yet?"

"No. I don't know what to say to her. She's already upset with me, and once she finds out how much more trouble I've gotten myself into, I really don't know how she's going to respond."

"Jay, you know better than anybody that Nokea is the most kindhearted, understanding, and forgiving person that we know. She ain't going to trip as much as you think she is. If anything, she gon' trip because you haven't called her. I suggest that you call her, soon."

"I will," Jaylin said, reaching for the glass. "First, I need a nap. Then, I'll call to see if she'll come to St. Louis until I get this shit resolved."

I agreed that she should be here, and allowing him to get some rest, I went back to my room to change. Keeping it simple, I kept on my faded jeans, and put on an ice-blue button down shirt that clung to my muscles. I thinly trimmed my beard and gave my twisties a shine. When Scorpio came out of the bathroom, she approved my look.

"Don't you look handsome. I'm not in the mood to be fighting any women off of you tonight."

"And if you plan on wearing this tiny skirt," I said, holding her silk peach skirt in my hand. "And this shirt to go with it, we both gon' be in jail tonight."

She snatched her outfit from my hand. "We got boundaries, baby. You got my back and I got yours."

Scorpio dropped the towel from around her and rubbed herself with some glittery lotion. Afterwards, she slid into her skirt. It hung low on her hips, showing off her curves and sexy ass midriff. When she put on the fitted silk shirt, it barely made it over her breasts and showed the thickness of her nipples.

"What do you think?" she said, turning around so I could get a good look at her.

Before giving my approval, I studied her entire body. "And here I thought Beyonce had it going on. All I can say is don't bend over too far. You might cause me to slip something into you."

While I sat on the edge of the bed, Scorpio placed her arms on my shoulders. "Beyonce? You know I'm jealous that you think she's got it going on, especially when you have all this to look forward to."

"Trust me, I'm grateful for what I have," I confessed while rubbing my hands up and down her smooth legs. I reached up her skirt and she moved back. "Why don't you have on any panties? Girl, that coochie gone get cold."

"Who needs panties when I got a strong and warm set of hands like yours to keep me warm? The Jazz Corner is always dark, and after a few drinks, who knows what will happen?"

Since Scorpio and I seemed to be on the same page, she swooped her hair in a ponytail and we headed for the door. By the time we made it to the living room, Jaylin was knocked out. I could hear him snoring, but I surely didn't bother to wake him.

The Jazz Corner was packed. Scorpio and I stood for a while, and when we saw a couple leaving, we held our drinks and made our way to a tiny two-seat table that sat in the far corner of the room. The table was covered with a red velvet table cloth and had a lit round scented candle in the middle. And even though the place was smoky, it remained one of our favorite places to chill. The soothing jazz music was spectacular, and Freddy and his band certainly knew how to set the mood.

From across the table, I looked at Scorpio and she seemed to be indulged with the sounds of Wallace Rhoney. She closed her eyes, and when she opened them, she noticed my stares.

"Why do I always catch you looking at me like that?"

"Because you're looking into the eyes of a man who loves you very much."

"I'm blessed. But, I hope that my man knows how much he's loved, too."

I placed my index finger on the side of my face as if I were in deep thought. "Sometimes. I often wonder if this relationship between us seems a bit rushed."

"Are you doubting my love for you? Is that what you're saying?"

"No. I just feel as if, at times, you're not ready for such a commitment."

"Shane, I have no idea where that came from. I thought we were over this. For months, I've been with no one but you. If this has anything to do with Jaylin being at your house, you need to get over it. Trust me, I've moved on and so has he. Now, can we not have this conversation anymore? This drink is making me tipsy and I'm in the mood to let my hair down and dance with you."

I shot the Grey Goose down my throat, stood up and took Scorpio by her hand. She escorted me to the crowded dance floor and we wrapped our arms around each other.

She laid her head against my chest and whispered. "I feel so safe and secure whenever I'm with you. How could you ever doubt my love for you?"

I didn't say one word. Time would surely tell me everything I wanted to know. Of course, I'd thought about asking Jaylin to catch a room at a hotel, but I wanted to see for myself if Scorpio could handle being in the presence of a man she'd once loved more than life itself.

The music, along with the drinks, had both of us feeling loose. Scorpio turned around and had her back to me. I held her waist and pecked my lips down the side of her neck. Since the lighting on the dance floor was dim, my hands started to roam. I touched the silkiness of her skirt and then made my way around to her inner thighs. When my hand touched her hotspot, she moved it away and turned to face me.

"Not on the dance floor," she whispered. "Do you have any idea how many people are looking at us?"

"Who cares? I'm not paying attention to anybody in here but you."

"Same here, but I don't want you to start nothing you can't finish."

Before I could respond, a voice interrupted.

"What's up, Scorpio Valentino," the brotha said.

Scorpio smiled, "Marcus? Is that you?" She paused and gave him a hug. He held her tightly.

"Yeah, baby girl, it's me. Long time no see."

"I know," she responded, and then, looked at me. "Marcus this is Shane. My significant other."

Marcus looked stunned by her words and checked me out tough before extending his hand. "You're a lucky man," he implied. "I hope you don't mind if I step in for a lil…for old-times-sakes dance, do you?"

"Not at all," I said, shaking his hand. I looked at Scorpio and then walked away.

Since I'd never been a man to feel insecure about my relationships, I had no problem with Scorpio dancing with Marcus. I went to the bar and ordered us another drink. Lexi, the bartender, knew us from coming in all the time. She was an older ghettofied woman with a light complexion. Her lips hung low, her tinted blonde braids looked as if they needed shampooing and her fingernails were about four or five inches long. I hated for her to wait on me because she was always up in somebody's business, including mine.

"Hey, Carmel Delight, what can I get you?" she asked, smacking on some gum. She placed a napkin in front of me.

She took another sip, and then another. And by the time we got ready to leave, I was fucked up and so was she.

"Baby, who gon' drive," I said, wobbling to my feet.

"For damn sure not you. Give me the keys," she ordered.

"Gurllll, your eyes are watered down. I bet you can't even see."

"Shane, I'm fine. Yes, I'm tipsy, but I think that I can handle getting us home a whole lot better than you can."

She reached in my pockets for the keys. Coping a feel, she grabbed my dick and squeezed it.

It tickled, so I laughed. "Ay, don't play, au-ight?"

"Where are the keys?" she laughed. She then reached into my back pockets for them. And unable to resist, she gathered my butt in her hands. I was all smiles, but she still didn't have the keys.

"Would you tell me where the keys are so we can go," she pleaded.

I moved in close to her and put my arm around her waist. I then leaned in to her ear, licked my lips and whispered. "You gotta unzip my pants and dig down real deep. Once you get to that point, I'll direct you to the keys."

Scorpio moved in closer to me. I stood with a seductive, yet serious look on my face, but she turned away with embarrassment. Seeing that I wasn't playing about her dipping into my pants, she looked down and unzipped my pants. She maneuvered her way through the slit in my boxer shorts and massaged my head. Instantly, my dick grew larger and she stroked it up and down.

"Which direction shall I go next?" she asked.

I closed my eyes and my head spun. "You're on the right path. Stay right there, and I'm sure the keys will pop up soon."

Scorpio cracked up and removed her hand. "I'm sure that if I keep at it, the keys won't be the only thing that pops up."

After she zipped my pants, I reached for my keys that were, at all times, in my back pocket. I dangled them in Scorpio's face and she snatched them out of my hands. She then took me by the hand.

"Come on, let's go. You've teased me enough for one night."

I followed behind her, as she made her way to the door. When we got to my Lexus, I opened the passenger's side door for her to get in.

JAYLIN
5

I was lying in the dark on Shane's couch knocked out, until I heard the front door swing wide open. I looked up and saw Shane and Scorpio blasted as they came in, slamming the door behind them. They were so messed up, and I don't think they even saw me.

"Shhh, sh, sh, shhh," Shane laughed, while placing his arm around her shoulders.

"Your drunk butt is the one who needs to be quiet," she whispered.

She removed Shane's arm from around her shoulders and made her way to his bedroom. Barely able to stand, he leaned against the wall and looked in her direction.

"Gimmie that," he sung out loudly, "Girl gimmie that, uhm, uhm...

Scorpio burst into laughter and so did Shane. They played around in the hallway for a moment, and then went into Shane's bedroom. I heard nothing but laughter, and after awhile, things got quiet. When the door squeaked, I certainly knew what time it was.

Since I'd gotten plenty of sleep, I felt well rested. I reached for the lamp and turned on the light. I still had on my wrinkled shirt so I pulled it off and laid it beside me. I undid the button on my pants and unzipped them. Thinking hard about Nokea, I looked at the clock on the wall and it showed almost 2:00 a.m. I got up, poured myself another drink, and then lay back on the couch. After taking a few sips from the glass, I reached for the cordless phone and held it in my hand. I dialed home, waiting for Nokea to answer. Almost immediately, she picked up.

"Did I wake you?" I asked. She didn't respond, but I knew she was still on the phone. "Nokea?"

"Where have you been?"

"I've been at Shane's place. I was arrested yesterday, and after Frick got me out of jail, I chilled overnight in a car, and then came to Shane's place to get some rest. I wanted to call you sooner, but I knew you'd be upset with me."

"So, I guess you decided to take matters into your own hands and not leave well enough alone like I asked you to do?"

"Baby, you don't understand. I can't let nobody come into our lives and try to destroy what we...

Nokea got loud. "No, Jaylin! You don't understand! I need you here with me and our children! At a time like this, leaving me was the worst thing you could've done. It's like you...you enjoy going back to St. Louis. If St. Louis is where you want to be, then stay there!" Her voice cracked. "I can't do this anymore, I can't!"

"Baby, please don't say that. You know that I want to be there with you. Maybe coming here was a big mistake, but I felt the need to come here and get this bullshit under control."

"So, is that what you did? You got everything under control? By getting arrested, it's obvious you lost control."

"Yes, I did. But more than anything, I gave Felicia exactly what she deserved. A good ass kicking."

Nokea was quiet, and then she spoke up. "I hope you're proud of yourself. And when all is said and done, I assure you that you're going to regret taking matters into your own hands. I just hope and pray that your stupid mistake doesn't affect your children in any way."

I frowned and Nokea knew that mentioning my kids was a sore spot. "What's that supposed to mean?"

"Since you have all of the answers, you figure it out. I'm too tired to even discuss this anymore."

We sat silently on the phone for several minutes.

"Nokea?"

"What is it, Jaylin?"

"I love you. I know that you may not understand my actions, but just know that my actions were because of my love for you. I can't come home yet because I have to be in court on Monday. If the judge doesn't consider me a flight risk, which I'm sure he probably won't, I'll be back home right after court is over. In the meantime, I was hoping that you'd catch a flight out of Miami tomorrow and...

"I have to see about *our* children, Jaylin. You got yourself into this mess and it's only fair that you do whatever you have to do to get yourself out."

"Can't you ask Nanny B to watch them for a few days? I'm positive that she won't mind."

"I will do no such thing. I'll just see you *whenever* you get back."

There was silence again. I stared at the ceiling, and then closed my eyes. I was hurt because Nokea had rarely spoken to me in such a coldly manner. I knew she was still upset about the CD and losing the baby, so I tried my best not to say the wrong thing to her.

"It would be nice to hold you in my arms, but I understand how you feel. However, our marriage vows said for better or worse. We're having a little down time right now, but I know things will get better. Right now, a lil 'I love you too Jaylin' would mean everything in the world to me and I need some hope. Again...I love you, Nokea. Always have and always will."

Again, there was silence. I wasn't saying nothing else, until she spoke up. Soon after, she did. "I love you too, Jaylin. But this time, you have to work this out on your own."

"Will do," I said, listening to the dial tone.

I sat up and placed the cordless phone on the table. I knew that I had my work cut out for me, and the faster I got myself out of this mess, the better. I couldn't wait until later so I could talk to Frick about my case. Hopefully, he'd have good news for me.

Ready to shut it down again, I reached over to the lamp and turned it off. I picked up the glass of Remy from the table and held it in my hand. Needing a comfortable bed to lay in, I made my way down the hallway to the guestroom. As I neared Shane's bedroom, I heard soft moans coming from inside. The door was slightly cracked and I knew Scorpio's moans like the back of my hand. She sounded overly excited, and just for the hell of it, I stood outside the door and listened.

For awhile, I didn't hear anything from Shane. And since my curiosity got the best of me, I slowly moved my head, peeking through the cracked door. I took a few more sips from my glass, and even though the room was dimly lit, I caught a glimpse of Scorpio as she lay naked on her back. Her head was damn near hanging off the bed and her thighs were resting high on Shane's shoulders. His face was buried between her legs, and by the sounds she made, it was obvious that he was sucking her correctly. Her eyes were closed and she bit down on her bottom lip.

"Ohh, babyyyy," she moaned while holding his head in place. I could hear the slurps and watched as he not only worked her pussy with his tongue, but massaged her breasts at the same time. "Shaaaaane, I…I'm coming, baby! I'm about to cummmm again!"

Scorpio's eyes popped wide open, and I'll be damned if they didn't connect with mine. After having an orgasm, she stared directly at me for a few seconds. Shane lifted his head and she rolled on top of him. Before going down on him, she made eye contact with me, closed her eyes and then placed his dick into her mouth. No doubt, she worked him well. I watched her take him to the back of her throat and listened to him give his approval. When she opened her eyes, they looked in my direction again. I was still standing there taking in every moment of the festivities that I could. My dick was rock solid hard, and even though I didn't feel good about watching, my feet wouldn't move.

Scorpio knew she had my attention. And once the head job was over, she straddled Shane's lap to ride him. Her rhythm was on key with his and that kind of connection only came with constant practice. After being rode very well, Shane decided to step it up a notch. He aggressively turned Scorpio on her stomach. She laid her head on the pillow and hiked her nicely shaped ass up a bit so he could straddle her from behind. That was one of my favorite positions with her. I loved to watch her ass smack against my thighs and the feel of her insides were like no other. I shot the remainder of the Remy down my throat and squeezed my eyes together. When I opened them, I witnessed Shane tearing it up. Both of their bodies dripped with sweat and enjoyment showed on their faces. Scorpio gave me one last look, and then turned her head to the other side. Her moans got louder, and that's when I walked away from the door. I went into the guestroom and closed the door. Feeling awfully horny, I stripped naked and made my way to the shower. I turned on the cold water and let it run down on me for as long as I could. Once my dick calmed down, I got in bed. I wanted to make love to Nokea so badly that I thought about saying to hell with this case and going home. Instead, I reached for the phone and called her again. This time, she didn't pick up until at least the fifth or sixth ring.

"Did I wake you again?" I asked.

"No. I can't sleep."

"Then, what took you so long to answer the phone?"

"I was sitting outside on the balcony thinking."

"Good thoughts or bad thoughts?"

"I'd rather not say."

"Well, I was laying here thinking, too. My thoughts were good though. Would you like for me to tell you how good they were."

"I'm almost one hundred percent sure that I know what your thoughts were all about."

I cracked a tiny smile, as my wife knew me all too well. "Yeah, they were about making love to you, but that's because I miss you. Don't you miss me?"

"Of course I do, Jaylin. I just wish like hell you would have listened to me, that's all. More than anything, I'm seriously worried."

"There's nothing for you to worry about. I promise to work this out, and from now own, whatever you say goes. Okay?"

Nokea chuckled. "Yeah, right. The man I married doesn't listen to anybody. And even though what you said sounds really good, I know better. You listen to no one."

Nokea's chuckle made me smile again. "Naw, for real. I wouldn't lie to you. I swear. From this moment on, I will listen to everything you tell me to do."

"Jaylin, you are just saying that because your behind is in hot water. Besides, I don't want a husband who takes orders. I'd like for you to compromise with me and not run off like you did. If you can promise me that, then we'll be okay."

"I promise," I said, yawning.

"Good. Now get some rest and hurry back home. I need you."

I placed my hand over my dick. "Shit, I need you, too. Badder than a motherfucka. You should see and feel how hard my dick is. A lil dirty talk to your husband sure would be nice."

"Do I look or sound like a phone sex specialist to you?"

"You are a phone sex specialist. But your services are for my pleasures only. Besides, don't be on this phone pretending like that thang ain't over there wet and missing me, woman."

Nokea chuckled again. "As a matter of fact, it's dry as a bone."

"Well, as soon as I see you, you better believe I'm gon' take care of that little problem for you. I wish that I could take care of it now, but I guess the thoughts of me sliding my hardness into that pussy...

"Jaylin, please. I think it is so tacky for two people to sit on the phone and indulge in such conversation. Besides, I'm too mad at you to get wet. And, too darn sleepy."

I was tired too and yawned again. "Alright, Miss Tacky. Get some sleep and I'll call you later to let you know how things went."

"Don't forget. And, before you go to bed, I was thinking about making love to you when you called. My insides stay moist whenever I think of you, and it's not the dirty talk that turns me on, but the man himself that does."

"That's my girl," I smiled. I blew Nokea a kiss over the phone and she returned the love. I felt so much better and pulled the covers over my head so I could get some rest. Hopefully, I'd be able to see my family soon.

FELICIA
6

This hospital was driving me nuts! How in the hell was I supposed to get any rest, if the nurses kept running in throughout the night poking at me. I'd had enough, and when I saw this nurse come in with several glass tubes in her hands, I looked at her like she was crazy.

"What now?" I asked.

"I need to take some more blood from you."

"Like hell. I've given enough blood already. You need to go find blood elsewhere because you won't get anymore from me."

"Please, Ms. Davenport. This is the last time. Your doctor gave the order...

"I don't give a rat's ass what my doctor said. I'm going to make a suggestion that you take blood from him and not from me. So, how's that? His blood for my blood."

The nurse placed the tubes in her pocket and walked out. All the mess they were doing was totally unnecessary. I knew that the more test they ran on me, the more money the hospital made. I was so anxious to get out, and since Frick hadn't called me back yet, I reached for the phone to call him. Finally, he answered.

"That's right, kick a sista when she's down," I joked.

He laughed. "Feliciaaaa, I was just getting ready to call you."

"Sure you were. But, now that I have you on the phone, did you get my messages yesterday?"

"Yes, I did. And I have to be very upfront and honest with you. I can't take your case, hun, I'm sorry. It's too risky."

"Risky? How is your defending me being a risk?"

"Felicia, you know that Jaylin's been my client since...forever. I've already taken care of some matters for him pertaining to this case, and it's not in my best interest to assist both parties."

"Mr. Frick, do you have any idea what you're up against? The man who you intend to defend severely assaulted me, nearly tried to kill me, and almost left me for dead. If the prosecutor takes this case, Jaylin will go to jail for a very long time. There will be nothing that you can say, or nothing that all the money he has, can buy him out of."

"Felicia, I wouldn't be so sure of that. Either way, he's not going to be my client and neither will you. As of today, I'm removing myself and I'd be happy to recommend another attorney who might be able to help."

"Does Jaylin know this yet?"

"I'd rather not say."

"Will you be recommending someone else for him, too?"

"Can't say."

"Then, what can you say to me, Mr. Frick? Other than, sorry Felicia, you pay me big dollars, but now, I can't help your black ass out of this situation? I guess Jaylin's dollars go a longer way than mine, huh?"

"This has nothing to do with money."

"Like hell! That's such bullshit and you know it! You will regret...

"Felicia, I won't stand for your verbal abuse. I will have Mr. Glasgow call you shortly. Hopefully, everything will work out for you."

"You'd better hope...

The sucker had the nerve to hang up on me. I was going to call him back, but instead, I called Stephon. He said he was in route to the hospital, so I asked him to hurry up.

When Stephon arrived, he walked in looking prepped out in his Sean Jean blue jean outfit and Timberlands. His baldhead was cleanly shaven and light brown eyes were covered with tinted glasses. I could tell that rehab had done him justice because he was starting to look better and better each day.

He smiled and his pearly whites were in full affect. "Why did you rush me up here?" he asked. Before I could respond, he gave me a peck on the lips and pulled up a chair beside me.

Ashamed of my looks, I placed my hand in front of my face. "I hate for you to see me like this. I haven't even looked in the mirror yet. But, I can tell that I'm not going to like what I see."

"It's just a lot of swelling, baby. Trust me, before you know it, it'll go down. But before it does," Stephon reached into his pocket and pulled out a camera. "We need to gather as much evidence as possible."

"You know what, I hadn't even thought of that. Good looking out, baby."

I posed for the pictures and Stephon took plenty of shots. He said that he'd have them developed soon and he placed the camera back into his pocket.

"So, when are you going home?"

"I haven't a clue. Hopefully soon. In the meantime, I have a serious problem."

"What's that?"

"Frick is refusing to represent me. You know he's one of the best damn lawyers in St. Louis, and if he assists Jaylin with his defense, this thing could get real ugly."

"You got that right," Stephon said, slowly standing up. He placed his hands in his pockets and walked over by the window.

"What shall I do, Stephon? Frick suggested another attorney for me, but I don't even know this man."

"I know somebody who would be more than happy to take your case. He is the bomb, trust me."

Stephon dialed out on his cell phone and asked for Timothy Tydus.

"I'll be back," he said, and then stepped into the hallway. Moments later, he came back and said that Timothy was on his way to talk to me.

"Thanks," I said. "I hope he'll be able to help me."

"Aw, he will. Until he gets here, can I get you something to eat or drink?"

"Yeah, I'm a little hungry. This hospital food is making me sick. I think there's a café in the lobby and anything you can find would be appreciated."

"Alright," he said, walking towards the door. I took a glimpse of his muscular ass.

"Stephon."

He turned. "What's up?"

"Come here for a minute."

He came over to the bed and stood next to me.

"Why are you being so kind to me? If I didn't have you right now, I don't know what I'd do. I know Jaylin is your cousin, and I hope like hell that I can trust you."

Stephon reached for my hand and held it with his. "You have the nerve to ask me that, after all you did for me? Jaylin allowed pussy to come between us. I might have been tripping with those drugs, but I was calling out for his help. Instead, his only concern was me fucking Scorpio. I know I made some mistakes, but he should've been there for me. After all we'd been through, he left me hanging dry and I'm damn mad about it. So, Miss Lady, if it wasn't for you seeing about me, I don't know where I'd be. Probably dead, who knows, but consider yourself my guardian angel."

I smiled and Stephon leaned forward, giving me another kiss on the cheek. "We gon' handle this together, alright?" he said. I nodded, and soon after, he left the room.

As Stephon and I were chomping down on our food, Timothy Tydus walked in. I was not only in total disbelief, but also in shock. If he wasn't the most grimy looking, non-talking, unprofessional brotha I'd ever seen, then I don't know what he was. He couldn't get two words out of his mouth, before I sat up in bed and tried hard to be polite. I caught a glimpse of his busted up shoes, and could no longer hold my peace.

"Who are you planning on representing?" I asked.

He had the nerve to talk with his tongue. "Stephon said you needed a lawyer."

"Yes, I do. But not one who requires a speech therapist."

"Damn, baby, hold on," Stephon said frowning at me. "You ain't gotta be tripping like that."

I folded my arms in front of me. "Is this some kind of joke? Stephon, if it is, please don't play with me."

"Man, what's up with her," Timothy asked. "I come all this way to help you out and yo woman dissing me?"

"Oh, I haven't *dissed* you yet. But, I'm about to, if somebody don't tell me what's going on."

Frustration was written all over Stephon's face. "Felicia, this brotha is here to help you. He knows the courts system and has won many cases. You've got to give him a chance."

I rolled my eyes at Stephon, and then searched Timothy from head to toe. His suit was cheap, his beard was too fuzzy, and the gold watch on his wrist was faded. Since I had such a hard time looking over the rips in his shoes, I had to decline. Besides, I could visualize Jaylin laughing his butt off in court, once he got a look at him.

I extended my hand. "Thanks for coming, Timothy, but no thanks. I am in dire need of a professional and not some one of your caliber. Honestly, I don't know who in their right mind would allow you to step in court looking as you do."

He threw his hand back at me and looked at Stephon. "I see why she all fucked up like she is. She got a mouth on her that...

"Stephon, please escort him out of my room before I call security."

Stephon shook is head, but left the room with Timothy. A few minutes later, Stephon returned and had the nerve to be upset with me.

"All that was uncalled for, Felicia. I'm trying to help you and...

"If you're offering me that kind of help, thanks, but I don't need it." I pulled the covers back and swung myself around to get out of bed. "I see now that I need to get out of this bed and go take care of my own business. If I don't, Jaylin will walk without any repercussions. I'm not about to let that happen."

When I stepped on the floor, my body was a bit stiff from lying down for so long. I took slow steps to the closet so I could get my clothes and go. As I neared the mirror, I stopped. I turned, looked at my face and covered my mouth. Not only was my face swelled, but it was covered with bruises. The sight of it made me cry, and that's when Stephon rushed over to comfort me. He kissed my forehead.

"It's gon' be alright," he assured me. "I promise you that Jaylin will pay for everything he's done to you, and to me."

JAYLIN
7

As tired as I was, I couldn't get back to sleep. My mind was cluttered with the thoughts of Nokea, my case, and even though I hated to admit it, Shane and Scorpio were on my mind as well. I couldn't really say that I was jealous, because I knew for a fact that if I wanted Scorpio again, she'd drop her panties in a heartbeat. Basically, there was no need for me to be envious of something I for damn sure knew I could have.

Since I couldn't get any rest, I got out of bed and opened Shane's closet. I searched around for something to put on, and when I saw a pair of burgundy sweat pants, I reached for those. I slid into them and went into the bathroom to freshen up. Afterwards, I made my way down the hallway, looking into Shane's bedroom that had a wider crack. Scorpio was laid across the bed knocked out. If my memory served me correctly, after a good night's fuck, she'd be asleep at least until noon. I thought about where Mackenzie was, but I guess it really wasn't any of my business. I knew Shane was somewhere in the house, so I stepped away from the door to go find him.

I found Shane doing sit-ups, while lying on the floor in his home office. Not only was it his office, but he had workout equipment in the room as well. The whole room was rather junky and cluttered to me, so I looked for the quickest place to sit, which was on a weight bench.

"Good morning," he said, straining and continuing with his sit-ups. "Did you sleep all right?"

"A lil bit. The couch was comfortable, but the bed could stand a new mattress."

Shane laughed and stopped his workout. He sat up on the floor and wiped the sweat off his body with a towel. "If the mattress is that bad, then why don't you consider buying me a new one?"

"Negro, please. You got plenty of money. Your ass just cheap."

"Cheap? Just because I don't blow money out of the window like you do, that doesn't make me cheap. That makes me smart."

"Whatever," I said leaning back on the weight bench. I lifted the weights in the air and started to pump.

"What time are you meeting with Frick?"

"As soon as I have a new suit sent to me from Brooks Brothers. When they open, I'm gon' call to see if they'll deliver me a few pieces of clothing to wear for the next few days."

"You see. That's what I mean about blowing money. It's going to cost you a fortune to do that, when you can find something in my closet to put on."

"Fool, you are out of your mind. It's killing me now to wear these country ass sweat pants I got out of your closet. Besides, I don't wear other people's shit. You know me better than that."

"Hey, I'm just trying to help. But, let me know what time you plan to hook up with Frick."

"Why's that?"

"Because I want to go with you. You need some support, don't you?"

I put the weights back on the bar and sat up. "I guess so, especially since Nokea won't come here to be with me. Can you believe her lil stubborn ass told me to work this out myself?"

"Naw, not really. But she must be really upset."

"Yeah, I guess." I sat quietly in deep thought.

Shane stood up and stretched. "Well, I gotta go make a few runs. Today is my mother's birthday, so I'm taking her to breakfast. I promised her I'd paint her porch, so I plan to knock that out for her too. I shouldn't be long, but hit me on my cell and let me know when you're ready to go see Frick."

"That sounds like a plan. But, uh, if you don't mind me asking...are you taking Scorpio to meet your mother or has she already met her?"

"No, I'm not taking her to meet my mother, and no she has never met her. Why'd you ask?"

"I was just wondering." I paused for a moment. "So, you don't have a problem with me being here?"

Shane raised his brows. "Should I have a problem with you being here? You my best friend, Jay. Of course I don't have no problem with you being here. Now, if you're trying to ask if I trust you being alone with my woman, I can't answer that yet. Scorpio knows what she's got, and if she don't recognize, then only time will tell."

"Cut the theoretical bullshit, man. You know damn well that the thought of Scorpio and me being in your house alone is going to eat at your ass all day long."

"It ain't that serious," he said, walking towards the door. "I'm gon' hit the shower, and then hit the door. Like I said, whatever happens, it just happens."

Shane left to go change and I went into his kitchen to get a cup of coffee. It was only 8:00 a.m., and since Brooks Brothers didn't open until noon, I decided to sit back on Shane's covered patio and chill. I turned the TV to *Meet The Press* and listened to all of the political bullshit that was going on.

When Shane came into the room, I was focused on the TV. He cleared his throat and talked about me for being so indulged.

"Do you watch this stuff at home?" he asked.

"Sometimes. They be talking about some informative things, man. Trust me."

"Yeah, I know. I'm hooked on CNN and MSNBC, but for now, I'm out. I didn't want to wake Scorpio, but tell her to hit me on my cell when she wakes up."

"By the time she wakes up, you'll probably be back by then. And after what went down last night, don't expect to see her face until two or three o'clock in the afternoon."

Shane chuckled. "Let me guess...you remember from prior experience, huh?"

"Fasho," I grinned.

Shane stepped further into the room. "How do you know what went down last night and I vaguely remember?"

"Hey, it wasn't my fault that you were too messed up to remember. Let's just say that, by the sounds of it, you really had a good time."

Shane laughed again. "Man, I was messed up. I don't even remember coming in this motherfucka last night. When I woke up, I was naked and so was Scorpio. I assumed we must—
Shane paused.

I held out my hands. "Hey, it doesn't bother me at all. Things have changed and time has ticked away. I'm over it, Shane, trust me."

"We good friends, Jay, and it...it feels so awkward talking to you about her. At times, I want to share with you how I feel about her, but I can't. Not just yet."

"Whenever you're ready, I'm here. I'd be lying if I told you that I support your relationship with her, but I won't be lying when I say that I respect it."

Shane slammed his hand against mine. "I gotta jet. My mother probably cursing my ass out for being late."

He took several steps towards the door and I continued to watch the TV. Soon, he interrupted me again.

"What is it now, fool?"

He grinned. "Don't fuck my woman while I'm gone. I will mess you up if you even look at her."

"You'd better tell your woman don't be trying to get at me. I'm an irresistible, big dick Negro, and she's the one who will have to maintain her composure. Now, get yo ass out of here, tell your mother I said Happy Birthday, and trust me, alright? I can handle this."

We both laughed and Shane jetted.

Not even intending to, I dozed off again. When I woke up, I looked at the clock on the wall and it was 11:05 a.m. Having mega shit to do today, I reached for the phone to call Frick. He didn't answer, so I left a message on his voicemail for him to call me. I knew Brooks Brothers wasn't opened yet, so I continued to sit around in Shane's burgundy sweats. After I flipped through the channels, realizing nothing was on, I headed for the kitchen. To my surprise, Scorpio was sitting in a chair with her head lying on the table. Her long hair was spread out and her eyes were closed. When I stepped back to exit, she lifted her head and looked at me.

"So we meet again," she said.

I felt very uncomfortable. "What's up, Scorpio. I thought you were asleep and I came in to get a cup of coffee."

Wearing a white button down silk pajama top that barely met up with the cheeks of her ass, she stood up and walked over to the coffee machine. She poured two cups of coffee and handed one of them to me. I thanked her, and without saying anything else, she left and made her way to the patio covered hearth room. Getting comfortable, she sat back on the wicker sofa and placed the tips of her toes on the edge of the table. I sat back on the chaise and looked over at her.

"Shane told me to tell you to call him as soon as you woke up."

She wouldn't even look my way. "Thanks, but I already talked to him."

What's with the attitude, I thought. Instead of asking, I picked up the remote and flipped through the channels. Her head snapped to the side.

"Excuse me, but I was watching the *Lifetime* channel, if you don't mind."

"Well, I do mind. I was in here before you were and I don't want to watch the *Lifetime* channel."

She got up and stood in front of the TV. Her back was to me and it was hard not to notice her perfect heart shaped ass. My eyes lowered and scanned her silky smooth shapely legs. She switched the TV back to the *Lifetime* channel and turned around.

"Now, leave it," she demanded and walked back to the sofa.

To aggravate her, I switched the channels again. She folded her arms and cut her eyes.

"Would you please stop? I bought this TV for *my man*, and I have every right to watch whatever it is I want."

On that note, I stood and stretched my arms. My hard dick made an eye catching print in the sweat pants, and Scorpio's eyes dropped right to it. I tossed the remote into her lap and left the room. After I made my way to the guestroom, I closed the door and sat on the bed. In deep thought about my life, I fell backwards and placed my hand behind my head. More than anything, I felt guilty for admiring Scorpio's body so much. It had always been my weakness, and the sad thing about it was she knew it. I guess that any man in his right mind would look, and as long as I didn't touch, then I didn't have much to worry about.

Within moments of returning to the guestroom, there was a light knock at the door.

"Come in," I said, while still lying back on the bed.

Scorpio came in and stood by the door. "Can we talk?"

"About what?"

"About why we have so much anger for each other."

"Not interested in discussing that."

"Why not," she said making her way over to the bed. She sat on the edge and looked down at me still lying flat on my back.

"I'm not interested because it's obvious that you are attempting to fuck with my head again."

"Jaylin, you said it yourself, this game over. I have no idea what you mean when you say I'm trying to fuck with your head."

"Stop bullshitting, Scorpio. I know you better than you think I do. That shit you pulled with Shane in the bedroom was your first attempt. Walking around here half fucking naked is your second attempt, and sitting this close to me in bed is another attempt."

She pointed her finger at me. "Wait a minute...you're the one who stood outside of the door, watching Shane and me make love. I didn't ask you to watch us in action, nor did I think we would entertain you for as long as we did. Secondly, I didn't have much else to put on, and lastly, I am not sitting that close...

To prove my point, I shut Scorpio up when I pulled her back and rolled on top of her. Her heart beat fast and she couldn't even move. I then placed her hands above her head and squeezed them together with mine. We lay face to face, eye to eye, and lips to lips.

"Is this what you want from me? If not, then tell me what it is because I'm not understanding your motives."

"I don't have any motives," she whispered. "I want nothing from you, Jaylin, nothing at all."

"Then, why can't you just leave me alone and allow me to be satisfied with the decision I made?"

"I have allowed you that, but I want you to know that I think you made the wrong decision."

"You'll never convince me. If anything, having sex with Shane reveals what kind of woman you really are."

"Is that your way of calling me a whore?"

"No. It's my way of telling you that I have very little respect for you. I think you are using Shane to get back at me and this game you're playing is going to blow up in your face."

Scorpio had a blank expression on her face and stared into my eyes. Her legs slowly widened, causing my manhood to grow. "And, you want to know what I think Jaylin? I think you have the most seductive grey eyes, and along with the pressure I'm feeling between my legs, those things are capable of getting you anything you want from a woman. I also think you're jealous because I'm in love with Shane, and no longer in love with you. You would be on cloud nine, if those sweat pants would disappear and your dick could dip into my pussy like you want it to. I can see the lust in your eyes, right now, and just like I saw last night. If you could have me every morning, day and night, the way you did in the past, then that would make you one happy man."

"Fortunately, I have what I want every morning, day, evening and night. Just in case you forgot, her name is Nokea. You can talk all the bullshit you want, but I can see right through it. Right now, I feel your heart beating, I see the sweat forming on your forehead, and I feel the warmth between your legs. If I put my dick inside of you, there would be no denying me and you know it. Instantly, Shane would become history, and you know for a fact that I speak the truth."

"Why don't you stop talking shit, try and let's see."

"Ah, you would like that, wouldn't you?"

"Not as much as you would."

Neither one of us made a move or said another word. If anything, we both had something to prove, but we continued to lay there in a very compromising position. After several more seconds, the phone rang and we looked at it. That was my cue to move from between her legs, so I did. Scorpio pulled her shirt down and stood up. She walked over to the phone and picked it up.

"Hello," she said in a soft spoken voice. "Yes, he is. Hold on." She handed me the phone. I didn't hesitate to take the call because I thought it was Frick. Instead, it was Nokea.

No doubt, she couldn't wait to ask. "Who was that who answered the phone?"

I had a lost for words. I watched Scorpio as she left the room, closing the door behind her. "That was Scorpio."

"Who…who did you say?"

"I said Scorpio. She's Shane's guest, not mine."

"Well, where is Shane?"

"He's at his mother's house."

"Oh, really? And just for the heck of it, he left you and Scorpio alone at his house? Is that what you want me to believe?"

"Damn, baby, it's the truth. Scorpio and Shane are now dating, and you don't think I'd…

"Jaylin, after seeing that CD, I don't know what to believe. I do know that before I called, you and her must have been close because, within seconds, you were on the phone. Baby, I am seriously mad about her constantly being a part of our lives. When is it going to stop? Please tell me. I really need to know."

"You are just so, so wrong. If you don't believe me, why don't you come to St. Louis so that you can see for yourself what's going on? I need you, please!"

"I'm not coming to St. Louis," she shouted. "To hell with St. Louis, Jaylin! Since you're having such a spectacular time, why don't you just stay there!"

I was taken aback by Nokea's tone. Even more when she hung up on me. I tried to call her back but she wouldn't answer. After a few more calls, I got a busy signal. I knew she was mad, but damn! What the hell was I supposed to do? If Scorpio wanted to answer her man's telephone, who was I to tell her not to pick it up?

Frustrated, I hurried to call Frick so I could get the hell out of here. My marriage was at stake, and I wasn't about to lose Nokea over no bullshit. I needed to get home and fast!

This time when I called, Frick answered. I quickly asked why he hadn't returned my calls and he told me to meet him at his office around 2:00 p.m. I ended the call, and then phoned Brooks Brother so they'd get my clothes to me as soon as possible. My measurements and credit cards were on file, so the process went pretty smoothly.

In an effort to distance myself from Scorpio, I stayed in the guestroom until the doorbell rang. I thought about talking to her about going to see Mackenzie, but I decided against it. I also wanted to know where Mackenzie was, but I kept telling myself that it was no longer any of my business.

I hurried to the door, and Damion from Brooks Brothers came in, handing over a black garment bag.

"Jay, you are going to like this suit and the other items I picked out. I'm very familiar with your taste and it's good doing business with you."

I knew Damion was working on a tip, so I already had two-hundred dollars in my hand. I gave it to him and he was all smiles. He thanked me and left.

Seeing how well he knew me, I unzipped the bag and sure enough, the dark gray pin-striped suit that he accessorized with a black, lighter gray and fire red tie was one hell of a combination. And when I moved the suit aside, the casual tan and black linen pants sets worked for me, too. He hooked up shoes and socks that matched everything, and even threw in several belts. Just for the hell of it, I looked at the receipt. I chuckled and balled it up in my hand. In Shane's opinion, that much money would've been money out the window.

On my way back to the bedroom, Scorpio saw me and called my name. When I looked into Shane's bedroom, she held the telephone out to me.

"Shane would like to speak to you," she said.

I held the garment bag over my shoulder and went into the room to get the phone.

"What up?"

"I thought you were supposed to call me when you made arrangements to go see Frick."

"I was anticipating on calling you, but you beat me to it. My appointment is at two. Can you make it by then?"

"I'm on my way there now. It shouldn't take long for me to shower and change."

"Well, put the pedal to the metal and hurry it the fuck up, alright?"

"I am. And I hope when I get there, I don't have to kick no ass before we leave, do I? I hope you've been nice to my woman."

I looked at Scorpio who was for damn sure listening to our conversation. "Yeah, I was real nice to her. Maybe even too nice. But let's just say that while you were away, things got pretty Hot Hot Hot. If you don't make your way back here soon, I anticipate them getting even hotter."

Shane laughed and cleared his throat. "I anticipate you getting your hot ass out of my bedroom." I turned around and he was behind me.

"Negro, your woman invited me in here to use the phone. If you got a beef, you'd better chat with her about it."

Scorpio stood up and walked over to Shane. He looked a bit uncomfortable with what she had on, but he would never let me know it. She gave him a peck on the lips and eased her arms around his waist.

"Baby, can you drop me off at Jay's before you go with Jaylin? I'll get a ride home from Jamaica. We have inventory to do today and I should have been there hours ago."

"I don't think Jay and I will have time. You can use my car and I'll just ride with him."

She nodded and stepped away from him. Giving me one last look, she walked into the bathroom and closed the door.

Shane placed his keys on the dresser and pulled the blotchy painted white t-shirt over his head. His painter pants were messed up too, along with his boots.

"This shouldn't take long," he said. "Give me about fifteen minutes and I'll be ready."

"If you use the same bathroom that Scorpio is in, you could be hours. In fifteen minutes, I'm out the door."

Shane nodded and agreed. He headed towards the bathroom in the hallway and I made my way to the guestroom. Frick had better be talking what I wanted to hear, and if not, I was leaving town. Warrant or not, St. Louis would soon be history.

SHANE
8

Yes, I hated to do it, but it had to be done. As much as I cared for Scorpio, I wanted to know for sure if she could remain true to me with Jaylin around. I wasn't completely safe with the situation, but a part of me felt as if I could trust Jaylin, more than I could trust her.

There was still just a little fire in her eyes for him, but I guess that was to be expected. As for Jaylin, personally, I think the thought of losing Nokea was affecting him more than he was willing to admit. He told me about how coldly she'd been towards him and when he told me about Scorpio answering the phone, I told him that was a bad situation to be in. There was no way for him not to look at it from Nokea's point of view. She had to be frustrated with the whole damn thing, and at this point, he was one lucky man that she hadn't already given up.

We sat in Frick's office, waiting for him to end a call. As soon as he did, Jaylin made it clear that he was anxious to get this over with and back at home with his wife and kids.

Frick tapped a silver pen on his desk and looked overwhelmed with the whole thing. "Jaylin, this is not going to disappear overnight. I wish I could make it go away, but as of today, Felicia has filed charges against you. The prosecutor is going to try you for carrying a weapon, but I don't think the attempted murder charges will stick. Assault charges may be filed, and even though your gun was licensed, the building you were in doesn't allow it."

Jaylin arrogantly stood up and placed his hands in his pockets. "Assault and carrying a weapon? Man, make arrangements to pay somebody off so I can get the hell out of here. Those are tedious charges and I've seen people get off with those charges every single day of my life."

"I'm hoping that you'll get probation, but I don't know. You were carrying a loaded weapon, Jaylin, with the intentions of using it. As for Felicia, she's very persistent, and she's not going to let this...

Jaylin's brows scrunched in and he darted his finger at Frick. "Fuck Felicia! She deserved what she got and I'm not going to be apologetic about it. If she wants to meet me in court, then so be it. Any jury will see right through her bullshit and she'll be the one doing time in jail, not me!"

I cleared my throat. "Mr. Frick have you considered that Felicia illegally taped us in Davenports? You know the CD is what caused all of this mess."

"Shane, of course I've thought about that. But, it didn't give Jaylin the right to come here and do what he did to her."

Jaylin snapped at Frick again. "Are you defending her?"

"No, I'm just being honest with you. And the truth is, I have to remove myself from this case. There's too much—

"Wha...what the fuck did you just say?" Jaylin was furious and I personally didn't blame him. Frick appeared to be bullshitting around. "Remove yourself?"

Frick took a hard swallow. "Yes. Only because of the position I'm in. I will refer you—

"Refer, me, my, ass!" Jaylin yelled. He leaned forward and placed the palms of his hands on Frick's desk. "How fucking long have you known me?"

Frick looked away and didn't respond.

"Let me refresh your memory, Mr. James Cortell Frick. You've known me since I was seventeen years old. Back then, you were a white man with a dim future. Because of me, my connections, and for damn sure my money, you've become one of the most prestigious and wealthiest attorneys in St. Louis. Now, I've gotten myself into a lil trouble. Trouble that I am positive you can get me out of. After tomorrow, if I'm not back at home with my wife and kids, shit gon' get real ugly. So, my only question for you is, what time shall I meet you in court?"

Frick was pissed. His forehead wrinkled and his green eyes shot daggers at Jaylin. He spoke calmly and pointed his finger. "Don't you ever, come in here, and speak—

Jaylin slammed his fist on Frick's desk and spaced his words as he yelled. "What, time, do, you, want, me, in, court!"

Frick remained calm. "You're not listening to me Jaylin. I...

Jaylin reached for his checkbook and started to write. He ripped the check out and slammed it in front of Frick. Frick picked up the check and was taken aback by what was written on it. He then looked at Jaylin and cracked a tiny smile.

"You know my wife and I could use a new yacht," he said.

Jaylin stood up straight and rubbed his goatee. "And all my wife wants is a really good fuck. I can't give it to her if I'm still here, can I?"

"I guess not," Frick said standing up. He reached out for Jaylin's hand. "Nine o'clock Jaylin. And don't be late."

Jaylin just looked at his hand and turned his head towards me. "Let's get the fuck out of here. I'm getting screwed by everybody but Nokea, ain't I?"

I stood up and reached for Frick's hand. "See you tomorrow, Mr. Frick."

"Goodbye Shane. And, take your friend somewhere for a drink. I need him on good behavior tomorrow, alright Jaylin?"

Jaylin cut his eyes and walked out. I knew everything would be cool with him and Frick, but at times, they had their moments.

On the way out of Frick's office, Jaylin and I felt like a million dollars. Two Black men, sharply dressed, clean shaven and smelling good was enough to turn many heads. No doubt, I loved the attention and so did Jaylin. It was rather funny to see so many folks with big bright smiles, but underneath it all, we knew some were fake.

Since Jaylin had a big day ahead of him, I suggested going to get a bite to eat and heading back home. He agreed so we stopped at Morton's of Chicago for dinner.

The waiter seated us quickly, and when Jaylin's cell phone rang, he stepped away to take the call. I looked at the wine menu and ordered a bottle of expensive wine. When Jaylin returned he sat across the table.

"That was Frick ole punk ass. He wanted to ask me a few questions so he could have everything prepared for tomorrow."

"That's cool. Are you worried?"

"A lil bit, man. I just be glad when it's over."

"I feel you. After tomorrow, everything should be cool."

The waiter came back and we ordered our food. After he took our order, he leaned down and whispered.

"There's two lovely young ladies sitting nearby who would love to join the both of you for dinner. I told them I would ask, but it's completely up to you."

Jaylin didn't bother to look. I turned to the side and noticed two attractive Black women sitting at a table behind us. They waved and I waved back.

"What do you think, Jay?"

"Haven't you already got me in enough trouble? Besides, I don't think Scorpio would appreciate you having dinner with another woman, would she?"

I turned again, taking another glance. "Naw, she wouldn't approve. But, take a bottle of wine to their table," I suggested to the waiter. "Tell them that we appreciate the offer, but maybe some other time."

The waiter nodded and walked away.

"I had no idea you were still a playa," Jaylin said. "I thought you'd chilled, since things have taken off with you and Scorpio."

"I ain't no playa. I haven't been inside of another woman for quite some time."

"Hey, who needs another woman when you got somebody like Scorpio? She makes herself available to you twenty-four-seven, and all she likes to do is fuck, doesn't she?"

I wasn't too pleased with Jaylin's tone and I tried not to trip. "You know, I really wish you wouldn't make those comments about her. It's kind of like a low-blow, don't you think?"

"Low-blow or not, I'm just being honest. When I was shaking her down, I recall you and Stephon saying all kinds of shit about her. But as soon as we ended it, it didn't take either of you long to pick up where I left off."

"Listen, I thought you were cool with the situation. You sound bitter, or if not, jealous. That's the reason why I choose not to discuss her with you. You wouldn't understand how I felt if your life depended on it."

"So, how is it that you feel, Shane? Is she the woman of your dreams? Do you see yourself married to her, having more children? What about Mackenzie?"

"I haven't figured all that out yet. Our relationship is still young, and that's why we decided to not involve Mackenzie. Scorpio doesn't want her hurt again, and neither do I. As for being the woman of my dreams and marrying her, all I know is that I have feelings for her that I've never had for any other woman. In love? Yes. Also, I'm very protective of her. So, when you make your comments, I'd rather you keep them to yourself."

"Shane, whether you take it or not, I'm gon' give you some words of advice. There are some women who simply can not be in a committed relationship. For months, maybe even years, they do alright. But, there comes a time that one man is never enough. Scorpio just happens to be one of those women. She is slick and she uses her body and that magic she's got between her legs to manipulate men. If you lose focus, and it's obvious that you have, you will find yourself in a fucked up situation."

"You know what's funny, Jay. Exactly what you just said is a description of you. I don't think one woman is enough for you, and you're the one who's always referring to your thang as a "magic stick." I don't need to, nor have I ever allowed my dick to keep me in a relationship. I come with the ultimate package and aside from all of that, I treat my women with respect. It goes a long way, and my advice to you would be to stop stressing yourself about my relationship with Scorpio. If it doesn't work out, then so be it. Love will come and go, and as long as I stay true to myself, I will always have someone decent to look forward to."

Jaylin took a sip from his glass of wine and so did I. No doubt, the tension was thick. "Very good answer, Shane. And even though we are very good friends, you really don't know much about me. And the most insulting thing of all is your doubting my loyalty to Nokea. I've had more pussy than ten...fifty men put together. At times, I allowed pussy to be my driving force, my decision maker...just about my everything. But, when I decided to make Nokea my wife, she became all of thee above. That's what you do when you love somebody, and I, in no way, shape, form or fashion, see Scorpio as being your driving force, your decision maker, or your everything. I see her as being your sleep-in pussy. Nothing more, nothing less. Dispute it all you want, my brotha, but you will soon find out what I mean."

"Excellent come back, but I guess only time will tell. We are incapable of predicting the future, so we just got to sit back and let shit happen."

Jaylin lifted his glass of wine and we clinked them together. My insides were boiling, and if Scorpio ever betrayed me, especially for Jaylin, I would hurt her.

FELICIA
9

After being deprived my rest, starved and ordered to give more blood, I walked out of the darn hospital last night. I had Stephon come pick me up and he took me home so I could get some for-real rest. He left around 1:00 a.m., and I slept like a baby.

I couldn't wait for Monday to arrive, even though I had no intentions to show my face in court. It was too messed up and for the time being, I didn't want Jaylin to see how much damage he'd done. On my behalf, the attorney that Frick recommended came to see me. He decided to take my case and promised me that I had nothing to worry about. With that in mind, I woke up early and waited to hear from him. I knew the court hearing was at 9:00 a.m., but I was so anxious to find out how things would turn out. So anxious, that after looking at my watch a million times, I decided to go see for myself. Of course, with how messed up I was, I had to disguise myself. I figured I could wear some dark shades and wrap my head neatly with a scarf. I did just that, and when I looked in the mirror, I knew no one would recognize me.

By the time I reached the courtroom, several cases were already in session. The courtroom was crowded, so I took a seat in the far back. I sat between a fat White woman who looked like trailer trash and a Black man who could have easily been a bum on the streets. As I looked around, I didn't see Jaylin. My watch showed 10:15 a.m., and it was evident he was late. I did see my attorney, which was very good news to me, but he appeared to be quite nervous. He kept looking back at the double wooden doors, continuing to adjust his tie. The judge was an older White woman and she apparently wasn't up for a bunch of bullshit. Several times, she ordered people in the room to be quiet and got frustrated with an attorney who didn't have his shit together.

Soon, in walked Frick and I'll be damned if Jaylin wasn't right behind him. They had to be the most arrogant team I'd ever seen, and damn that fool Frick for lying to me about taking Jaylin's case. When they took a seat up front, he was all over Jaylin. Whispering in his ear, grinning and kissing his ass. Jaylin didn't seem nervous at all, but he sure as hell did look spectacular. So spectacular that even the judge had stopped to take a peek. His curly black healthy hair was trimmed and lined to perfection. The gray suit he had on fit every curve in his muscular frame and the goatee he wore had every woman in the courtroom nudging the person next to them. I listened to two ghettofied sistas in front of me, as they giggled and talked about taking him home with them. The silliness seriously worked my nerves, and when their heads turned to the back of the courtroom, that's when I saw Shane. They giggled some more and gave each other high-five.

Shane searched around for somewhere to sit, and when he looked in my direction, I dropped my head and started to lightly cough. Hopefully, he'd think I was contagious, and when I looked up again, thank God he took a seat on the other side of the room. The courtroom got a tad bit louder again, and the judge slammed down her gavel.

"Quiet, please," she yelled.

What a bitch, I thought. I hoped that she had PMS and was ready to give Jaylin exactly what he deserved.

Rushing the judge, once she finished laying down a $5000 fine to a felony shoplifter, Frick stood up and approached her. Whatever he said to her, she rolled her eyes and asked for the paperwork on Jaylin's case. For only a few minutes, she scanned the paperwork over, then called my attorney up front. There was a lot of whispering going on, but I really couldn't hear much. When Frick talked, she peered over her black framed glasses at Jaylin and then looked back at Frick. Her eyes scanned the paperwork again, and then she asked for Jaylin to come up front. When he stood up, somebody whistled. The judge's head snapped up and she looked over at the Bailiff.

"If that happens again, find out who it was and throw them out of here. I said quiet," she yelled.

Once Jaylin was upfront, the prosecutor rose up and stood beside Jaylin. It was a double whammy to have both the prosecutor and my attorney working on this case. That sucker Frick had his work cut out for him, and when I heard Jaylin's voice rise, I knew all hell was about to break loose.

"Flight risk," he said loud enough for everyone to hear. Frick placed his hand on Jaylin's chest and said something to my attorney and the prosecutor. The judge tuned in, shaking her head from side to side.

"I'm not going to deal with this right now," she also said loud enough for everyone to hear. "Your client will receive no special treatment, Mr. Frick, and he will have to wait."

Just then, I could have fainted when I saw stand-by-your-man, no matter what, Nokea. The bitch was too proud to take a seat, so she stood by the door with her arms folded. The only thing I could say was...the ho was clean. She wore a dark blue suit with a short skirt that hugged her curvaceous hips. Underneath was a hot pink silk blouse, a matching scarf was thrown around her neck and she wore strappy dark blue stilettos. Her layered hair was cut short and spiked a bit in the front. Makeup was flawless and the ring on her finger was blinding. As his wife, she didn't have to let it be known, because property of Jaylin Jerome Rogers' was written all over her. *Bitch*, I thought. Years of lying on her back had surely paid off.

Frustrated, I turned my head and things got even more heated. Apparently, Jaylin's interruptions were out of line and the judge made it perfectly clear to him that if he didn't shut his mouth, she would ask him to leave.

"Well, if I leave I'm going home," he said.

The prosecutor quickly spoke up. "This is why Mr. Frick's client is considered a flight risk. If he leaves, I assure you that he's going to become a fugitive."

Normally, Frick would've spoken up, but he didn't say nothing. Jaylin was fired up, and when he turned around to calm himself, he looked to the far back and saw Nokea. He stared without cracking a smile and so did she. When she rolled her eyes and looked away, he turned back around. I was cracking up inside because this was so hilarious. It was obvious that Nokea was mad at him, but I was sure that it wasn't nothing that a little...big dick wouldn't cure.

Either way, Jaylin got what he deserved. His mouth kept running, and not only did the judge deny his request to go home, but she also threatened to have him jailed for a long time if he didn't, "play by the rules."

Nokea was so angry that she walked out, and rushing to get to her, the judge stopped Jaylin before he stepped away.

"When I see you again, Mr. Rogers, make sure you're on time in my courtroom and do not interfere when I'm speaking. Do you understand?"

Jaylin didn't respond, so Frick spoke up for him. "He understands, Your Honor."

She got loud and ignored Frick. "Mr. Rogers, do you understand what I just said?"

The courtroom was so quiet that you could hear a pin drop. Jaylin turned to the judge, held his arms in front of him and looked at her. "Sorry, but I don't take orders."

There were more than a few snickers, so she slammed down her gavel and quickly called for the Bailiff. "Get him out of here. I don't have time for nonsense today. Next!"

I wanted to stand up and jump for joy, but I had to contain myself. The Bailiff took Jaylin away in handcuffs and Frick followed behind him. I leaned forward and whispered to the ghettofied chicks in front of me.

"Y'all won't be taking him home tonight," I laughed.

They looked at me like I was crazy and I stood up to exit. As I made my way to the door, so did Shane. I quickly dropped my head, held my fist to my mouth and coughed. He made the exit without noticing me. I stood for a few minutes, and then left.

No sooner had I made it to the elevator, Shane and Nokea stood close by talking. I would've given anything to be a fly on the wall, but I didn't want to get too close to them. Instead, I observed her playing her normal role, the pure and innocent wife. She appeared to be shaken up by what Shane said to her and it surely didn't take him long to make his next move. His arms eased around her waist and she moved in close, very close to him. It was almost sickening to watch, and if Jaylin stayed behind bars for long, I could only assume what would happen.

SHANE
10

Jaylin sure in the hell messed up the perfect opportunity to go home. I couldn't believe his arrogance, but then again, what did I expect? Nokea was just as furious as I was and she expressed her anger while sitting in my kitchen drinking coffee.

"Sometimes, I don't understand him, Shane. All he had to do was cooperate and he couldn't even do that. You have no idea how sick I am of all of this. At this point, I don't know what to do."

"Well, you can't go giving up on your marriage. Like I told him, sometimes things happen that are beyond your control. Every thing will work out, trust me."

Nokea sipped the coffee and dropped her head back. She closed her eyes, as if she was in deep thought. "What is going on between you and Scorpio? I didn't know the two of you were dating and it was serious."

"Yes, our relationship is pretty serious."

"Are you in love?"

"Yes, I'm in love."

She shook her head, and looked at me with disgust. "How did a man like you manage to hook up with such a...a—I don't even want to disrespect her in front of you."

"I appreciate that, and I know you ain't trying to hear this, but Scorpio has many good qualities, too. If she didn't, you know that Jaylin wouldn't have been with her for as long as he was."

"Jaylin was pussy whipped, Shane. Scorpio never gave him the security I've given him and that's what a man like him needs."

"Maybe, but you're speaking for Jaylin. You can't speak for me or for how I feel."

Nokea stood up and walked over to the sink. She washed the coffee mug and placed it in the cabinet. She then turned around and folded her arms in front of her.

"Why did you leave the two of them alone in your house? Don't you think something may have happened?"

"I left them alone because I trust the both of them. Are you saying that you don't trust Jaylin?"

"At this point, I don't trust him. When I called, they were close. The way Jaylin spoke, I could tell something wasn't right. Didn't you sense something...anything?"

I didn't want to upset Nokea, but she was right. Hell no, I didn't trust either of them, and something still didn't sit right with me. "Nokea, I don't know what to tell you. At times, I see a little something, but that's to be expected. I know Scorpio loves me and that's what I have to hang on to. You know how Jaylin feels too, so don't waste too much time tripping off their past feelings for each other."

"I guess you're right," she said. She came over to the table and picked up her purse. "I'm going to the hotel to get some rest. I'm so upset with Jaylin that I can't even speak to him right now. If he calls...

"If he calls, I'll let him know where you are, okay?"

Nokea nodded and I walked her to the door. It bothered me to see her so upset and I hoped like hell that Jaylin got his shit together.

Before leaving, Nokea turned to me while at the front door.

"Shane, what if Jaylin and Scorpio decide to be together? Have you given any thought to that scenario? I know you have."

"I...no, I haven't. It amazes me, though, that you're so insecure. Maybe losing the baby has you like this, but Jaylin loves you Nokea. He doesn't love Scorpio, and if he did, then he would be with her. Even though I'm his friend, I can't convince you that he loves you. That's something you have to know and feel for yourself."

"Well, right about now, I'm feeling betrayed." Her eyes watered. "I'm losing him, Shane, and we have fought for so many years...

I reached out for Nokea and comforted her in my arms. "You're not losing each other. Damn, baby, I wish you would understand...

"Nobody understands," she hurtfully said. "You don't understand unless you've walked in my shoes. I hate Scorpio. I hate what she's done to Jaylin and I hate what she's going to do to you." She pulled her head back, looking up at me with her watery eyes. "Don't you know what she's going to do to you? Can't you see that you deserve better?"

Before I could say another word, shockingly, Nokea's lips touched mine. They tasted too sweet to back away from, so I indulged myself, while holding the sides of her face and wiping her tears with my thumbs. It didn't take long for me to back away and come to my senses.

I placed my hands behind my head and spun around. "Damn! What in the fuck am I doing?"

Nokea stood and watched me panic.

"I'm sorry," she said. "I'm so, so sorry."

She hurried out the door, leaving it wide open.

JAYLIN
11

"Bullshit," I yelled at Frick as he waited to speak with the judge about releasing me. "This is bullshit and you know it! You stood there and didn't say shit! What in the hell is—

"Jaylin, we are not going to get through this unless you calm down. If you let me do my job, I promise to get you out of this mess. Felicia's attorney and I are very good friends. I assure you that we will work this where everybody is going to be happy. In the meantime, you need to sit tight, until I have a chance to speak with the judge. If she asks to speak with you, you'd better buckle down and change your attitude fast. Right about now, a bit of ass kissing might not hurt."

I didn't say nothing else to Frick because he knew I wasn't about to kiss anybody's ass. Now, if an apology was needed, I didn't have a problem with that, and the only reason I didn't mind was because I was anxious to get to Nokea.

When I saw her, damn, something just went all through me. I wanted to hold her so badly, just to let her know everything would be okay. I guess I fucked that up, but as soon as they released me, I planned to find my way to her.

By the time Frick made his way back to me, it was almost 6:00 p.m. I'd been released again, but Frick said the judge wouldn't accept an apology. All she wanted was to hear the case on Thursday, then decide what needed to be done. He made it clear that she was highly upset with me and Frick recommended trying to settle the issue out of court, especially the assault charge against Felicia. Frick felt as if the prosecutor charged me with carrying a loaded weapon, maybe I could get probation. But with both charges on the line, he was sure that the judge would stick it to me good. I told Frick to do whatever he felt was necessary and to not make any decisions without speaking to me first. He agreed. I went my way and he went his.

No sooner had I got in the car, I called Nokea's cell phone. She didn't answer, so I called it again. Still no answer, so I called Shane's house. He picked up and quickly tore into me.

"I can't believe how incredibly stupid you are. You had a chance to be back at home with your wife and children, but you blew it!"

"Man, I was doomed the moment I stepped into that bitch's courtroom. Her attitude was messed up and I wasn't about to kiss her ass."

"If it meant being with my family, I sure in the hell would have."

"That's the difference between you and me, Shane. You's a fake nigga, and I'm a real nigga. Now, forget all this shit. Is there any chance that my wife is there with you?"

"Nope. She was with me earlier, but she went to a hotel to get some rest. If you'd wait a minute, I'll tell you which hotel she's at."

Shane placed me on hold for a minute, and then came back to the phone. "She's at the Downtown Marriott. I can't quite make out the room number but it's, 42 ssssomething."

"Thanks. I'll call you later."

I hung up and headed to the Marriott.

A while later, I pulled up to valet parking in my rented Mercedes and the valet gave me a ticket. I rushed into the hotel and went to the counter. The desk clerk looked at me and smiled.

"May I help you, sir?"

"Yes. I was hoping that you could tell me what room number my wife is in? Her name is Nokea Rogers."

The desk clerk typed Nokea's name into the computer and came up empty.

"Then, check Nokea Brooks. That's her maiden name."

She checked again, but then said that she couldn't provide me with any information.

"What do you mean, you can't provide me with any information?"

"What I mean, sir, is she requested not to be disturbed."

I let out a deep sigh and stroked my goatee. "Listen, I'm having a bad motherfuckin' day. Would you please tell me what room number my wife is in so I can see her?"

"Sir, I'm sorry. It is our policy...

"Fuck your policy! Get me a manager, now!"

"I'm afraid that he's going to tell you the same thing."

"We'll see about that," I said, seething with anger. This day was just unbelievable! How many fools was I gon' have to disrespect today? Damn!

As I waited for the manager, I called Nokea's cell phone again. She didn't answer, but I told her I was in the lobby. I begged her to stop tripping and to call me back.

When the manager came to the counter, thank God, he was a brotha. I pulled him aside and briefly explained my situation to him.

"Mr. Rogers, if your wife hadn't requested her privacy, there would be no problem giving you her room number. Unfortunately, ...

"Tell me how much it'll cost me. Whatever you want, I'll give it to you."

The manager hesitated, but when I heard Nokea call my name, I turned around. She didn't say anything, just walked away and I followed behind her. We walked in silence to the elevator, and when we made it to her room, she still wouldn't say anything to me.

"I guess silence is golden, huh?" I said, as we went inside. Ignoring me, she stepped out of her high heels and took a seat at the round table. She crossed her legs and stared at me from across the room. Looking awfully beautiful, I felt as if now was the perfect time to kiss a little ass—literally.

I stepped out of my shoes and walked over to her. I kneeled in front of her, rubbing her hands with mine.

"Aren't you as happy to see me as I am to see you?" I asked.

She held a blank stare on her face. "Why does Scorpio have a salon named Jay's? And, are you living a double life and I don't know about it?"

I let out a deep sigh. "Baby, I—who gives a fuck what Scorpio has? I am just glad to be here with you at this moment, this day and this time."

"So, you knew about Jay's, didn't you? Or, did you purchase the place for her? It's kind of obvious because I know she can't afford to run an establishment like that unless somebody with your money...excuse me, but with *our* money provided it for her."

Again, I was taken aback by Nokea's tone and demeanor. Not only that, but her referencing *our* money kind of pissed me off. Don't get it twisted, what's mine is hers, but if she ever decided to trip with me, well...let's just say that she very well could be left without.

This time, I was the one who ignored her. I stood up and pulled my suit jacket away from my chest. She reached for my tie and yanked it to pull me to her.

"Answer me, Jaylin. I want to know right now about this lie you've been living."

I pulled my tie away from her hands, straddled my hands on the arms of the chair and spoke calmly to her. "How in the hell have I been living a double life when I've been in Florida with you for the last two years? I visited St. Louis three times, Nokea, and unfortunately, one of those visits didn't go too well. I only learned of Jay's a few months ago, and if you would like to know where Scorpio got the money from, then maybe you should ask her. Now, are you planning on allowing her to ruin what we have or can I count on you to see things for what they really are?"

"You want me to see things for what they really are, or would you like for me to see things for what you tell me they are? If anything, you are dead wrong to expect me not to question you about this...this messed up situation." I searched deep into Nokea's eyes and her voice started to crack. "I saw with my own eyes, Jaylin, a CD that showed how hungry you were for her. You couldn't resist her, or her lips when she kissed you. Don't expect me to forget when she went down on you, and you didn't even ask her to stop. You didn't come home until midnight the next day, and the look of shame was written all over your face. Then, yesterday...let's not even go there. You place yourself in a house, alone, with her. And you expect me not to trip?" Nokea closed her eyes and dropped her face into her hands. She started to cry. "How can you keep doing this? How could you?"

After seeing her cry, I was crushed and my heart ached. Since we'd been married, I promised myself that I would never, ever cause her hurt again. I inched backwards and sat on the edge of the bed. I massaged my hands together and shamefully lowered my head.

"Baby, where did I go wrong? That's all I want to know," I said swallowing hard. "Since we've been married, I have never cheated on you. Have I thought about it? I...I would be lying to you if I said that I hadn't. Just because I've thought about another woman, it doesn't mean that I love you any less. And it for damn sure doesn't make you any less of a woman. It's a man thing, and even I, myself, don't sometimes understand why we do some of the things that we do. But, I assure you that I will never act upon those feelings. Those feelings are only momentarily and they are never worth losing what I have. Trust me, I'm no fool, Nokea, and neither are you. I know your gut is telling you the truth about us, isn't it?"

She didn't answer. She wiped her teary eyes and continued to look down at the floor. I kneeled over to her and lifted her chin.

"Tell me, Nokea. What is your gut feeling about trusting me? I know you do, you've got to. We wouldn't have made it this far without trust." I slowly stood up.

She moved her head from side to side. "I don't like the idea of you thinking about sex with another woman. That frightens me because I never think about having sex with other men."

"Baby, but men and women, we are so different. Like I said, I can't explain it, but you have nothing to worry about. Come here," I said, and then pulled her up from the chair. I held her tightly in my arms, and like always, her body next to mine felt good. She eased her arms around my waist and I placed my hands on the sides of her face. I kissed her tears, and then placed my mouth on her sweet quivering lips. Soon, my tongue left my mouth and entered hers. That alone excited the both of us and it was a rush to the finish line as we quickly removed our clothes.

As Nokea stood naked, I picked her up and straddled her on my hips. She wrapped her arms around my neck and rubbed the back of my head.

"I love you," she whispered.

"I love you, too. That's why I say to hell with them doctors. Every opportunity we get, we gon' try to make another baby, alright?"

Nokea nodded.

I backed up to the table and placed her on top of it. As she continued to rub the back of my head, I lowered it and circled my tongue around her chocolate and severely hard right nipple. After I worked the right one, I made my way to the left. Nokea's arms left my shoulders and she dropped her hand down below. She held my dick in her hand and started to massage it. She stroked it so good that it instantly grew long and navigated its way between her legs. We both held it in place, but before I went inside, I had a dying need to taste her. I took a few steps back, turned her on her stomach and separated her legs. She bent over and I squatted down behind her. I kissed all over her ass and gazed between her legs. It was a pretty ass sight and all I could do was smile.

"You are in major trouble," I said, as my curled tongue entered her from the backside. I leaned in and licked her slit wide open. I tasted her from every angle that I could and used the tips of my thick fingers to massage her clit. On fire, she started to heavily breathe and her legs weakened.

"Do…do you know how anxious I've been for you?" she moaned in a passionate, oh-I'm-getting-ready-to-cum voice.

I slowed my licks, used more of my fingers to bring down her juices and held my dick to get it ready. "Don't, tell me how anxious you are, show me."

As I felt her insides tighten, I stood up and slid myself right in. Nokea reached around my ass and dug her fingernails deeply into it. I pumped hard, and the faster I pumped, the more she came. She pressed her ass against me and called my name like I rarely heard her call it before.

"Yes, Mrs. Roger," I said, holding her waist. "Are you alright?"

"I'm more than alright," she said, backing me up to the bed. I laid back and she crawled backwards to straddle my face. She fell forward to go down on me, but I stopped her.

"Head is good. But, daddy would like to feel the insides of his pussy again."

Nokea smiled and scooted down. "Whatever it is that daddy wants, daddy gets."

Nokea for damn sure didn't lie. She put an arch in her back and did overtime work on me. Her insides were filled with juices, and the sounds that it made every time that she jolted down on me, turned me on. I couldn't stop coming, and sex between me and my wife had been long overdue. By the time we finished, I was one happy man and she was a sore, completely satisfied woman. Hopefully, I'd keep her that way.

NOKEA
12

Making love to my husband was the best, but it still didn't cause my insecurities to go away. There was no doubt he loved me, but there was still something about Scorpio that was bugging the hell out of me. When I talked to Shane, yes, he told me about his relationship with her. He explained why she and Jaylin were at his house alone, and even though he told me what was up, he still seemed unsure about the whole thing, too. When I asked what Scorpio was doing with herself these days, that's when he told me about Jay's. I couldn't believe it. She had the nerve to name an establishment after my husband? What was wrong with this chick? Didn't she realize what they had was over? To me, for a woman to hold on to a man for as long as Scorpio had, either he was telling her what she wanted to hear, or else she was crazy.

By morning, I was worn out. My insides felt good when Jaylin was inside of me, but after going at it for so many hours, I surely felt exhausted. While at home, I missed his touch, his kiss and his loving. I hadn't planned on coming to St. Louis, but when Scorpio answered Shane's phone, something told me to get up and get packing. Of course, I wanted to show him some support too, but I really felt as if he needed to learn a valuable lesson from his mistake. Yes, I was upset about him putting his hands on a woman, but I was more upset with Felicia for continuously poking her nose where it didn't belong. She and Scorpio, both, needed to get some serious business and move on with their lives.

Jaylin was sound asleep. I eased out of bed and went into the bathroom to take a shower. Once I finished, I planned to pay Ms. Valentino a visit at Jay's. Jaylin told me if I wanted answers to ask her, and that was what I intended to do. For whatever reason, I wanted to know, from her, if she was really over Jaylin. Even though Shane and Jaylin said she was, the CD revealed otherwise.

As I was in deep thought about meeting with her, Jaylin startled me when he stepped into the shower behind me. He wrapped his strong arms around my petite frame and kissed my cheek.

"Good morning," he said. "Why didn't you wake me so that I could join you?"

"Because you were looking so peaceful and I knew you needed your rest."

"I do, but I thought we were going to stay here all day and rest together? I saw your clothes laid out on the bed. Where are you going?"

"Nowhere special. I haven't seen my best friend, Pat, since Lord knows when, so I'm having dinner with her today. Before that, I'd like to stop by my old job and visit some of my ex co-workers. And when I leave here, I'm going to my parents' house."

"You hadn't planned on taking me with you?"

"Of course, but...but I thought you might want to get some rest. Being in jail so much might have tired you out."

Jaylin laughed and turned me around to face him. He pecked my lips and lowered his hands to my butt. I felt his goodness press against me and backed away.

"You couldn't be serious," I said. "After all I gave to you hours ago, you have the nerve to get hard?"

"I'm not hard, Nokea, but I'm getting there. Besides, what's so wrong with me getting turned on after seeing my wife in the shower naked? If I wasn't hard, you'd be complaining."

I rubbed the side of his handsome face and sucked his wet lips with mine. "Okay, listen," I said. "We need to cut a deal, right here and right now."

"What's the deal?"

"On Thursday, if you promise not to show your butt like you did yesterday in the courtroom, and to respect the judge when she speaks to you, I'll promise that when I get back, we'll make love as much as you want to."

"We gon' do that anyway, but only because I love you will I make such a deal. I know I be tripping, but I just get so angry when anybody try to talk down on me. I had enough of that when I was a kid and...

"And you miss your children so much that you'll do whatever it takes to get back to them—soon."

"And, that too," he said, kissing me.

After we washed and dried each other off, Jaylin got back in bed and I got dressed. He said that he wanted to stay and talk to Frick, so that relieved me from not being honest about my traveling plans today. I wasn't sure how he'd feel about me going to see Scorpio, but I knew he wanted me to get over what had happened. That, of course, was easier said than done. All I wanted to do was protect what was mine and what for surely belonged to me.

Dressed to impress, I wore my Dolce & Gabbana red linen strapless dress that hugged my curves. My hair was neatly layered and my already long lashes required little mascara. My lips were glossed with Mac, and my sweet smell had Jaylin shaking his head.

"Where did you say you were going?" he asked.

"I already told you," I said, grabbing my D & G red and black handbag that matched my ribbon-tied stilettos. "I shouldn't be that long, but I'll call to check in on you from time to time."

"Yeah, you do that. Every hour on the hour," he joked.

I snickered and kissed my husband goodbye.

Since Shane told me where Jay's was, I went straight to it. I sat for a moment in the rented BMW and looked at the fancy letters, JAY'S, painted on the glass windows. *How dare her*, I thought. And seeing Jay's for myself made me madder. I got out of the car and headed inside. When I pushed on the door, it chimed. I was immediately stared down by four pretty decent Black women and an Asian woman who was giving a pedicure. Everybody had a customer, so the one who appeared to be the oldest, invited me to have a seat.

"Thanks, but I'm not here to get my hair done. I'm looking for Scorpio Valentino. Is she around?"

"Whom shall I ask is here to see her," the woman asked.

"Nokea. Nokea Rogers."

The woman who questioned me took a quick glance at another woman beside her. "Jamaica, would you buzz Scorpio and tell her Nokea is here to see her?"

Jamaica touched an intercom button and talked into it.

"Miss Boss Lady, are you there?"

"Yeah, I'm here Jamaica. What's up?"

"There's a Nokea out here to see you. Shall I send her back or send her away?"

"Who?"

"Nokea RAH-JERS. She said her name with emphasis so maybe it means something to you and not to me."

Scorpio didn't respond, and within seconds, she appeared near the back of the shop. Always trying to show off her body, she had on a pair of tight hip-hugging jeans. Her leopard print blouse was sleeveless and the middle of it draped down to show her cleavage. She was braless, and as low as her jeans were, probably pantyless, too. Since the last time I'd seen her, her curly bouncing hair had grown even longer. And just by looking at her, HELL NO I didn't trust Jaylin alone with her! Something had to have happened.

"May, I help you," she said, walking towards me in her high stilettos.

"Do you mind if we go somewhere private and talk?"

Without saying a word, she turned around and I followed behind her. I checked out her place and was getting angrier by the minute. It was put together rather nicely, but I had a feeling as if my husband's money had paid for the entire place.

Scorpio opened the door to her office and it was laid out. Leather couch and sofa, plasma television on the wall, silver and glass desk, flat screen monitor and a Jacuzzi room in the corner. I had a loss for words and took a seat on the couch, as she'd already asked me to. She got comfortable in a chair across from me.

"Nokea, as you can see, I don't have a lot of time on my hands so make this quick."

"What is going on between you and Jaylin, Scorpio? Why is it that you continue to interfere with what we have? Once you answer both of those questions for me, I'll be out of here."

"Memories are all that I have of *your* husband. I'm not trying to turn back the hands of time, because I've found true love elsewhere. As for interfering, you'll have to explain that one to me. How is it that I'm interfering with your marriage?"

I sighed and figured she would BS around. "Scorpio, look. By now, I'm sure you know I've seen the CD. If that wasn't your attempt to interfere, I don't know what was. You knew Jaylin and I were married, yet you tried to seduce him, and went down on him. What kind of woman are you? After that night, I don't know what transpired between the two of you. I need clarification, from you, that nothing happened."

"Jaylin is known for being an honest man. Have you asked *him* what transpired between us after that night?"

"I'd rather hear it from you. That's provided, you don't mind being honest about it."

Scorpio leaned back in the chair and crossed her legs. "Nothing happened between us Nokea. It was supposed to, and you'd better believe I intended to give myself to Jaylin that night. After he left Jay's, I thought I could make things as good as they used to be. I prepared myself for one hell of a night, and so did he. However, for whatever reason, we got cold feet. For one thing, I wanted a future with him, but all he wanted was sex. One night with him wasn't good enough for me, so I guess that's why I changed my mind. The next thing I knew, Shane brought me a letter from Jaylin that basically said, "Sorry, maybe some other time." Yet again, he hurt me. But, that was then and this is now. Now, I'm happy and that's what's important to me."

"So, are you saying you're over Jaylin? And since you're being so honest, how did it feel being alone with him the other day? You can't expect me to believe old feelings didn't rekindle."

"I'll never be over Jaylin, Nokea." She placed her hand on her chest. "He's in my heart and that's where he will forever stay. And every time I see him, yes, a part of me yearns for him. It's hard not to think about what we once shared, but I've made up in my mind that we could never go back. Shane has shown me…

"What if there was no Shane? What if Shane didn't exist? Pursuing Jaylin wouldn't be a done deal for you, would it?"

"If there wasn't no Shane, then I'd say you'd have a big problem on your hands. Remember, though, I can pursue Jaylin all I want. You'd just better make sure he can't be persuaded. And from my experience, just within the last few days, that might not be as difficult as I thought it might be."

Now, it was clear that she was screwing around with my head. "What is that supposed to mean? How close did you and Jaylin get at Shane's place?"

She got up from her chair, leaning in close to my face. The tip of her nose touched mine. "This close," she whispered. She moved back and stood up. "Now, your two questions have turned into ten. I'd like to get back to work, if you don't mind."

I grabbed my purse and slid the straps on my shoulder. "Speaking of work, would it be too much to ask why this place is not named after your current lover, instead of your past lover? I'm sure that might cause trouble in your current relationship, especially since you've claimed to have moved on."

"Jay's is here to stay, Nokea. He's not...this place isn't going anywhere. Besides, why would I change the name after *all* Jaylin has done for me? It's the least I could do for a man who has given me so, so much."

I snickered and headed for the door. Having just one more thought, I quickly turned and raised my finger. She couldn't help but notice the pink tinted, princess cut diamond ring on my finger. "Before I go, Scorpio, I want to make one thing clear. I might appear to be a bit insecure about my marriage, but I trust Jaylin with everything that I have. It's women like you who I don't trust, and if you were looking for me to come up in here and clown, sorry, but clowning is only for a woman who is afraid of losing her man. I fear nothing, especially when I know, as I've always known, that it takes more than a woman opening her legs to remove Jaylin from where he belongs. If he can ever be persuaded by your advances towards him, then I'd consider him one big fool. A fool is a person I refuse to be married to, and if he ever falls into that category, I'd be more than happy to sign him away to you. For the record, that's never going to happen. So, for your sake, I hope things truly work out for you and Shane. To me, he can do better, but that's just my opinion, of course."

She gave me a fake smile, "And, your opinion doesn't mean a damn thing to me. And for your records, don't be so sure of yourself. I took Jaylin away from you once, and if I wanted to, I very well could do it again."

I smiled and stepped into the hallway. "All you did was take his dick away from me and I refused to make use of it while it was in yours and other women's possession. You never took his heart away from me, Scorpio, and if you did, you'd be his wife, not me."

Not saying another word, Scorpio reached for the door and was about to slam it in my face. I pushed it open and couldn't help but slap her across the face. Her head snapped to the side and she stunningly held her cheek with an annoying grin on her face.

"That's for causing me to lose my child. I owe you way more than that, but in the meantime, a slap will have to do." I walked away from the door and headed out.

When I made it back to the car, I sat inside for a moment and leaned my head back on the headrest. I felt good about my *chat* with Scorpio, but her description of being "this close" to Jaylin had me thinking. The thoughts of him touching her and continuously being around her kept stirring in my head. I tightly closed my eyes, trying desperately to erase my thoughts. I pulled off, and almost immediately, my cell phone rang. I looked to see who it was, and it was Jaylin calling from the hotel.

"Hey," I said in a soft voice.

"Didn't I tell you to call me every hour on the hour?"

"I didn't think you were serious."

"That's because I wasn't. I just called to see what you were up to. I miss you."

"Well, I just left my parents' house. I'm on my way to my ex employer, then I'm going to have an early dinner with Pat at Café Lapedero. I'll call you after I leave there."

"Okay. But, are you alright? You sound as if something is wrong."

I placed my hand on my forehead. "I'm fine, Jaylin. I'm just a bit tired, that's all."

"Then hurry back so I can rock you to sleep."

"I will," I said, and then hung up.

My throat ached, because even though I hated to admit it, some of the things Scorpio said made me sick to my stomach. I tried hard to gather myself and waited patiently for the light to turn green. After it did, I drove for about a half a mile and then parked beside a parking meter. I looked at the name on the building to my right and it showed Jefferson & Associates. It had been two years since I walked away from Collins. My marriage to him was a huge mistake. I knew I loved Jaylin, but I thought marrying Collins would make the feelings I had for Jaylin go away. What nerve did I have to show up at his doorstep? He was devastated by my decision to divorce him, and his final words to me were, "as long as you're happy."

I got out of the car, dropped some change in the parking meter and headed inside. I waited until the receptionist ended her call and then approached her.

"Is Collins Jefferson available?" I asked.

"I think he's still in a meeting, but let me check. If he's not, who shall I say is here to see him?"

"Nokea. He'll know who I am."

She dialed Collins' office and told him I was there to see him. After she hung up, she looked up at me.

"He said he'll be right up."

"Thank you," I said with a queasy feeling in my stomach. I continued to stand by the receptionist and could see Collins making his way down the hall. *What a man*, I thought. Almost two years had gone by and he still looked the same. Him and Denzel Washington could pass for twins and the way he walked with so much confidence was admirable.

When he saw me, his face lit up and he gave me the biggest smile ever. I smiled back, even harder when he wrapped his arms tightly around me.

"You just made my day," he whispered and rocked my body with his.

I let go of our embrace and looked up at him. "And how's that? Were you having a bad day?"

"Let's just say that it's been chaotic." He took my hand. "Come on. Let's go back to my office."

The hand holding gesture was a bit much, but I went with the flow. We walked into Collins' office and he closed the door behind us. He told me to have a seat and I sat in the chair in front of his desk.

"What did I do to deserve this blessing today?" he asked, taking a seat across from me.

"I was in town, so I stopped by to see you. I often wonder about how you're doing. Wasn't sure if you moved back to Detroit or not."

"Naw, we wound up closing the office in Detroit. After you left, I was having some personal, as well as financial problems. For the last year or so, I jumped back on my feet and things are good, Nokea."

"I'm glad to hear that. I know our divorce was hard on you, but it was hard on me, too. More than anything, I regretted hurting you so much."

Collins clinched his hands together and stared at me. "Is that so called husband of yours treating you right?"

"Yes, Collins, Jaylin and I are doing well."

"Your eyes tell me a different story. You know darn well that you don't have to front for me."

"No, honestly, we are fine. I'm here because I wanted to stop in to say hello. I often said that if I ever came back to St. Louis, I'd have to stop in and check on you."

Collins shrugged his shoulders. "Okay, if you insist. But, why are you here? On business, to see your parents, what?"

"Business. Jaylin has some business to tend to and I came along with him."

"So, how's ole Pretty Boy doing these days? I hope and pray that he realizes how lucky he is."

"Like I said, Jaylin is doing well. We have another child, a girl, and her name is Jaylene. I would love to show you her picture, but it's inside of my other purse."

Collins was quiet for a few seconds, then cleared his throat. "So, you all have two children now?"

"Yes. It would've been three, but I...I lost the third one."

"Say it ain't so." He was really trying to feel me out, and when he sat up straight and rubbed his waves, he pushed more. "How'd you lose the baby?"

I was barely able to look at him. "I had an accident. I fell down the stairs and injured myself and the baby."

"I'm sorry to hear that. I'm sure the loss was devastating for the both of you."

"You couldn't even imagine."

Collins pushed his chair back and stood up. He walked around his desk and sat on the edge of it in front of me. He folded his arms, looking down at me. "Something is not right with you, Nokea. Just in case you forgot, I used to be your husband. I won't pressure you into telling me, but I want you to know that if you ever need me, and I do mean ever, I'm here. I know you don't want to hear this, but I have to say it. I think when you ended our marriage that was the biggest mistake of your life. Pretty Boy can't love you like I do, because he doesn't know how to. Most likely, he's still in the process of trying to figure it out, but in the meantime, if comfort is what you came here for." Collins snapped his fingers. "I'd be there in a snap."

I stood up and reached out to Collins. We wrapped our arms around each other and then I let go. "Thanks for the talk. I have to go," I said, making my way to the door. "It was really good seeing you, Collins."

As I placed my hand on the doorknob, he rushed up behind me. He reached up and held the door closed with his hand.

"Before you leave, can I take you to dinner? I might not ever get this opportunity again, and I still have so much I need to tell you."

"Then, tell me now. I'm not sure about dinner...

Collins leaned in further and placed his lips on the side of my neck. I inched over to stop him. "Please don't do that," I said.

"I can't help it. I swear to God that Jaylin doesn't deserve you. What I want to tell you is that I still love you. I want to make love to you and never let you out of my sight. My relationships have not been right, because I find myself comparing every woman to you. I've tried hard to get over you, but the way you left me still hurts...

I turned around to face Collins. "I'm sorry, but I'm a different woman...

"Dinner. Just have dinner with me. That's all I ask. After that, you can go home to your husband and live happily ever after."

"I'll call you later, Collins. I'm not sure if that's a good idea or not."

He dropped his hand from the door and pulled the knob. "Dinner, Nokea. It would truly mean a lot to me."

I walked out, and on that note, I left. I headed back to my car and was pissed off when I saw I'd gotten a ticket. I snatched it from the windshield, putting it inside of my purse. I wasn't sure about having dinner with Collins, but suspected that it wouldn't hurt a thing.

FELICIA
13

My face might have been jacked up from Jaylin, but it surely didn't affect me in no way down below. After I told Stephon about what had happened in court, we got a good laugh and wound up in my bedroom tearing it up. He was so supportive of the whole situation, and once all of this mess was taken care of, I was going to make sure that, financially, he got what he deserved.

Since my attorney called and told me that we needed to meet, I made Stephon stay in my bedroom and put on my game face as a devastated, I'm-for-damn-sure-damaged-for-life victim. As soon as he rang the doorbell, I stalled before answering. I gathered my pink cotton robe in the front and slowly walked to the door with a cup of hot tea in my hand.

"Hello, Mr. Glasgow. Please come in."

He smiled and walked inside. He followed me to the kitchen and I offered him a seat.

"I know you said that everything went okay yesterday, but where do we go from here," I asked.

"Well, how you want to move forward will determine the outcome. If you decide to drop the case against Jaylin, Frick and I can settle this matter out of court. Or, you can take it to trial with his other case, and hope that the jury finds him guilty. That could turn into a long process. However, if you would like to see him go to jail for what he did, then I'd suggest you pursue this case to the fullest."

"But, what if the jury doesn't convict him? Is there another way?"

"Felicia, honestly, I'd hate to see you waste the courts time."

My voice switched to a higher pitch. "How would I be wasting the courts time? This man tried to kill me. As a citizen, I thought that's why the courts were put in place to protect...

Glasgow touched my hand. "Calm down, Felicia. My only concern is Mr. Frick. He's got a way of twisting things around, and when I spoke with him earlier, he's prepared to get Jaylin out of this mess. I think it would be in your best interest to settle this matter out of court. From what Frick said, you could stand to gain a lot of money by going that route."

Finally, he was talking what I wanted to hear. "Well, how much money are we talking?"

"Apparently, Jaylin is anxious to get this over with. I'll go in with a high amount and let him negotiate from there."

"High end? What do you consider high end?"

"One hundred thousand dollars."

My mouth hung open. "Are you serious? Do I look like I'm prepared to accept one hundred thousand dollars! Look, I am a successful businesswoman, Mr. Glasgow. Davenports earns one hundred thousand dollars plus in a year's time. The money you're offering is chump change for what I've been through. In case Frick hasn't informed you, Jaylin Rogers is worth M-I-L-L-I-O-N-S. He's got plenty of money and I want a piece of it."

"Felicia, maybe there's some kind of mix up here. Frick informed me about Jaylin's financial status, but he never classified him as being a millionaire. Maybe you're...

I snapped, as Frick was playing Glasgow. "Frick is playing you for a fool. I, on the other hand, know better. I've known Jaylin for a very long time, and trust me when I tell you that he is loaded with money. Now, why don't you and Frick collaborate on this again? One hundred thousand, minus your fees, will not suffice."

Glasgow scooted the chair back and picked up his briefcase. "Give me another day or two, Felicia. I'll be in touch."

I didn't say another word. I walked him to the door and he left.

Surely, I was about to cancel his ass and get me another attorney that I could trust. I'd already considered suing Frick for how badly he dissed me, and once all of this settled, I sure in the hell planned to. What he did to me was low. I don't care how much money Jaylin paid him. Frick should have stepped away from the entire case and been done with it.

After Glasgow left, I headed back into the bedroom where Stephon was. Even though he'd given up the drugs, cigarettes became his alternative. Not only did I hate the smoke, but I hated the smell even more.

"How did it go?" he asked while sitting up in bed. I pulled the covers back and eased in next to him.

"It didn't go so well, Stephon. He wants me to settle out of court, and if I do, the money he's proposing wouldn't be enough to satisfy my addiction to Saks Fifth Avenue for a year."

"How much was it?"

"One hundred thousand dollars."

Stephon smashed the cigarette in an ashtray and pulled his head back in disbelief. "You wouldn't settle for a hundred thousand? That's a lot of money, Felicia."

"Stephon, don't play yourself, alright? If I settle for a hundred G's, I have to pay Glasgow 20% of that. Then, the rest will be split between us. Forty thousand dollars ain't no money. You tell me, how quickly can you blow forty G's?"

"If I was thinking about remodeling the barbershop, then I can forget it. And, I've had that BMW for quite some time. Yeah, I guess you're right. Besides, I'm sure that Jaylin can do much better than that."

I nodded. "Ya, see. Now, that's what I'm saying. He can do a whole lot better than that."

The phone rang and I reached over to answer.

"Felicia," Glasgow said.

"Yes."

"Are you up to meeting with Frick, Jaylin and myself tomorrow?"

"I thought you could handle this without me?"

"I thought so, too, but Frick and I agreed that a meeting between all parties involved would be better."

"I guess. But, I surely hope you get a backbone before our meeting tomorrow. Frick seems to have Jaylin's back pretty well and I need you to have mines even better."

"That's what you're paying me for, Felicia. I'll see you at Frick's office at 10:00 a.m. sharp."

I hung up and turned to Stephon. "Are you busy tomorrow?"

"Nope. Why?"

"Because I want you to go with me tomorrow. You haven't seen Jaylin in a long time and I think it's about time that the two of you got reacquainted."

Stephon nodded and displayed a devilish grin.

JAYLIN
14

When Nokea came through the door, I had just ended my call with Frick. He said that Glasgow had convinced Felicia to settle, and that we'd meet to discuss it at 10:00 a.m. tomorrow. I was surprised to see Nokea back so early. And when I asked what happened to her dinner plans with Pat, she said they decided to cancel them until tomorrow.

"Why? You and her still cool, ain't y'all?"

"Yes, we're very cool. It was me who cancelled. I just felt like coming here and spending the rest of my day with you. I know you have to be back in court on Thursday, but I miss our children. I spoke to Nanny B and she said that LJ's been asking for us. I talked to him and I promised him I would be home on Thursday. I hope we can wrap this up soon so things can go back to the way they were."

I lay in the bed and held my arms out for Nokea. She really seemed as if all she needed was a hug. She kicked off her shoes and got in the bed with me. "Baby, I talked to Nanny B and the kids today, too. I know they miss us and I apologize for keeping us away from them like this. If this thing drags on beyond Thursday, go back home. I just can't see it taking up weeks at a time, but LJ and Jaylene need you as well."

Nokea agreed and laid her head on my chest. Within minutes, she was asleep. Thinking about tomorrow, I sat up for a while and messed around on my laptop beside me.

By morning, I was the first one to wake up. Nokea still had on her clothes from yesterday, so I kissed her forehead numerous times to wake her. She slowly opened her eyes and looked up at me.

"Is it morning already," she yawned.

"Six o'clock to be exact. And it's time for both of us to get up."

Nokea took a deep breath. "It's too early, Jaylin. What do we have to do this early in the morning?"

"Hey, a deal is a deal. If my calculations are correct, sex between us could take about two hours, we'll most likely spend one hour cleaning up, and then spend one hour getting dressed for my meeting with Frick today."

"No thanks to all of thee above. I'm too tired for sex, I don't feel like putting up with Frick's arrogance today, and besides, Pat took the day off so we could spend some time together. I told her I would meet her at her house by 9:00 a.m., we'd have lunch by noon, shop until three, four, or five, and then, you can have me all to yourself. I promise."

"Alright, that's cool. But, don't be too late getting your fine self back to me. If things don't work out for me tomorrow in court, you might not have me next to you for...

"I'm going to remain optimistic. And so should you. Just remember what this terrible mistake of yours has cost us, and never, ever do anything this stupid again, okay?"

"Never," I agreed.

By 9:00 a.m., Nokea was heading out to her adventurous day with Pat.

"See you later, baby," I said. "Have a superb day and call me if you need me."

"Same here," she said, rising up on the tips of her toes to give me a kiss. We smacked lips for a long while, and afterwards, she left.

After searching for my sock, I sat on the edge of the bed to put it on. I heard a cell phone ring, and knowing that mine was in my pocket, I knew it had to be Nokea's. Apparently, she'd left it. I followed the sounds of the ringing phone and realized they were coming from her purse she carried yesterday. I opened her purse and reached for her phone.

"Hello," I answered.

"Jaylin, this is Pat. How are you, darling?"

"I'm fine. How about you?"

"Just dandy. Where's my girl at? I told her to be here at 9:00 a.m., and not to be late."

"She left not too long ago. Give her another fifteen or twenty minutes, she should be there soon."

"Okay. And, I hate that I didn't get a chance to see you. Why don't you catch up with us later? We're having lunch at Café Lapadero around noon."

"Pat, I have too much on my plate. I'm not sure how long my meeting with Frick will be, but if I don't get a chance to see you this time, you can always come visit us in Florida. Nokea really misses you, and I wish you could visit more often."

"Me too, but money is tight. Now, if you send for me, that's a different story."

I laughed. "I just might have to do that, especially if it makes my baby happy."

"Well, let me know. In the meantime, take care and if I don't see you today, I'll see you soon."

Pat hung up and I reached for Nokea's purse to put her phone back inside. When I did, I pulled out a parking ticket she'd gotten yesterday. The jurisdiction said Clayton, Missouri and when I looked at the nearest address, it was very familiar to me. I rubbed my goatee and was in deep thought. Soon after, a thought kind of hit me. Jefferson & Associates was in the same vicinity. I rushed over to grab the yellow pages, and when I compared Jefferson & Associates address to the address on the ticket, they were exactly the same.

WTF, I thought. What the hell did she go see Collins for? I replayed yesterday and this morning in my mind and Nokea had been acting real strange. Yesterday, I called her three times and she never called me. When she came in, she didn't even take off her clothes. And then when I wanted to make love to her, of course, she declined. Knowing how important my appointment was to me, she showed no interest in going. And most of all, now all of a sudden, she was anxious to get back home.

I looked at my watch and quickly called Pat back to speak with Nokea. I got no answer and closed my phone. Seeing that it was almost 10:00 a.m., I knew how important it was for me to get to Frick's office, but I needed some answers.

I left the hotel in a hurry. Slow Pokers got cursed out by me, especially the valet who moved like a turtle. I almost ran his ass over, as I quickly drove off the parking lot. Frick's office wasn't too far away, but Collins' office put me well out of my way. I waited at the light and tried to decide...Frick, Collins, Frick, Collins. By the time my decision was made, I was already in the parking garage to

Frick's office. I was fifteen minutes late, so I rushed upstairs to get this shit resolved—fast.

As soon as I got off the elevator, Frick's receptionist stood up. "They're waiting for you, Mr. Rogers. Mr. Frick wants me to show you where the boardroom is."

"I already know where it is, so thanks."

I headed to the boardroom, and as soon as I stepped in the doorway, Felicia, Stephon, Frick and Glasgow sat at a circular table with leather chairs around it. Frick stood up and told me to come right in. My eyes stayed locked with Stephon's, as I couldn't believe that he was so close to Felicia's side. This was almost like the shock of my life, but for the moment, I remained calm and took my seat next to Frick.

"Jaylin, I'm sure you already know Stephon and Felicia. She asked that he be here on her behalf, and if you don't have a problem with it, then we can proceed."

I sat back, placing my leg on top of the other. "Of course I don't have no problem with it." I eyed Stephon again. "Stephon is free to do whatever he wishes."

"Good," Frick said, looking across the table. "Now, I called this meeting because I would like to see this entire case go away. The only way that's going to happen is if we can settle this right here and right now. I spoke to my client yesterday and he's prepared to offer you, Ms. Davenport, one hundred and fifty thousand dollars for your trouble. If you accept...

Felicia quickly spoke up. "And I don't. If that's all *your* client can come up with, then there's no need for us to sit here and try to work this out." Her voice rose to a higher pitch. "I was battered...

"Calm down, Felicia," Glasgow said, placing his hand on top of hers. Stephon had the nerve to place his hand on her back and rub it.

What a fucking joke, I thought. However, I still remained calm.

Frick spoke up. "Felicia, considering the fact that you contributed to the events that took place on the night in question, I'm not sure if my client is prepared to offer you anymore. If this case goes to trial...

Glasgow cut in. "If it goes to trial, Frick, the jury would chew your client up and spit him out." He tossed several pictures on the table. "After getting a look at those, it would prove that your client maliciously and irresponsibly came to St. Louis and tortured...

Frick fired back. "That's bullshit, and you know it! I have tapes and evidence that your client harassed, stalked and...

"What?" Felicia yelled. "If you have that much damn evidence, then let's take it to trial. I'd rather see Jaylin behind bars...

"Watch your mouth, Felicia," Frick warned. "Everything that comes out of it is on tape."

"I don't give a shit about no tape." She mean mugged me and cut her eyes. "I want what is due to me."

I reached out for one of the pictures of a battered Felicia and held it in my hand. "You got what was due to you, didn't you," I said. "The only thing that's due to you now, Felicia, is another good ass kicking. If I wasn't so anxious to get back home, I'd jump over this table and beat your ass again."

"Jaylin," Frick yelled, and then turned off the tape. Glasgow pulled a tape out of his pocket, placing it on the table.

"No, just keep on talking. We need that evidence to keep on piling up."

Stephon had the nerve to grin.

Now, I was pissed. "What the fuck you grinning at, nigga?"

He stood up. "Your punk ass, that's what!" He cocked his head from side to side and held out his hands. "So, what's up? I've been waiting for this moment..."

When I stood up, Frick reached for the intercom. "Jada, get me security. Now!"

Frick stood in front of me, and Glasgow held Stephon close to his seat.

"Mr. Stephon Jackson, either you leave, or else take a seat in the far corner of the room. I refuse to have anymore outburst or distractions, and if another one happens, this meeting is over," Frick said.

By the time security came, Stephon was in the far corner and I was back in my seat. Frick apologized for the inconvenience and the hearing proceeded.

I guess I'd gotten off on the wrong foot again, when I held Felicia's picture in my hand and snickered. The person I saw in front of me was not the person in the picture. She was still badly messed up, but a huge part of me felt good about what I had done.

Frick snatched the picture from my hand. Truth be told, I was in another world and had not paid much attention to what he'd said.

"Excuse me, what did you say?" I asked.

He was frustrated. "I asked if you would be willing to accept the demands of Felicia's offer?"

"Look, I really don't want to be here right now. My mind is not up for this shit this morning, so the faster I can get out of here, the better." I looked over at Felicia. "I am never going to apologize to you for what I did, and I have very little regrets. What you took from me and my wife was devastating to us. Someday, you will be dealt with by a much higher power than me, and I assure you that you will suffer much more than what I did to you. Until that time comes, what in the hell is it that you want from me!"

The room was silent. Felicia looked over at Stephon and then she looked back at me. She sat up straight, clinching her hands together.

"ONE MILLION DOLLARS," she said in a sassy voice. "Nothing more, nothing less."

Frick spoke up before I did. "You are out of your freaking mind. My client is not prepared to offer you that much…

I snatched up Frick's gold pen in front of him and reached for the papers underneath his hands.

"What are you doing?" he asked.

"If I want to settle, are these the papers I have to sign?"

"Yes, but we're not going to settle for…

"Give me the motherfuckin' papers! If this bitch thinks that a million dollars gon' leave me high and dry, she is sadly mistaken! I don't have time for this shit anymore!"

Frick let go of the papers, I filled in the amount and scribbled my signature. I dropped the pen and stood up.

"Done deal," I said. "Now, we can all go home happy. So happy, that we just might have to pick up a crack pipe and celebrate—ain't that right, Stephon?" I looked over at him. "For the record, you just bought your ticket to hell. And, I just happened to be the man who signed it away to you." I chuckled and looked at Felicia. "Your good days are behind you. Your worst days are yet to be seen."

I shoved my chair to the side and got the hell out of there. Frick yelled behind me, but I just kept on walking.

Deep down, my blood was boiling. One million dollars gone down the drain over some bullshit! I knew the bitch would demand a lot of money, but never in a million years did I expect her to ask for that much. Either way, I really didn't have much choice. Through the entire meeting, my mind had been on Nokea and I was anxious to find out about her visit with Collins. I thought paying him a visit would be rather tacky, so instead, I pulled my car over to the side of the road and called the operator to get Jefferson & Associates phone number. After the operator connected me, I wasted no time in asking for him.

"Mr. Jefferson is on another call. Would you mind holding?"

"Sure, I'll hold."

Only a few minutes later, Collins answered the phone.

"C. Jefferson," he said.

"J. Rogers," I replied. "I'm not calling to get on your bad side, but I would surely like to know what my wife was doing at your place yesterday."

"Who is this...Pretty Boy? Now, after ruining my marriage, I know you don't have the nerve to pick up your phone and call me. But, because you did, I guess it's only fair that I inquire about the reason for your call."

I swear I hated to do this but I was desperate. "Like I said, all I want to know is...

"Oh, yeah. You wanna know what Nokea was doing here yesterday, right?" He snickered. "Well, Jaylin, it appeared that you terribly failed again. The look in her eyes said it all, and you should have seen the way her eyes lit up once she saw me. I'm not gon' speak long because I'm already late for a meeting, but, uh, she still got those same ole sweet lips, her body still feels warm next to mine, and if we would have spent a little more time together, I would be able to share some other things with you. She's supposed to meet me for dinner, so how about checking with me and I'll let you know how it goes."

Collins hung up and I listened to the dial tone. Having a major headache, I dropped my head back on the seat and closed my eyes. I felt like crying, but I couldn't. Whether Collins told me the truth or not, Nokea should've known better going to see him. We were already walking on eggshells and she was going to make sure that we cracked through them. I wasn't sure what her purpose was for going to see Collins, but I sure as hell was anxious to find out. I looked at my watch and it was a little after noon. I knew her and Pat was probably at Café Lapedero, so I made my way to the restaurant.

When I got there, I saw Nokea's rental car parked outside. I took a deep breath, placed my tinted shades over my eyes and headed inside. I looked around and spotted Nokea and Pat chit-chatting at a round table. Before I made my way over to them, a waiter stopped me and told me to wait to be seated. Today was not my day to take orders, so I quickly waved him off and walked towards Nokea.

Before I approached them, Pat spotted me. She smiled, stood up and opened her arms to greet me.

"I'm so pleased that you made it," she said. Without a smile, I hugged her back and looked over her shoulder at Nokea. She was all smiles and blew me a kiss. I backed away from Pat's and my embrace and Nokea stood up. My eyes searched her over. She was dressed in a stretch black fitted dress that did hella justice to her curves. Not one strand of hair was out of place and it looked to me as if she was preparing to go out on a date. The most interesting thing about it, was when she left the hotel this morning, she had on something completely different.

She moved closer to me and reached out for a hug. Only my right arm went up to embrace her and I quickly took a seat.

"Where did the dress come from?" I asked.

"Pat bought it for me. I tried it on and loved it. Loved it so much that I decided to wear it. Do you like it?"

I nodded and gazed down at the floor. "I love it. It looks really nice on you."

Nokea noticed my demeanor and reached her hand out to touch mine. "Baby, is everything alright?"

I kept my head down, removed my glasses and moved my head from side to side. "I don't know, Nokea. You tell me if everything is fine."

"Of course. Why do you ask?"

I swallowed the huge lump in my throat. "Do...don't you want to know how things went today? Or, do you even care?"

She squeezed my hand. "Yes, I care. I was just about to ask you, but you asked me about my dress first. Did everything go okay?"

I stared at her with hurt in my eyes. "If you call signing away a million dollars okay, then that's what I did."

Her arched eyebrows rose. "You did what! Jaylin, tell me you did not give Felicia one million dollars!"

"Maybe, I should let the two of you talk alone," Pat said, scooting back in her seat. "Nokea, I will be over by the bar, okay?"

Nokea didn't say a word. She continued to wait for a response from me, but I couldn't even open my mouth to get out what I came here for.

"I...I can't believe you would throw away money like that. No wonder you're upset. I told you this was going to affect your children...

I cut her off. "What did you do yesterday? From the time you left the hotel, to the time you came back, I want to know your every move."

She snapped. "Why? I told you what I did."

"No, you lied to me about what you did and who you saw yesterday. Now, either tell me the truth or I'm about to embarrass the hell out of both of us."

"Now is not the time or the place for us to have this conversation. And, if this is about me going to see *your* lover, then yes, I did go see her. I assume she couldn't wait to call and tell you about my visit, and if you have a problem with me confronting your mistress, then I suggest you learn how to keep your dick in your pants."

Nokea hopped up and started to walk away. I grabbed her wrist and squeezed it. "Don't you walk away from me when I'm talking to you! I guess your visit with Scorpio prompted your visit to Collins. After whatever the fuck she told you, you wanted revenge, didn't you?" I stood up, twisted her wrist back and gritted my teeth. "I swear to God that if I find out you fucked him, kissed him, or even thought about it, I will break your damn neck!"

Nokea snatched her wrist away from me. "Let go of my wrist, Jaylin! After all of the crap you've put me through over the last month, I should have fucked him and fucked him good!"

My hand went up, and before it landed on Nokea's face, Pat grabbed it.

"No, no, no. We're not going out like that," Pat said. Nokea snatched up her purse and ran off. I dropped to the chair behind me and Pat ran after Nokea. Feeling terrible, I covered my face with my hands. Within seconds, somebody walked over to me and asked me to leave. I removed my hands from my face and saw that it was the waiter who approached me when I walked in. More than angry, I picked up the chair, glanced at the huge picture window and at several people sitting by it. I guess they knew what I was about to do, and many of them had already ducked out of the way. As hard as I could, I threw the chair and it crashed through the window. After that, I straightened my suit jacket and walked the hell out.

SHANE
15

It was rather late, when I heard the doorbell ring. I looked over Scorpio, at the alarm clock, and it showed 12:45 a.m. I reached for my robe and stood up to put it on.

"Who could that be?" she mumbled.

"I don't know," I yawned. I made my way to the door and looked out the peephole. It was Jaylin. Since I'd been calling him all day, and got no answer, I hurried and opened the door.

"Man, what's up with you not answering your phone?" I asked.

Jaylin stepped inside. His forehead was wrinkled and no smile was on his face. "Is Scorpio here? If she is, I'd like to speak to her."

"Yeah, she's here. Have a seat and let me go get her. But, is…is everything alright?"

Jaylin stroked his goatee. "No, it's not alright. But, I'm here to make it right."

I didn't like the tone of his voice, so I invited him in the living room to sit.

"Shane, I don't want to talk to you right now. Would you please go and get Scorpio before I go get her myself."

"Jay, I can tell that something…

Scorpio walked up from behind me and interrupted. "It's okay, Shane. If Jaylin wants to talk to me, I'm fine with it."

We all stepped into the living room and took a seat. Scorpio sat next to me on the couch and Jaylin sat in the chair beside us.

"All I'd like to know is, when Nokea came to see you, what did you tell her?"

I looked over at Scorpio. "When did Nokea come to see you? She didn't pay you a visit, did she?"

"When I was at Jay's yesterday she did. She inquired about that day at Davenports and accused me of interfering with her marriage. I told her that I had a hard time letting go, and once I found a way to move on, I did."

"And that's it?" Jaylin asked.

"Yeah, pretty much."

"Then, why is it that she now believes you and I had sex?"

"I never told her we had sex. I told her the day after the incident at Davenports, we almost did. But I also told her you had a change of heart that day and left. I didn't want to lie to her because she deserved to know the truth."

"Under the circumstances, I think you were wrong for sharing as much information with her as you did. And I know for a fact that given the opportunity, you said more to her than just that. But since everybody deserves to know the truth, did you just happen to tell Shane about our close encounter the other day?"

I sat back on the couch and placed my hands behind my head. Scorpio caught a quick attitude with Jaylin. "There was nothing to tell. How dare you come over here and try to mess up...

"Jay, why don't you be a bit more specific?" I suggested. "If you got something to say, just go ahead and say it."

"Let's just say that not once did Nokea save me, but twice. When she called your house and Scorpio answered the phone, if Scorpio would've had it her way, shit would've been on and popping. I was between her legs, Dog, and she had spread them this far apart for me." Jaylin opened his hands and gave me an example. "Basically, all one of us had to do was make the first move. But you see, that never happened. Nokea called and the pursuit was over."

"You're damn right it was over," Scorpio fired back. "Like I told you that day, Jaylin, I don't want you anymore. You act as if you're some kind of prize or something and no woman can resist you. The only thing I did to you that day was prove you wrong. Now, you can see it however you want to, but that's your imagination playing tricks on you."

Jaylin stood up. "Shane, my friend, there's always two sides to every story. I told you my side and I'm gon' finish it off by saying that she came to *my* room, definitely where I was, chilling back and minding my own business. Whether you continue your relationship with Scorpio or not, you still gon' be my nigga. As for you, Ms. Valentino, please do not converse with my wife again. If she ever questions you about us, just refer her to me. It's as simple as that. That's the least you can do, especially after putting me in a messed up position that day at Davenports. I hadn't considered you as being the sole person responsible, but not once have you apologized for the damage your actions caused me. Maybe it was your intentions to hurt me, and if it was, I applaud your efforts. They were good, and you won." I'd never seen Jaylin look so hurt as he spoke. "I don't know where my wife is, I don't know what our future holds, and I don't even know if she loves me anymore...

I had to interrupt. "Man, you know damn well you and Nokea will work this shit out. Married couples have ups and downs and it is not the end of the world. Stop..."

I'm not sure if Jaylin listened to me or not. By the time I finished speaking, he'd already made it out the door.

Scorpio looked at me and I looked at her. Saying nothing to her, I left the living room and hit the lights. Maybe being in the dark would give her a little more time to think about her actions.

NOKEA
16

No doubt, it was simply time for me to go. After I left the restaurant, I said goodbye to Pat and went back to the hotel to gather my things. I didn't even bother to check out because that would have delayed my time. Instead, I drove the rental car back to the airport and waited for my plane's departure.

It wasn't long before I sat on the plane and had time to think about all that had happened. My only question was, where did Jaylin and I go so wrong? For almost two years, things had been good. Good until he'd gone back to St. Louis and connected with Scorpio again. I never thought he'd allow her to come between us like he did. And to treat me like I had no say-so about the matter was what hurt more than anything. Then, to top it off, he had the nerve to be upset with me because I paid her a visit? What was wrong with him? Was he still in love with her and didn't know how to tell me? I was so confused, and when I thought about him raising his hand at me, that truly brought tears to my eyes. I was starting to wonder if he'd even changed. It was just a matter of time that the old Jaylin returned, and at this point, I had to decide what was best for my children and me.

I turned my head, gazing out of the plane's window. I thought about Felicia and her one million dollar pay-off. She had surely been the victorious one here and I knew something had to be seriously wrong with Jaylin to make that kind of deal. I knew if I was there, that surely wouldn't have ever happened. Maybe it was a good thing I didn't go, then again, maybe it wasn't. Either way, whether he was willing to admit it or not, a million dollars put a dent in our financial situation. Not only that, but Frick had to be paid, Jaylin's bond had to be paid, and Lord knows how much more money Jaylin had to put out in order to clear up this mess. None of it was worth it, and there was no way he would ever convince me any differently.

I looked at my watch and had less than an hour before my plane arrived in Florida. I couldn't wait to hold my babies in my arms and poor Nanny B had to be exhausted. The thought of seeing them all made me smile, so I reached for my purse to look for our family picture in my wallet. I flipped right to it and placed it on my lips. A few tears fell and I turned to both Jaylene's and LJ's baby pictures. We had a lot to be thankful for, and even at a rough time like this, all I could do was look up to the Lord and thank him for my many blessings.

I flipped through a few more pictures and came to a picture of Collins and me that was hidden away in my wallet. I pulled it out, holding it in my hands. My visit with him was rather interesting. Of course, I had a purpose. I often heard that when you loved someone, the memory of them always stays in your heart. And since Jaylin seemed to have such difficulty being around Scorpio, I wanted to see for myself if being around Collins again made me feel something...anything for him. Maybe, I'd feel the need to make love to him, or want to be with him again. Maybe even have a queasy feeling inside because he was in my presence. But, for me, none of that happened. Yes, I was happy to see Collins. I was even more delighted that he was doing well. However, there was nothing inside of me that wanted to love him again. I had no desire for his touch, and when he placed his lips on my neck, my first thought was Jaylin. But, the funny thing was, even though we shared a different kind of love, I felt secure when Shane held me in his arms at the courthouse. I felt even more secure when we made it back to his house and talked that day. And upon my departure, our tender juicy kiss went a bit too far. It was me who leaned in to it, and I hoped he accepted my apology for being the aggressor. I guess I felt the need to get my many frustrations off my chest, but when I thought more about it, I realized that I could never love another man like I love Jaylin. However, since the kiss between Shane and me happened, it was easier for me to understand Jaylin's thoughts of another woman. Shane had been on my mind and I was so disappointed about his relationship with Scorpio.

Just as I placed the picture back into my wallet, turbulence from the plane caused my body to shake. A few moments later, it shook again. The third time it shook, things started to get a bit frightening. The passengers around me had worried looks on their faces, and the stewardesses asked for everyone to remain calm. The pilot made an announcement that there was a small problem and it would *hopefully* soon be fixed. He ordered everyone to stay in their seats and reminded us where to locate the safety equipment. That, in itself, was not good news to me, especially since the plane seemed to be flying a bit out of control.

Soon, things got more intense. Two passengers started yelling and screaming, and as one stewardess tried to calm them, I saw the frightened look of another, who quickly sat behind me and dropped her head to pray.

I did the same and the white lady who sat next to me placed her hand over mine. I glanced over at her, noticing she had tears in her eyes as well.

"I saw you looking at those pictures. Was that your family?" she asked.

"Yes. How about you, do you have a family?"

"An awesome husband, two boys and two girls. Let's just pray that we make it to see them."

She squeezed my hand tighter and we both dropped our heads and prayed some more. When the pilot mentioned an emergency landing, I panicked. At this point, I begged the Lord to allow me to see Jaylin again. The way we departed should have never been. I needed to tell him so much and I didn't want our lives to end on this note. I was so sorry for not being there with him at that meeting. I was sorry that my anger had gotten the best of me. More than anything, I was sorry for allowing others to destroy what God put together. We'd come too far for it to be over with so soon. My children, Lord, what about my children, my parents, Nanny B, Pat, I thought. Not now, no! Especially when I had so much more to live for.

JAYLIN
17

I lay in bed at another hotel in downtown St. Louis, staring at the striped wallpapered walls. I waited for Nokea to come back to the Marriott, and when she didn't show up, I walked out without checking out. I couldn't stand to be in a room that carried her scent and the thought of making love to her the other night cluttered my mind. Not only that, but the thought of Collins making love to what belonged to me frightened the hell out of me. I wasn't sure if she'd gone to see him last night or not, but I had a good damn feeling that she had.

So, yes, it was already Thursday. The big day, the decision day, and I couldn't even get out of bed to go handle my business. At this point, I didn't give a fuck what happened. When I talked to Frick this morning, I instructed him to go to court on my behalf and informed him of my little incident at Café Lapedero yesterday. He was pissed off, but I asked him to work both situations out as best as he could. He assured me that, most likely, I had a warrant out for my arrest. I agreed, but as much as I'd paid him, a little more effort on his part shouldn't be a problem. I told him just that, and decided to wait around for his phone call. No matter what the outcome, after today, I was going home.

Near one o'clock in the afternoon, the hotel's phone rang. The only person who had this number was Frick, so I knew it was him. I almost hated to answer, but I knew that my future was at stake.

"Hello," I said slumped down in the bed.

"Jaylin, this is Frick. Why haven't you been answering your cell phone?"

"Because I threw it and it broke. I gave you this number to reach me at, so why would you call my cell phone?"

"Don't know...but now that I have you on the phone, I need you to cooperate and be patient with me. When I ask you these questions, I need you to be as accurate and honest as possible. Do not answer my questions with questions, and once I place you on the intercom, you need to speak loud and clear. Alright?"

"Yeah."

"State your full name."

"Jaylin Jerome Rogers."

"How old are you, Jaylin?"

"Thirty-five."

"Married or Single."

"Married."

"Occupation."

"Retired Millionaire."

"Children?"

"Yes."

"Parents?"

"Deceased."

"Siblings?"

"Stepbrother and sister."

"Ever been convicted of a misdemeanor?"

"No."

"Felony?"

"No."

"Ever been arrested?"

"Yes."

"For what?"

"Being an asshole." Frick was quiet and waited for another response. "For assault and carrying a loaded weapon."

"Is that the only time?"

"Yes."

"Wrong answer...think hard."

I was in deep thought. "Uhm, I...I can't recall. Oh, the other day for not listening to the judge."

"Are you sorry?"

"Uh, yeah."

"Is that an apology?"

"Yes. And a very sincere one."

"Good. Right answer."

"Three combined questions...Are you still in St. Louis, if so, where are you and why were you unable to make it to court today?"

"Yes, I'm still in St. Louis, I'm at the Four Seasons in Downtown St. Louis, and I did not come to court today because I paid my attorney very well to go there on my behalf."

"At least he's honest," I heard a female's voice say.

"Jaylin," Frick said. "Will the Four Seasons be able to verify your stay?"

"Absolutely."

"I'll call you back in ten minutes."

Frick hung up and I really wasn't sure what that was all about. I waited and waited for him to call, and didn't hear from him until almost forty-five minutes later.

"Okay, J.R.," Frick said. "I have good news and bad news...which would you like to hear first?"

"You might as well hit me with the bad news."

"Because of the vital and honest information you provided, the judge found you to be credible. She issued a ten thousand dollar fine for carrying a loaded weapon, community service in your hometown, and you must attend anger management classes for six weeks. If you fail to complete the classes and not do the community service, the judge promised to hit you with 90 days or more in the slammer. For the window incident, all the owner wants is to have the window fixed. He's willing to drop the charges, but a lady who was sitting by the window claims to have been injured. He can't guarantee that she won't sue, but I told him to take it up with his insurance. I don't know the outcome, but I promise to keep you posted."

"Seems to me that my credibility wasn't worth a damn. Now, what's the good news?"

"You can go home...tomorrow."

"Tomorrow? What about tonight? I was hoping to leave soon."

"There's too much paperwork involved and the judge and prosecutor won't be able to get to it until then. I need your original signature on everything and it has to be returned to them no later than tomorrow evening."

"Frick, listen, I gotta go. Another day I do not have. My marriage is at stake, and I haven't seen my kids in days. Forge my signature, Fed-Ex the shit, or whatever. Do what you gotta do, but when I check out of here today, I'm checking out of St. Louis for good."

"You drive a hard fucking bargain, Jaylin. Besides, I wanted to see you before you go."

"Shit, haven't you seen me enough? What's the purpose for seeing me again?"

"I...I wanted to personally apologize to you for declining to take your case. It was a stupid move, and I do not feel pleasant about the outcome with Felicia. I wish like hell that would have never happened but...

"But it is what it is, Mr. Frick. And if you're feeling so unpleasant, then a generous thing to do would be to return some of the money I paid you."

Frick laughed out loudly.

"Yeah, that's what I thought," I said. "Money talks and bullshit walks, doesn't it? Until next time, holla."

"Holla back," he said and we both laughed.

My shit was already packed because I knew that after I spoke to Frick, I was taking my butt home. I wanted to stop and say goodbye to Shane, but I said fuck it. I called for a bellhop to assist me with my things and jetted. By the time I made it to the airport, I was moving so quickly through it, that if you'd blinked, you missed out. I went to pick up my ticket, but they informed me there was a short delay. I was cool, and since I knew I was on my way home, I sat down in a chair and chilled.

Within the next hour or so, my plane was ready to depart. I took a seat, closing my eyes in deep thought. I hoped and prayed that Nokea would be home so that we could talk. The last time I spoke to Nanny B, she said she hadn't heard from Nokea. A part of me didn't think she'd be stupid enough to go back to Collins, but I knew if she wasn't at home, then that was exactly where she was. Bottom line, she had some serious explaining to do. She might have run out on me at the restaurant and hotel, but when I got her in Jaylin's territory, there would be no where for her to run.

As soon as the plane touched down, I was already out of my seatbelt. Slow Pokers were getting cursed out again, but this time, it was underneath my breath. The moment I grabbed my luggage, I thought about using the payphone to see if Nokea had made it home. Instead, I grabbed the nearest taxi and asked him to hurry me home.

Seeing my house felt like standing at the gates of heaven. I paid the driver and hurried out of the taxi. I walked to the front door and took a deep breath before opening it. I kept thinking... God help Nokea if she wasn't home, and God help her even if she was.

When I pushed the door open, the first person I saw was Nanny B. She was on the couch, while soaking up air from the fans that hung from the cathedral ceilings. When she saw me, she gave a half grin and stood up to greet me.

"I'm so glad you're home," she said, hugging me tightly. I dropped my luggage and held her back.

"Where's Nokea and the kids?" I quickly asked.

"The kids are resting and Nokea is in the bedroom. Please go see about her Jaylin. I'm really...

I didn't give Nanny B time to finish. I tossed my jacket on the leather chair and made my way to our bedroom. When I opened the double French doors, I saw Nokea standing by the doorway to the balcony while looking out. She wore one of my white crisp buttoned down shirts and quickly turned to me.

I defensively held my arms apart. "Why in the hell did you leave me like that? You just gon' walk out on me...this marriage just like that?"

Nokea rushed over to me with red and puffy eyes. She reached around my waist, placed her head on my chest and held me tight.

"I've never been so happy to see you in my entire life," she admitted. She then reached up and grabbed my face with her hands. She covered my lips with hers and aggressively stuck her tongue in my mouth. "Make love to me," she demanded. "I want to...need to feel you now!"

I broke our kiss and held her shoulders with my hands. "Sex is not the answer to this problem, Nokea. Do you think that just because you get all emotional and shit, I'm supposed to forget about your visit with Collins? And then not trip off of you saying you should have fuck...

She moved her head from side to side and spoke in a teary voice. "I don't care about Collins. To hell with him and Scorpio. It's over, baby, it's all over. I...I'm sorry for leaving you. Please forgive me. I should have been there for you, no matter what."

"Why are you saying all of this to me now? Are you feeling guilty or something!" I snatched away from her and took a few steps forwards. My heart raced. "Baby, if you slept with Collins, this marriage is over! There is nothing that you can say or...

Nokea reached for the sleeve to my shirt and pulled me to her. She grabbed the back of my curly hair and squeezed it tightly. Her lips found mine, and again, her persistence to make love continued. "This marriage is not over," she said, aggressively moving me back towards the bed. "I did not have sex with Collins, and I would never betray you."

I fell backwards on the bed and Nokea rushed on top of me. She ripped my shirt open and reached for my belt buckle. Once she had it undone, she unzipped my pants. I held my hand over hers to stop her. We looked deep into each others eyes.

"Swear to me you didn't sleep with him, Nokea. Tell me that I am all you will...

"I swear to God I didn't sleep with him and you have my word that I will never, ever allow another man to have me. You are all I want, need and desire. All I want is the same in return. Can you promise me the same in return?"

I reached up and moved Nokea's sweaty bangs from her forehead. "Yes, baby, yes. You are my everything. Since we've been married, I have never had sex with another woman."

"Please don't lie, Jaylin. Now is the time to tell me. Please be honest with me about Scorpio."

I held Nokea's face and spoke sternly. "It never happened. I swear on everything I love that sex between us never happened."

She leaned forward and wet my lips with hers. I started to feel excited and Nokea could feel my dick on the rise. She eased her way down and pulled the zipper over the hump in my pants. She then reached for what she wanted and gulped it far down into her mouth. What a good ass feeling? I thought while removing my pants. But before I even had a chance to enjoy the feeling, my toes curled and I let loose. I grabbed Nokea, flipping her upside down. Her legs straddled my face and I stood up. She knew the routine, as I made my way over to the wall and laid her back against it. Her legs tightened around my neck and it was time that I returned the favor.

For a long while, Nokea's juices quenched my thirst. I had her pussy on fire, and when she came, I damn near dropped her on the floor. Instead, I gently laid her down. She got on her knees and I kneeled behind her. I reached my hands around to her perky tight breasts, massaging them together. And as my hands were in motion, she turned her head to the side, pleasing me long and wet kisses. Kisses that made me reach my hand down to her clit. I stroked it a few good times, and then used my middle finger to moisten her hole. It was more than ready for me, so after a little more finger action, Nokea bent down and separated her knees. I wiped my goods along her wet slit, before searching inside. She gasped from the feeling and leaned forward. Realizing that I'd most likely hit bottom, I put my hands on her hips and pulled her back to me.

"Is that better," I said, giving it to her Jaylin's way. Only those who'd had it, knew what it felt like. And for those who'd missed out, they obviously had to use their imagination.

"Better," Nokea moaned. "Oh, you have no idea. No idea how much I love this...and love you more."

"I love you too, baby."

Nokea and I made up for lost time. She said that I didn't know how much she loved me, but now, I for damn sure did. Not only that, but I knew how much I loved her more. There wasn't no competition between us, pertaining to who loved who the most, but just the tiny thought of her not being in my life, was causing me to lose my mind. Peace had made its way back into my home, and I hoped like hell that it stayed there.

SHANE
18

After getting ignored by me, Scorpio gathered her things and left. I just wasn't up for no arguing and I was tired of her always having to explain. The apologies were enough to drive me crazy and I felt as if you hadn't done anything wrong, then what was you apologizing for?

No doubt, I wanted to hear her full side of the story, because I thought it was fair that I, at least, heard her out. But today, was not the day. Since Jaylin had left, I'd visualized the whole encounter in my head. I allowed them a few hours alone and she couldn't even control herself. First, to be running around half naked was definitely inappropriate and disrespectful. She could have easily grabbed my robe and covered herself, but that would mean Jaylin couldn't see all that he'd been missing. I'm sure that was her intention for wearing what she had on, and she knew for a fact, him being married or not, being dressed like that would arouse him.

I guess Nokea's phone call saved everybody. Whatever was about to go down before she called, those two hot-heads probably would've fucked. And then, in my house? On my bed? Underneath my sheets? Of course I was mad. Maybe that's why Nokea and I felt as if our kiss wouldn't hurt nobody. I was surprised when she brought her lips to mine, and even more surprised when I didn't back away. Yes, it was wrong, but I was upset with Jaylin about his remarks. Whether I was making a big mistake by being with Scorpio, or that he could still have her whenever he wanted to...his words left a bad taste in my mouth. Getting back to Scorpio...she knew better. I'd been nothing but good to that woman and she had no reason to open her legs up to any man. I didn't give a shit about her past with

Jaylin, it had been time to move on, and the both of them very well knew it.

Instead of lying around all day fucking, I was kind of glad Scorpio was gone. I had mega work that needed to be done, and for the last few weeks, Alexander & Company had been put on the back burner. I knew that if I wanted to make more money, I'd better get busy. So, I went into my office and continued on my sketch for the Mayor's Group. Since picking up my account with them, I'd already gotten another one. It was recommended to me by one of my previous clients through Davenports. Since Felicia and I parted ways, I'd taken a wealth of the business with me. I was surprised that I hadn't gotten a phone call from her about an attempt to sue me.

I guess everything must have worked out with the situation between her and Jaylin. He didn't say anything about it, and frankly, I was tired of calling him to find out. I figured he must have been busy, and I hoped that the reason he wasn't calling was because he was behind bars.

By 1:30 p.m., I could see the progress I'd made on my client's design. I had a few setbacks, as I remembered I'd left some of my expensive art tools at Davenports. I had planned on going back to get them, but it never seemed to be the right time. And, since I still had a key to let myself in, I put on my Mahogany velour track suit and made my way to Davenports.

I hoped that Felicia was still in the hospital, but when I pushed the door open and saw her from a distance, my thought was short lived. She was casually dressed in some khakis and a royal blue button down shirt. Her micro braids were pulled back, hanging several inches from her shoulders. The further I walked in, I could see her mouth moving with someone who sat in front of her. I didn't expect it to be one of her clients because she aggressively pointed a pen in the person's direction with every word that came from her mouth.

When I finally made it to her doorway, I was shocked to see Stephon sitting in front of her. Even more than that, I was surprised to see how bruised her face was. She dropped back in the chair and placed a pen in her mouth.

"Well, well, well. Look what the devil done dragged in," she said.

Stephon turned, glanced at me, and ignored me. His bitterness was obvious, but I wasn't the motherfucka stabbing friends and family in the back because of a drug habit, he was.

Wasn't no love lost for me, so I turned to Felicia, telling her my purpose for being there.

"If you don't mind, I need to gather some of my art tools I left behind. I promise you I won't be long."

"Just make sure I see everything you leave here with. And please don't take anything of mine because I know what I own, piece by piece."

I didn't say a word, just walked away. A bully must have taken that bitch's lunch money when she was a kid, because I can't ever remember a time she wasn't angry at the world. What in the hell made me give my dick and heart to a woman like her in the past, I will never know.

I spotted several of my tools lying around here and there, and then entered my old office and opened the drawers. After seeing a few more items I'd left behind, I took a seat and rummaged through the drawers. As I placed the items on the desk, I peered up and saw Stephon standing in the doorway. Since the last time I'd seen him, he did look a lot better. Last I'd remembered, he anxiously stood in an alley, making an exchange with a dope dealer. I walked up and snatched the drugs from his hand. He wanted to fight, and when I didn't give the dope back to him, he sucker punched me. Being a concerned friend, I didn't hit him back, and after giving him a piece of my mind, I went to the crib. Hours later, he showed up acting a complete fool. He begged me for, not only the drugs back, but also, for some more money. He tried to make me feel guilty because Jaylin and I had moved on with our lives. When I told him how much bullshit that was, he jetted. But not before stealing an expensive ring that my grandfather had given to me. I was furious, and when I called to ask him about it, of course, he didn't know where it was. After that, our friendship was over.

I snapped out of my thoughts. "What's up, Stephon?" I said.

He walked in and stood in front of the desk. "Nothing much, Shane. I wanted to come in here and thank you for turning your back on me. Now, though, thanks to your partna, and my long lost cousin, Jaylin, things are looking up again."

My forehead wrinkled. "I'm glad things are looking up for you, Stephon. But I'm not really sure what Jaylin has to do with it. I'm sure he doesn't want credit for, and I quote, 'bringing you back to life.'"

"A million dollars is enough to uplift anybody spirits." He placed his hand on his chest. "Even though I'm only entitled to half. But I knew that someway, somehow, or somewhere, I would get what was owed to me."

"Stephon, your grandfather left Jaylin that money because I'm sure he was a wise man. You didn't deserve one penny of it, and thank God that your grandfather was in his right mind when he died. He must have been able to predict the future, and right at this moment, so am I. I predict that whatever money you're talking about, it is more than enough to send you back to your previous unfulfilled, dark shadowed life. After all, Stephon, Felicia's back. With her around, you can't possibly come in here smiling at me as if your future is so bright."

Stephon leaned on the desk and winked. "Shane Alexander, you don't know shit. Your words sound like Jay's, so it's obvious that his bullshit has rubbed off on you. For the record, though, my grandfather was a wise, rich man. But he had the same problem that many of the men in our family had, and that was his major love for pussy. Nanny B was the one who inherited his estate. Not Jaylin. She was kind enough to turn it over to him, but he decided that he didn't want to share. I lost respect for him then, and I don't have any left for him now. As for Felicia, the pussy doesn't control me, I control it. You can say what you want about me, but you can never say I let a bitch come between me and my friends."

Stephon took a step back and stared me down. "When it comes to you and Jaylin, losing friends is a ritual. Friends dropping off like flies, because the bitches that both of y'all had were out of control." Stephon held his hand out and started to count his fingers. "Nokea? Been There and Done That. Scorpio? It was fun while it lasted, but I could damn sure use some more. And Felicia...well let's just say that a freak can't never get enough. In case you haven't noticed, this love triangle than turned itself into one big circle. Jaylin ole punk ass too afraid to admit how hurt he is by you shaking down his ex-whore, and when the truth comes to the light, that opens the door for you and Nokea. So, tick-tock-tick-tock, the clock is ticking away. If Scorpio doesn't destroy your, and I quote, 'friendship' with Jaylin, whenever you lay the pipe to Nokea, that for damn sure will."

I laughed and shook my head. "You are really, really one sick man, Stephon. This obsession that you have with Jaylin has gone overboard. Please don't hate, my brotha, it's truly an ugly thing. If money is the key to your success, then gon' and do your thang. I ain't tripping, and I assure you that neither is Jaylin. Because you see Stephon, the past is the past. Nokea, Jaylin, Scorpio and I are all living in the present, striving hard for a better future. Mistakes have been made and nobody's been perfect. Not even you." I picked up my belongings on the desk and walked past Stephon. I gave him one last look. "Pertaining to your life, the history books have already been written. You have the opportunity to change some things around. From a good friend, to the most backstabbing ass Negro I've ever known, I suggest you start making some for-real plans to change your life around. To me, it still stinks, and I can smell bullshit all over you."

Stephon smirked. "Fuck you, you slave driven ass nigga. You ain't nothing but another one of Jaylin's bitches...

As Stephon continued to rant, I snickered and went into Felicia's office to show her the several items in my hand. She examined them.

"I don't have much to say to you, Felicia, but you'd better watch your back. I hope like hell you know what it is you're dealing with."

Another stubborn ass person, she tooted her lips. My business was finished, so I went on my happy-go-lucky way.

Before I returned any of Scorpio's calls, it had been almost a week. I did, however, leave her a message to tell her how awfully busy I was. The truth of the matter was, yes, I was busy, but I was also still upset with her. No doubt, I was the type of man who didn't have time for apologizes, especially if they came every other week from someone who claimed to love you. Besides, Scorpio said she'd been missing Mackenzie, so I felt as if time apart would do both of us some good.

Since I spoke to her earlier, I was on my way to Jay's to see her. She sounded so damn pitiful and when I asked her what was wrong, she wouldn't elaborate. As I was on my way out the door, the phone rang. I checked the caller ID and was surprised to see Jaylin's phone number. Since he hadn't responded to my previous phone calls, I hesitated, and then answered.

"You got me," I said.

"What's up? Why ain't a brotha heard from you? I know you ain't tripping off...

"Man, I ain't thinking about you or Scorpio. I called you several times, but you've been the one missing in action. If anything, I thought your ass was locked up."

"Damn, if I was, you sure as hell didn't inquire, did you?"

"I told you I called your cell phone, but a brotha get sick and tired of hunting you down. You knew I was anxious to find out what happened in court, and when I saw Stephon the other day, I would say that things didn't go too well."

"What? Things went very well. I'm back at home...been back at home with my wife and kids. What happened in the Lou, stays in the Lou. Stephon and Felicia racked up on one mill of my money, but ain't no trip. You know a brotha like me gon' be alright."

Stunned, because I'd finally heard it from Jaylin's mouth, I grabbed a stool in the kitchen and took a seat. "That's a whole lot of money, Jay. I thought Stephon was bullshitting around with me when he told me."

"Naw, he wasn't bullshitting. I wish he were, but fuck it. Money is money, and there's plenty of more where that came from. Nothing beats being back at home with Nokea, Nanny B and the kids."

"So, I see the two of you worked things out. I'm glad to hear that and I might have to work my way down there to take another vacation. I surely could use it and it would take me away from all the bullshit around here."

"You mean between you and Scorpio?"

"Yeah, we gon' work shit out, but I was referring to a funny feeling I got when I saw Felicia and Stephon the other day. I got a bad feeling inside and the way he talked was almost kind of creepy."

"What did he say?"

"He's just so obsessed with you Jay. Not only that, but the brotha is bitter with a capital B. He dogged me out too, and you know Nokea was included as well. Just make sure you be on guard and protect what's yours."

"Don't I always? Besides, Stephon doesn't put fear in me. I would love to bust a cap in his ass, and family or not, I would have no regrets. Anyway, what did that motherfucka say about my wife?"

"He talked about his past relationship with Nokea. Said we all go around screwing each other and it would be just a matter of time that Nokea and me...

"You and Nokea? Man, what the hell is wrong with that fool? Why would he say something that fucking stupid?"

"C-R-A-Z-Y," I looked at my watch. It was getting late. "But, uh, let me get back at you a lil later. Tell Nokea I said what's up and give her a kiss—a hug for me."

"Will do," Jaylin said. "Give me a holla later."

I grabbed my keys from the top of the fridge and jetted.

Since it was the weekend, I knew Jay's would still be crowded. I had a difficult time finding a place to park, and when I found one, it was almost two blocks away. I walked inside and my eyes searched around for Scorpio. As they searched for her, it seemed as if all of the women were searching me.

"That's the Boss Lady's man," Bernie said. "So, close your mouths and shoot for the next man who walks through the door."

I smiled, giving Bernie a hug. "Where my girl at?" I asked.

"She's in her office. But, you'd better be nice to her. She's been kind of moody all week and I have a feeling that you're responsible."

"That Skeeza ain't been getting no dick," Jamaica said. "Bernie, you know she gave you the DL on her and Shane. Baby, if you want a woman who doesn't run her mouth to her friends, I suggest you hook up with me. I promise to keep all that carmel chocolate...

"Jamaica!" Scorpio yelled as she walked into the work area. "Don't get thrown out of here on your butt, okay?"

"Now, I'd like to see you do that. Ain't no damn woman that bad where she gon' throw me out on my ass."

Scorpio folded her arms. "Keep talking."

Jamaica rolled her eyes and turned her head. She mouthed something underneath her breath and Scorpio gave her a soft shove.

Without saying a word to me, she turned and headed towards her office. Looking awfully good in her pleated mini skirt and knee high boots, I followed.

No sooner had I walked inside the door, she approached me with major attitude.

"So, it took you almost a week to respond to your woman's phone calls, huh?"

Before responding, I took a seat on the soft yellow leather sofa. Knowing that we'd probably be here for awhile, she sat in the chair in front of me. "I did call you, Scorpio. I called and told you how busy I was. Didn't you get my message?"

"Yes, I got it. But that was only after I called you—at least, ten times."

"Scorpio, every time you ring my phone, it doesn't mean I have to jump to it and call you back. I told you I was busy with work and I'd call as soon as I had some free time."

"Oh, so, now you only call me whenever you have free time? I thought we had a relationship Shane? One where we talk everyday to see how the other person is doing. We had it before, but I guess you're still tripping off of what Jaylin told you. Sadly, you haven't even listened to my side of the story. Yet, you claim to love me. What kind of love are you offering because I'm seriously not feeling it at all?"

"Are we going to sit here all night and argue, or can I take you out to dinner like I'd planned to."

"Dinner? I'm not interested in going to dinner. I'm more interested in why you have this nonchalant attitude about everything. You are truly too laid back for me, and I can't tell if you give a damn or not about this relationship."

"Is that how you really feel? Do you really think I don't give a damn about you, Scorpio?"

"Yes, I do. I feel like a stepchild or something when it comes to how you treat me."

I stood up, "Baby, if that's how you feel, then I can't do anything to make you feel any differently."

Scorpio looked away and ignored me. I walked to the door, and then stopped in my tracks. When I turned to look at her, her head was still turned in the other direction. She looked too good for me to walk away. Besides, I was horny as hell. "Honestly," I said. "Don't you feel my love for you?"

She moved her head from side to side.

"Not just a tiny bit?" I said, walking back over to her.

She moved her head from side to side again.

I bent over, put my face in front of hers, and straddled my hands on her chair. "Why you pouting? You look so damn beautiful when you pout. But, never forget that you have a man who loves the hell out of you. I apologize for not calling you back, but at times, I do require my space."

"Space my ass, Shane. You…

I quickly sucked her lips into my mouth and kissed her. She worked with me, so I knew the night wasn't going to turn out too bad.

"Mmmmm," I said, wiping my lips as we finished. "You have some of the sweetest lips, girl."

"Oh, you are so good. Look at you trying to work your magic. Now that you have my attention, though, where are you taking me for dinner?"

"Dinner?" I said, taking a few steps back to the couch. "Who said anything about dinner?"

Scorpio playfully cut her eyes at me. "I guess you're teasing me now? You previously mentioned dinner, or have you forgotten."

I shrugged my shoulders. "I don't know what you're talking about. I mentioned nothing to you about dinner."

She sat quietly for a moment and stared at me from several feet away. She then stood up, lifted the sides of her skirt above her hips, and eased her pretty pink lace panties to the floor. She tossed them on my lap and sat back in the chair. Once she took a seat, she lifted her right leg on the arm of the chair, stretching her legs apart.

"If teasing me is what you came here to do," she said. "Then I most definitely can play your game better than you."

She hiked up her skirt a bit more, placing her hand on her stomach. As her hand lowered, I turned to look away.

"Oh, no, baby. You've got to get a glimpse of this. *She's* been purring for you. It's only fair that, since you made *her* wait so long for you, you make your way over to satisfy *her* needs."

Unable to resist, I scooted back on the couch, lowered my eyelids and focused in on what was being offered to me.

Within seconds, Scorpio had me on cloud nine. She separated her neatly shaven slit with her fingers and massaged against her walls. They instantly got wet and so did her middle finger as she worked it inside. Her thumb circled her swollen clit and when she inserted more fingers, I could barely take it anymore. I placed my hand over the hard hump in my pants and got ready to release my monster. Scorpio saw how excited I was and she continued on with her festivities. She dropped her head back and moaned her words.

"Shaaaane. Baaaby, whyyy? Why would you make me do this to myself? Your...your fingers and dick inside of me would make me feel so much...

Before Scorpio could finish her words, I relieved her. I moved her fingers away from her slit, picking up where she left off. As my fingers entered her, I leaned my head down for a kiss. She moved her head back and placed her fingers in my mouth so I could taste her. No matter what form or fashion her pussy came in, it always performed at it's best. I widened my mouth, welcoming the taste. Soon, she brought her lips to my mouth and we both sucked her fingers.

"Mmmmm," she moaned as I worked her down below. "But, faster. I want you to go faster."

I knew exactly how Scorpio liked it, so my turning fingers put in the extra work. She tightened up and lifted her butt from the chair. Since she was about to come, I surely didn't want any good juice to go to waste. I buried my face between her legs and sucked down what belonged to me.

"I...I just want to cry," she smiled. I loosened her grip from my hair and stood up. I slid my Ralph Lauren belt from the loops of my stone washed jeans, and pulled my hooded sweatshirt, along with my white wife-beater over my head.

"You got all night to cry," I said. "Especially, after this whuppin I'm about to give you for being so bad."

"Oh, you'd better whup me good." She stood up and started to remove her clothes. "I have no intentions of being a good girl tonight, so make sure that you punish me to the extreme."

We got naked and I punished Scorpio all over the room. After smacking it up, I had no problem rubbing it down. As always, sex between us was off the chain and we didn't wrap it up until the wee hours of the morning. We'd had interruptions, but since the knocks on the door were ignored, they all went away.

FELICIA
19

Things were going along pretty darn smoothly. The money Jaylin had to hand over to me sure as hell helped out. It made up for loses at Davenports and I didn't give a care how many accounts Shane had taken from the business. If I wanted to, I could've sued him big time, but my newly founded income had me on cloud nine.

Stephon and I had been spending an enormous amount of time together. I had some pretty strong feelings for him, but I can't say love was what I felt. Since Jaylin dogged me out like he did, I've had a difficult time trusting and loving any man again. I never trusted him because I always knew he was a ho and he'll continue on being a ho. I hate to keep thinking about that *it* who calls herself his wife, but she has got to be the biggest damn fool I know. I was surprised she didn't show up at the meeting we had, but I was sure she knew how much money I got out of the deal. As usual, he probably threw his dick on her, and by now, it doesn't even matter. Bottom line, to hell with them all! Shane can keep on fucking the playboy bunny and Jaylin can have his mother goose that does nothing but lays his eggs. I'm happier than I've been in a long time and I have no one but Stephon to thank for supporting me.

I held up my end of the bargain and gave him half of what was left after my attorney's fees. Stephon paid off the second mortgage on the barbershop and bought himself a Denali. That sucker was cutting up so bad that it made me want to trade in my Lexus for an upgrade. Just so I didn't get ganked, Stephon told me he'd go to the Lexus dealer with me. But, when I called his house, I got no answer. I knew he was home, so I decided to go over to his place.

Within the hour, I made it to Stephon's house on the Northside of St. Louis. He lived in a newly remodeled house that was close by his shop in the Central West End. We'd talked about going to purchase furniture for his new place, but that had to be put on hold until I got my car. Since his Denali was in the driveway, I headed for the door. Nearly five minutes later, he opened it.

"Hey, Felicia," he said with a tired look on his face. He stepped back so I could come in.

"Were you sleeping?" I asked. "You look awfully tired."

"Nah, I wasn't sleeping. Just laying my head down and watching TV, that's all." He made his way back to his room and I followed.

When we stepped inside, his room had an interesting smell. He crawled back in bed, covering himself with a thick blanket.

Without any hesitation, I asked what the smell was.

"What smell? I don't smell nothing."

"Sex. It smells like musty sex and please don't tell me you've been having sex with somebody else. Is that why you didn't answer your phone when I called?"

He peered over the blanket and then pulled it back. He sat on the edge of the bed, while gazing down at the floor with his boxer shorts on.

"I didn't answer my phone because I wasn't feeling too well. I know I told you we'd go look for your car today, but my stomach hurts. I've been in and out of the bathroom...

"Uh, no need to elaborate. I don't care to hear about your trips to the bathroom." I fanned my hand in front of my nose and looked around his room. "Do you have an air freshener around here? I'm serious about the smell in this room."

Stephon didn't answer, so I made my way over to his closet. He watched my every move, and when I reached for the knob to open his closet, he quickly jumped up.

"Look, why don't you go have a seat in the kitchen? I'll get dressed so we can go. Alright?"

"I see you're feeling better already." I tossed my braids to the side and kept my hand on the knob. "Now, if you don't mind, I'd like to see for myself who or what is giving up ass that smells that horrible."

Stephon spoke sternly. "I said, go into the kitchen and wait until I get dressed. I will be there in a minute."

I ignored his demand and folded my arms in front of me. "I will go into the kitchen, once you open this door. Like I said before, you and I are only lovers. You told me that you weren't seeing anyone else, and all I ever told you was to let me know if you were. That way, Negro, I had a choice. Messing around with a woman whose pussy lights up an entire room, ain't no telling what I might have. So, either you open this door, and tell this...this funky *thing* to leave, or else you'll be added to my shit list. And trust me, Stephon, you don't want to be on my shit list."

Stephon placed his hand on the doorknob, rolling his eyes at me. "Will you go in the kitchen and sit down? I need to handle this, alright?"

"Tame it," I said, moving back to the bed and taking a seat. "It smells like an animal that needs to be tamed."

Out of the closet stepped a young, light skinned chick with green eyes and sandy brown hair. She barely looked over eighteen and Stephon knew better.

"Put your clothes on and go to my car," Stephon said, reaching in the closet for her clothes. She had a sheet wrapped around her and was afraid to look my way.

I sat frustrated. "How old are you?" I asked. She and Stephon ignored me, so I asked again. "I asked, how old—?"

"Twenty-two. Why?" she snapped.

"Felicia, cool out," Stephon said, moving her towards the bedroom door so she could go somewhere else to get dressed.

"Shut up talking to me. She ain't no twenty-two, because a twenty-two year old would know better than to bring her goodies over to a grown man's house like that."

She turned and Stephon blocked her in the doorway from getting to me. "Trick, who you talking to like that? You don't know me. I will bust a cap in your ass."

I threw my hand back at her. She wasn't worth my time. "Yeah, right. And, while you're busting a cap in my ass, squirt a douche in your vagina...

"Felicia and Honey, stop the bullshit!" Stephon yelled. He turned to Honey. "Go get your clothes on so I can take you home."

Honey cut her eyes at me and walked into another room. She slammed the door and Stephon turned to face me.

"You are so damn rude, Felicia. I can't believe...

I stood up. "No, Stephon. I can't believe you're rolling your women around in a truck that I bought for you. How dare you...

Stephon brushed me off. "Yeah, whatever. I've heard you loud and clear. Now, I'm gon' get dressed and take her home. If you still want to go see about getting a car, then wait here until I get back. If not, then go home and I'll meet you at your place."

My mouth hung open. "Are you out of your mind? You must be smoking again, right? There's no way in hell I'm going to stay here and wait until you take Ms. Chlamydia home. I need a new car, now! I've waited long enough."

Seething with anger, Stephon squinted his light brown eyes at me and walked over to his closet. He pulled a sweatshirt over his head and stepped into a pair of jeans. By then, Honey was dressed and stood in the doorway waiting for him. I leaned against the wall and waited as he groomed his bald head while looking in the mirror, combing his thinly shaven beard. He put the comb down and reached for his keys. Again, he ignored me and looked at Honey.

"Are you ready?" he asked.

She nodded and he made his way to the door. I grabbed his arm and squeezed his muscle.

"I won't be here when you get back."

"Good, because I'm not coming back," he said, and then snatched his arm away from me.

I wanted to go after him, but I wasn't about to make a fool of myself in front of his low-class hoochie. Instead, I slowly walked to the front door and watched as they got inside of Stephon's white BMW. I guess he tried to show me a tiny bit of respect by not driving the Denali, but I was pissed. He looked at me while backing out of the driveway, and so did she. She smiled and I couldn't help but give the both of them a finger.

Once they drove off, I planned to stay at Stephon's place and rummage through his things, but I decided against it. I already knew what kind of scum he was and there wasn't anything in his place that would reveal anything differently to me. Instead, I left without closing the door, heading back to my place. I wasn't up for car shopping anymore, and I had a feeling as if Stephon would show up apologizing soon.

Throughout the night, I tossed and turned. Stephon was on my mind, but so was everything else. I hadn't handled my business at Davenports like I normally did, and having so much money caused me to splurge more than I thought. Plus, I was starting to regret giving Stephon half of the money, especially how he treated me today. And then, not to call or come over really made me mad.

Furious, I looked at my alarm clock and it was almost midnight. I looked at the phone and thought about calling him, but I decided against it. Instead, I did the norm and rushed out of bed to get dressed. I hurried into my orange and white BabyPhat sweats and put my long braids into a ponytail. After sliding into my clean white tennis shoes, I headed out.

Stephon's house was pitch black on the outside and inside as well. His cars were both there, so that was a plus. Alone? I wasn't sure, but I really didn't care. I needed an apology from him, and as much as I did for him, he had to give it to me.

When I reached the door, I knocked several times, but got no answer. I rang the doorbell over and over again, still, no answer. I paused for a moment, and then, reached for the doorknob and turned it. The door came open, so I stepped inside.

"Stephon?" I whispered and reached for the light switch on the wall next to me. I flicked the switch several times, but the light didn't come on. I closed the door and tip-toed down the hallway to his bedroom. His door was closed, and as soon as I reached for the knob, somebody's hand touched the top of mine and squeezed it. Immediately after, a hand covered my mouth, and whatever that awful smell was, it caused me to pass out.

What seemed like hours later, I was awakened by the same smell. My head was spinning and all I could see was a blurred vision of Stephon sitting naked while on the couch. He had a cigarette dangling from the side of his mouth, and as I attempted to sit up, I couldn't because my body was sore. I heard him mumble something, but I couldn't quite make it out.

"What did you say?" I asked, while rubbing my eyes, looking in his direction. He removed the cigarette from his mouth and smashed it out in the ashtray in front of him.

"I said...it's about time you got your lazy butt up."

My body was cold, so I knew I didn't have on any clothes. And from the wetness between my legs, I knew I'd had sex with Stephon. For the moment, I couldn't remember a thing.

"Wha...what did you do to me? I don't remember anything and what is that smell?"

He stood up and walked over to me. He lifted my chin and looked down at me. "The only thing I smell is pussy. That would be yours, since we've been having sex for the last two hours. So, why don't you get up and go clean yourself up?"

He removed his hand from my chin and walked away. I slowly got up from the floor and felt extremely light-headed. I was so woozy, that before I fell, I had to quickly make my way to the couch. Stephon came back into the room and gave me some towels.

"Your bath water is running. Can you make it to the bathroom or not?"

After reaching for the towels, I laid them on my lap. I placed my forehead in the palm of my hand.

"I am really feeling ill. Now, I asked you before...what did you do to me?!"

"Woman, I didn't do nothing to you. You did it to yourself. Don't you know better than to walk into a man's house, or anybody's house, unannounced? Not only that, but leaving my door opened earlier wasn't cool. I was mad at ya, so you know I had to put a hurting on you. Right now, you're just feeling the after effects. Once you take a bath, you'll be okay. Then, we can finish where we left off," he said taking my hand and placing it on his dick. I wanted to yank that motherfucka from his body, but I didn't have the strength to do so. Aside from possibly raping me, I knew he'd done something else to me. Until I had it all figured out, I had to play it cool. I moved my hand away from him and slowly stood up. Like a turtle, I moseyed down the hallway, making my way to the bathroom. I locked the door and sat on the toilet to gather myself. I was still light-headed, and needing a bath like it wasn't funny, I dipped my hand into the water to feel it. It felt soothing so I stepped my body inside and lay back. I closed my heavy eyelids, and could hear myself snoring.

SHANE
20

Of course, since Scorpio had forgiven me so easily, I spent the next few days making it up to her. We'd been to the movies, to the Jazz Corner, to the mall to shop, and took a late night ride on my motorcycle through the park. Being at the park always led to sex, but I promised myself that our relationship wouldn't be based on that alone. And when I told her I had plans to go to Florida and chill with Jay for the weekend, she kept giving it to me as if I was never coming back. Whenever she was in my presence, it was hard for me not to want to make love to her. Many times, I had to control myself and so did she. We agreed that once I got back from Florida, we'd take a trip together, too. I even suggested that Mackenzie, Leslie and her kids come along, and Scorpio said it might not be a bad idea. Since we'd been together for awhile, I wanted a closer relationship with her family. I didn't want to rush her into anything, because I knew how protective she was of Mackenzie, since the break-up with Jaylin. She hadn't let any of her companions, including me, near Mackenzie. I respected her wishes, but I wanted to show her I was capable of loving her family, just as much as I loved her.

As for going to Florida, I hated for Scorpio to feel left out, but there was no way possible for me to take her with me. Nokea and Jaylin would be very uncomfortable and I wasn't in no position to make them feel that way, even though he was my best friend. So, for the time being, things had to be left as they were, and we all had to deal with this uncomfortable situation as best as we could.

On Friday morning, Scorpio took me to the airport. I was running behind schedule, so I rushed to get my luggage out of the car and to say goodbye.

"I'll call you when I get there, okay?" I said, standing with my luggage hanging on my shoulder, and another piece in my hand. She held my garment bag across her arm.

"Don't forget. And please have your phone on so I can call you."

"I will," I said, puckering for a kiss. She gave me a tiny kiss, and when I opened my eyes, she stared at me.

I backed away. "Is something wrong?"

She had a perplexed look on her face. "Not really. I...I just don't like the thought of you going to Florida to see Jaylin. He's always trying to feed you a bunch of bull and I don't know how much you trust and believe what he says to you. In addition to that, I'm afraid he might try to hook you up with someone because of his hatred for me."

"Baby, listen. Jaylin doesn't hate you. And, I'm not easily persuaded by my friends. I never have been and I never will be. Don't you know that by now? If not, then you still have a lot to learn about me. But, now ain't the time to discuss this. I'm late and I will call you the moment I get to Jay's house. Okay?"

She nodded and I barely had time to peck her lips again. I rushed off, even though I could see the ongoing concerned look on her face. I wasn't really sure what it was for, but Scorpio was good at keeping things bottled up inside.

Since I'd taken a long nap on the plane, the ride was short and sweet. By the time I opened my eyes, the plane was getting ready to land. Jaylin already had my flight information so I expected him to be there and to be on time. However, as I made my way off the plane and through the gates, I looked around and didn't see him. Soon after, I saw Nokea and LJ heading my way. He ran up to me and the excitement on both of their faces made me smile. I picked up LJ and held him in my arms.

"Hey, lil man, I can't believe how big you're getting." He smiled, while nodding his head. I tickled him and teased my fingers in his curly hair like Jaylin's. Nokea soon walked up.

"Hi, Shane," she said, reaching out for a hug. "Jaylin sent me to get you because him and our neighbor were putting up the decorations for the Hawaiian Luau on the beach tonight."

"Sounds like fun," I said, handing LJ over to her. He stood up and she took his left hand and I took his right hand.

"Uncle Shane," he said, looking up at me as we all walked together. "Are you going to live with us?"

I chuckled and looked over at Nokea. "No, but I plan to stay the weekend with you all. Trust me, by then, you'll be so sick of me that you'll be ready for me to go back home."

"I doubt it," Nokea said. "He was so excited that you were coming, but not as excited as Jaylin. At times, I think he gets lonely and I'm always glad when you come to visit us."

I grinned and we made our way to the baggage claim area to get my luggage. I thought Nokea drove to the airport, but I forgot that Jaylin had a driver named Ebay who drove them every place they wanted to go. He was waiting outside for us and loaded my bags up in his jeep. Once loaded, I opened the door for Nokea to get in the front seat and LJ and I got in the back. I couldn't help from noticing how pretty and classy she looked, even in a pair of blue jean shorts. She reminded me so much of Nia Long and Jaylin had to be one of the luckiest men in the world.

On the way to Jaylin's house, Ebay drove the shit out of his jeep. He quickly swerved in and out of traffic and the wind was tearing us up. LJ got a kick out of bouncing up and down, and even though I hated to admit it, I got a thrill out of watching Nokea's perky breasts bounce up and down as well. Hell, even Ebay had looked over at her several times. When he caught me taking a peek, he looked at me in the rearview mirror and winked. I turned my head and felt awfully guilty. It wasn't that I had never admired Nokea's beauty, but ever since she kissed me...we kissed each other, she'd been on my mind.

I could always tell when Jaylin and Nokea's house was near. The road got rocky, all you could hear was the ocean, and the palm trees were gracefully blowing. No doubt, this was the life. As I was in deep thought, Nokea turned sideways and looked at me.

"Why are you so quiet, Shane? You haven't said much of nothing all the way here."

I shrugged. "No reason. I'm just enjoying this amazing scenery and thinking about my future, that's all."

"It is beautiful, isn't it? Sometimes, Jaylin and I get up in the middle of the night and just walk until we can't walk anymore. It's so relaxing and the kids are so happy living here."

"I bet they are," I said, placing my hands behind my head. "Who wouldn't be happy living in paradise?"

Within the next few minutes, Ebay parked in front of the Rogers' house. The sight of it always blew me away and Jaylin was standing out front waiting to greet me. He walked up to the jeep, dressed in a white wife-beater and blue jean shorts. Tinted glasses covered his eyes and leather sandals were on his feet. Before he could even make it to the car, his twin, LJ, was all over him. Jaylin picked him up and carried him to the back of the jeep to assist with my luggage.

"LJ, hop down," Jaylin said. "Let me help Shane with his bags."

LJ hopped down and Nokea reached for his hand. They walked towards the house and left Jaylin, Ebay and me outside.

"How much do I owe you?" Jaylin said to Ebay while reaching in his pocket.

"You owe me nutteen if I can partay with you guys tonight."

"Ebay, you know you can stop by anytime you'd like to. How many times I got to tell you that you're like family to us around here."

Ebay smiled and showed his pearly white teeth. "Gud, gud," he said, patting Jaylin on his back. "But you gotta stop being so nice to me, man."

"I'm not being nice," Jaylin said, handing all of my bags over to Ebay. "Please take those to our guestroom and I will pay you on the way out."

Ebay saluted Jaylin and took all of my bags into the house. Jaylin then told me to follow him and we made our way around to the back and onto to the beach. There were several huge straw huts with bars inside. Palm trees and torches surrounded the huts and grass skirts and flowers were all over the place. Bongos and guitars were set aside for entertainment and I could already tell that tonight would be a night to remember. I stood and stared at how well everything was put together.

"This...this is the bomb. What's the occasion?"

"Occasion? My neighbors and I just get together sometimes and feel like celebrating our good fortune. Since there ain't no nightclubs close by, we make up our own forms of entertainment. Come night time, the whole place will be lit up. Yachts will be sailing in the ocean and people will be all over the beach."

"Then, I can't wait for tonight. Y'all rich folks know how to do it, and do it right."

Jaylin grinned and we headed back to his house. As soon as I entered, Nanny B was waiting to give me a hug. She wiped her wet hands on her apron and held her arms out to me.

"Give me some sugar, baby," she said.

I kissed her soft fat cheeks and squeezed her as tight as I could. "I came all the way here just to get a hug from you. And, to get a taste of your good cooking. I haven't had a good home cooked meal in a long, long time."

"And you for damn sure won't get one dealing with Scorpio," Jaylin added.

I ignored his comment and so did Nanny B. She rolled her eyes and pulled me into *her* kitchen. "If you're hungry, I got some left over meatloaf in the refrigerator." She opened the stainless steel double doors to the fridge, but I declined.

"Nanny B, I'll wait until later to eat. I don't workout as much as Jaylin do, so I gotta take it easy."

"Chile, I would never know. To me, you look like you workout every hour on the hour, but what does a thick old woman like me know. Whatever you're doing, keep on doing it. Someday, you're going to make some woman very, very happy."

I smiled and looked at Jaylin who was about to open his mouth again. Nanny B gave him a look that said, "Hush". Always listening to her, he kept quiet.

"Now, I've been here for almost fifteen minutes and I haven't seen Jaylene yet."

"That's because she's taking a nap," Jaylin said. "And I'm not about to let you interrupt the queen while she sleeps."

Just then, Nokea came into the kitchen sliding her feet on the hardwood floors in Jaylin's house shoes. "Well, the queen is awake. She's calling for her Da-Da, so you know the routine."

I don't think I've ever seen Jaylin move so quickly. He rushed out of the room, and within a few moments, came back with Jaylene. Her head was buried into his chest and her fingers were in her mouth. Her curly hair was separated into two afro balls and her grey big eyes matched those of Jaylin's and LJ. When I reached out to hold her, she turned her head and squeezed Jaylin tighter around his neck.

"You can forget about holding her," Nokea said. "She's Daddy's little girl and only Daddy's little girl. Depending on what kind of mood she's in, Nanny B and me might get a moment with her."

"That's cause y'all done spoiled these kids rotten," Nanny B said. "LJ clings to Nokea more, and Jaylene clings to Jaylin. I get my share of both of them, and if you'd really like to know who has the upperhand around here, you're looking at her."

"Nanny B, please," Jaylin said. "You or Nokea don't have nothing coming when it comes to mine. All they know is me and LJ will tell you that himself."

Without saying one word, Nanny B walked up to Jaylin and held out her arms for Jaylene. She hesitated for a moment, but then she jumped into Nanny B's arms.

"That's my baby," she said, rubbing noses with Jaylene. "That Daddy of yours don't know any better, does he?"

Jaylene giggled and continued to rub noses with Nanny B. She kissed Nanny B's cheeks and pulled on her gray hair.

"Can you believe that?" Jaylin said. "I can't believe that's how I get played."

LJ came in, walked right past Jaylin and Nokea and went straight up to Nanny B. It was obvious that since Jaylene had her attention, he wanted it, too.

"Nanna, will you make me a sandwich?" he asked.

"Baby, mama will make you a sandwich," Nokea said. "Go wash your hands and I'll put it together for you."

LJ dropped his head. "But...but I want Nanna to make it for me."

"And your Nanna will make it for you," Nanny B said, looking at Nokea.

"So, Mommy's not good enough to make a sandwich now, huh? I swear, Nanny B, it's you who do all the spoiling around here. You know I have no problem making him a sandwich."

"Well, me and my kids do. So, why don't you, Shane, and Jaylin go get things in order for tonight? We're going to eat, play some games, and watch cartoons. And don't interrupt us, Jaylin, because we don't want to be bothered."

"You are lucky I got company," Jaylin smiled and grabbed Nokea around her waist. "Come on, baby. We know when we're not wanted."

"Tell me about it," Nokea said, playfully rolling her eyes. She and Jaylin walked out of the kitchen and I followed. We made our way to the guestroom and Nokea took a seat on the king sized bed, while Jaylin stood next to her.

"Nanny B already hung your things in the closet, Shane," Nokea said. "If you'd like to take a shower, the bathroom has plenty of towels in it. And, some extra pillows are in the closet. The party doesn't get started until 8:00 p.m., so you still have a few hours to get some rest, if you need it. Normally, an event like the one planned will require you to be up all night. Any rest you can get will only benefit you."

"I'm afraid she's right, man. If you haven't had any sleep, now is the time."

"I'm cool. I slept all the way here on the plane, so I feel well rested. I will, however, take a shower in that bad-ass shower y'all got and make a few phone calls, if y'all don't mind."

Nokea stood up. "Make yourself at home," she said. "If there's anything else you need, let me know."

"Thanks, and I will," I said.

She left the room, but Jaylin stayed behind.

"Do you have something to wear for tonight?" he asked.

"I got some red swimming trunks. Do I need something else?"

"Naw. It's hot as hell, so I just wanted to make sure you didn't bust out in no hot ass jeans or nothing."

"I got plenty of those, but I knew I'd better pack some swimming trunks, being this close to the beach."

"Good thinking," Jaylin said heading towards the door. "Again, if you need anything, I'll be in my room."

I nodded and he closed the door behind him.

Since I told Scorpio I'd call her the moment I arrived, I looked in my bag for my cell phone. The battery was low, so I plugged the charger into a socket to let it charge. I then sat on the bed and reached for the phone on the nightstand. I called Scorpio's home phone number, but got no answer. I then called her at the shop, but

Jamaica said she'd gone to the bank. I left a message for her to call me back.

Afterwards, I stripped naked and went into the bathroom to take a shower. When I stepped inside of the oval shaped walls made of marble, I felt like royalty. The cushioned seat inside helped me relax, but not as much as the soothing water that poured from two waterfall faucets from above. All I could do was sit back with my eyes closed and enjoy the feeling. My mind started wandering about Scorpio's and my relationship. About Alexander & Company...getting married...having kids. I wanted a better life, and by all means, I deserved it. It wasn't that I was unhappy, but seeing what Jaylin and Nokea had made me feel as if I was missing out on something. As I was in deep thought, I heard Jaylin yell my name. I stood up and reached for the faucets to turn off the water. I grabbed a towel from the rail and wrapped the towel around my waist. As I stepped out of the shower, Jaylin stood in the doorway with a cordless phone in his hand.

"We need to talk about this," he said sternly. "I did not want her to have my phone number."

I held out my hand, but he dropped the phone to the floor and left the room. I picked up the phone, placing it on my ear.

"Hello," I said.

"You asked me to call you back, but didn't answer your cell phone. Since Jaylin's number came up on the caller ID, I thought you intended for me to call you back at his number."

"No, I didn't. But, you should have known better calling his house, Scorpio. It's disrespectful to not only him, but to his wife as well. Now, I have to go out here and apologize for...

"Then, you do what you gotta do. I am so sick and tired of you catering to Jaylin and Nokea. All I wanted to do was speak to my man. I kind of missed him, you know, and I surely didn't think that calling Jaylin's house to speak to *you* would cause any trouble. But, I guess, I fucked up again, right Shane? Just add another tick mark to my list and be sure to make me pay for it later."

She hung up. I laid the phone on the bathroom counter and snatched the towel from around me. I dried myself off and bent over to dab my ankles. When I heard Nokea's voice, I quickly stood up.

"Shane have," she paused in the doorway, took a quick glance at my goods, and quickly turned around. "Sorry, but have you seen Jaylin? I thought he was in here with you."

"He was, but not while I was taking a shower," I said, laughing and wrapping the towel around me again.

She chuckled and started to walk away. I reached for her arm to stop her, and she flinched.

"Are you alright?" I asked. "I just wanted to apologize for the phone call."

She turned, but looked to make sure I was covered up. This time, she seemed a bit at ease. "What phone call?" she asked.

"I called to let Scorpio know I made it, and your number came up on her caller ID. She called back, but Jaylin answered the phone. He was a bit upset, and I think I owe both of you an apology."

Nokea swallowed. "I didn't want her to have this number, Shane. I know she's supposed to be your woman, but I can't forget the hurt that she's caused me and my family. You know that I care for you a lot, but I will never agree to her coming to my home or freely calling here. I'm sorry if you don't understand...

"I do. And, I will never make you or Jaylin uncomfortable in your own home."

"Thank you," she said. She grinned at me and left the room. I was hoping to continue our conversation because I wanted to find out if she'd told Jaylin about our kiss. I figured if she had, he would have brought it to my attention. Then again, they didn't keep too many secrets from each other. Maybe, he was waiting on me to tell him about it. Up until now, Nokea appeared as if she'd forgotten all about it. By the way she flinched, I could tell that something was on her mind.

The Hawaiian Luau turned out to be a real bash. There was food for days: shrimp, crablegs, chicken, fruits, vegetables, and desserts lined up on tables around the beach. Throughout the night, loud bongo drums and music played. The barefoot Hawaiian dancers with grass skirts on had everybody on their feet, including me. I danced around tipsy with my red swim trunks on that went well with my carmel colored skin. The single ladies seemed to give me much approval, as well as a few married ones who couldn't keep their eyes off me.

As for Jaylin and Nokea, they seemed to be in their own little world. While others danced around them, they stood close in their swim gear, smiling and looking into each other's eyes. A few pecks on the lips came in from time to time, but I could surely tell they knew the meaning of true love.

Having my own fun, I stepped away and joined a group of Jaylin's neighbors as they sat near two fire burning torches and ate pineapples. One of the ladies patted her lap, asking me to lay on her lap so she could feed me. Since she was a beautiful brunette with dark brown eyes, I couldn't resist. I lay on my back and dropped my head right into her lap. Another lady, Sara, got up and said she was going to get us some drinks.

Sara came back with our drinks and I spent the next hour or so getting to know her and Christina. When Sara's husband came over and grabbed her to dance, that gave me a better opportunity to get to know Christina.

"Open your mouth," she said and dropped another juicy pineapple in my mouth. The juices squirted out and dripped on her shapely tanned legs.

"See," she said. "Now, you're going to have to lick those juices off my legs."

I sat up and looked into Christina's seductive eyes. They said that I could have her, if I wanted to, but I really wasn't sure. I reached for her hand.

"Let's go for a walk," I suggested.

Christina stood up and wiped the sand from her legs and backside. Of course, I helped, but only to check out the goods. She was slim, had a little curve action going on with her hips and ass was pretty decent for a White chick. Her bikini was turquoise and white and gave her breasts an extra boost. Before walking off, she signaled Sara and told her we were leaving. I looked around for Jaylin and Nokea, but from a distance, I could see them lip locked on their balcony. It looked as if they were naked, but since it was so dark, I wasn't sure.

Christina and I walked hand and hand along the beach. The wind blew her long hair all over, covering her eyes. She reminded me of Kim Kardashian, and I had to admit how pleased I was to be in her presence.

"So, Shane, are you going to tell me about yourself or do you intend to leave me guessing?"

"It depends on what you'd like to know and how important it is to you."

"For starters, what do you do for a living and where do you live? Without being too nosy, I'd like to know if you're married?"

"I live in St. Louis, I manage my own architectural firm and I'm not married."

She smiled and gave me thumbs up. "St. Louis, huh? I have family in St. Louis, but I haven't been there since I was a kid. Years ago, I moved here from New York to live with my father. Once he passed away, he left everything to me. So, I'm in the winery business. My brothers and I make wine and deliver it to many places throughout the United States."

"Wow. Sounds interesting. But if you don't mind me asking, are you married or single."

"I'm thirty-six and I've been married twice. Marriage isn't cut out for me, and I'm really enjoying the single life right now."

"I feel you," I said. "Marriage just ain't for everybody."

Christina and I walked for awhile longer, until she realized how quiet I'd gotten. She loosened her hand from mine and stood in front of me. She teased her hair with her fingers and gazed at me with her seductive pretty eyes.

"My house is the big one on top of the hill behind me. Won't you come inside, taste a few bottles of wine with me, and allow me to finish feeding you?"

I looked at the beautiful mansion behind Christina and was well aware of what kind of situation I'd get myself into if I went into her house. Instead, I held her hands with mine and kissed them.

"Christina, I think you may turn out to be an amazing woman. One who deserves more than a man who agrees to come into her house, have sex with her, leave and probably never see her again. I can't do that to you, nor can I do it to the amazing woman that I have back at home waiting for me."

Christina removed her hands from mines. She leaned forward and gave me a peck on my lips.

"Whoever she is, she's a lucky woman. And if things don't work out, you know where I live."

"Yes, I do."

She said goodbye, turned and made her way home. I watched her, until I heard laughter behind me. When I looked to see who it was, I saw Jaylin jogging down the beach with Nokea thrown over his shoulder. She was laughing her butt off, and when they reached me, he lowered her to her feet.

"What you doing way down here?" he said, out of breath.

"I was walking a nice young lady home."

"Who, Christina?" Nokea asked.

"Yes. Do you know her?"

"Yep. She is a very nice person. You can invite her to our house, if you'd like."

"Naw, that's okay. Besides, I'm quite happy with who I'm with."

Nokea and Jaylin looked at each other. Jaylin then cleared his throat.

"Say, baby. Why don't you meet me back at the house? I need to chat with Shane about some things, alright?"

"Alright, but it's getting awfully late. Don't come in waking me and your babies up, because we're getting some sleep tonight."

"I won't be long," he said, and then gave her a kiss before she walked away.

We stood silently for a moment, but I already knew what was on Jaylin's mind. He sat down close to the sudsy water and so did I.

"I...I apologize for responding the way I did when Scorpio called my house," he said. "It's just that for, over two years straight, Nokea's and my marriage had been drama free. She's my wife, Shane, and it's my duty to protect her and my kids. I know Scorpio's your woman, but I can't allow her to call my house whenever she wants to. I can't allow her to tease me and play with my mind like she did in the past, just to get back at my wife. I don't care what you say, but she knows that calling my house would upset me. Not only that, but she knows that calling my house for you would irritate me. Honestly, I don't know how much longer I can put up with this. You're my best friend, but I'm about to make you chose between her or our friendship."

I cocked my head back, looking at Jaylin in disbelief. "I can't believe you just said that. Scorpio's and my relationship is no distraction to you because we're all the way in St. Louis. I do not, nor have I ever discussed with you my true thoughts about her. You're supposed to be my friend, but you act as if you don't want to hear me out or understand what I've been going through with all of this. I can't control my feelings, and if I just happened to fall in love with your ex, then I'm sorry. Why would you be so bitter about it, if you have all the love and happiness that you have with Nokea?"

"Because I once had the same thing with Scorpio. I might not have loved her as much as I do Nokea, but I loved her as best as I could. You have to know, that even though I don't share how I feel with anyone, I'll admit, you being with her breaks my heart. It hurts because, as much as I try to forget about her and Mackenzie, the thoughts of them remain fresh in my mind, especially since I have this friendship with you. I call your house, she answers. I visit you, she's there. You visit me, she calls here. Man, I've already faced reality. And the reality of the situation is, I'm never going to accept you being with her. Since I can't, then I'm leaving the choice up to you. I've been thinking about breaking this down to you for some time now, and just by how upset I got from her call today, I know something has to be done."

"So, you're asking me to make a decision on our friendship and the woman I love?"

"Yes. But, that's only if you love her. I think you're infatuated, and when I make you this offer, only time will tell."

"What offer?"

"I want you to move Alexander & Company here. You and I can quickly turn it into a profitable business and start investing in some real estate property down here. I'm already invested in some property with my neighbors and my bank account is getting fatter and fatter by the day. I want you to share the wealth, my brotha, but that would mean giving up some things."

"Some *thing* like Scorpio, right?"

"You decide. I didn't say it, but you did."

I stood up and so did Jaylin. "The business deal sounds like a good one, and I know you ain't trying to hear me, but I can't leave my woman hanging like that."

Jaylin grabbed my shoulder. "Shane, do you trust me?"

"Yeah, why?"

"Then, you know I trust you, right?"

"Yes."

"Okay. Then, I trust that you'll make the right decision."

"I need time to think about it. When I get back to the Lou, give me at least a month. I'll call and let you know what's up."

"Sounds like a plan," Jaylin said, walking off. He took a few more steps and turned to walk backwards. "And, oh, by the way...you did say that I could trust you, didn't you?"

"Yeah, but I also asked why you're asking?"

He stopped in his tracks and so did I. "Because I trusted you would have told me about Nokea's advancement towards you."

I cleared my throat. "What advancement?"

"The kiss, Negro. She told me about the kiss."

I smirked and walked past Jaylin. I knew he wanted to hear my side of the story, but I took off running to his house. I didn't know if he was trying to catch up to me or not, until I reached the steps that led to his balcony. That's when he darted past me and quickly made his way up the steps. Out of breath, we both stretched out on the bottom deck to catch our breaths.

"I was a track star, fool," he said, heavily breathing.

"Was, is the key word. If you were a track star, you should have passed me up way back there."

"I wanted to give you time to get your lie together about why you tongued my wife."

I took a few more deep breaths, until they finally slowed. I looked over at Jaylin, still lying flat on his back.

"I don't know what Nokea told you, but your best friend or not, it wasn't my place to tell you about our kiss. If she didn't tell you, you wouldn't have ever heard it from me because I don't believe in interfering with people who are married. On that day, that time, and for that moment, I'm sure Nokea had her reason for approaching me like she did. I might have had mine, too, but it's over and done with. I can't take it back and neither can she. I'm just surprised that you've kept it under wraps for this long."

Jaylin rose up on his elbows. "Man, as much shit as I did to Nokea in the past, I'm surprised she didn't jump your bones and try to fuck you. Hell, yeah, I was mad. I didn't speak to her for a couple of days. But then, she told me about her almost losing her life in an airplane crash. Shane, we got too damn much to be thankful for. If I had lost her, over my bullshit, I never would've been able to forgive myself. If anything, her kissing you was a wake up call for me. It lets me know that if I don't keep my shit in order, my wife don't have no problem being with another man. As easy as she went to you, she would for damn sure find someone who will open his arms up to her as you did."

"No doubt," I agreed. "As beautiful as she is, inside and out, she will never have a problem...

"Yeah, yeah, yeah. Just make sure you don't make yourself available to her again. If so, I might have to bust you upside that big ass head of yours."

"Your head ain't all that small, nigga. I know you ain't...

"You damn right my head ain't small," Jaylin said, grabbing himself. "Motherfucka so thick, it has a hard time prying its way into the pussy."

"Jaylin!" Nokea yelled. She stepped outside and must have heard our conversation. "And whose vagina are you out here discussing with your friend?"

"Not you, baby. I was talking about some shit that happened a long time ago."

"Don't make me hurt your feelings. And, not that Shane really cares, but it isn't as big as his ex women make it out to be."

"Daaaamn," I said, laughing.

"Come on now, baby. It might not be big to you now, because you've been getting tapped quite often. We won't talk about back in the day when you...

Nokea placed her hand over Jaylin's mouth. "That was then and this is now. I've excelled to a new level and you don't have to pry into anything...

Jaylin placed his hand over her mouth. He moved his mouth away from Nokea's hand.

"We going to bed. If you hear her screaming, don't think I'm killing her. But I'll be for damn sure plugging her."

Jaylin kept his hand over Nokea's mouth and tried to ease her inside. Resisting, she bit his hand and laughed when he snatched it away in pain. He chased her to their bedroom and when the door slammed, I could hear all the laughing, giggling and screaming going on. Soon, things got quiet and the lights went out.

I lay outside on the hammock all night. I'd thought about going back to Christina's house, but decided against it. Jaylin's ultimatum was heavy on mind, and before I knew it, I dozed off about

4:00 a.m. Less than an hour later, I was awakened by a shake on my shoulder. When I looked up, it was Nokea.

"Shane, come inside. It's getting ready to rain."

I got off the hammock, making my way down the hall to the guestroom. Nokea brought me an extra blanket and laid it on my bed. She got ready to leave the room, but I stopped her.

"Can I ask you something?" I said.

She turned. "Sure."

"Wha...why did you kiss me? Did you even think about what harm it would've caused if I'd developed some feelings for you?"

Nokea shamefully looked into my eyes. "I don't know what I was thinking Shane. I was hurt by Jaylin's actions and I felt as if I was losing him. I'm sorry if I led you on, but that was never my intentions."

"Did you feel anything...I mean, was there a connection after the kiss or have you thought about it since then? I'm asking because I don't want to continue being used by the past or present women in Jaylin's life. Sometimes, I feel as if Scorpio used me in the beginning of our relationship to get back at Jaylin. I don't understand women and—

"Shane, I don't know what Scorpio's intentions are, but I wish that you'd be with someone who can make you happy. She's not capable of accomplishing that, and the sooner you realize it, the better off you'll be. Our kiss was...it was a special and unforgettable kiss. I needed it, and at the time, it felt so right. Yes, I've thought about it over and over again, but I only connect with Jaylin. I always have, and no matter what, I always will."

"Thank you for being honest," I said. "And, sweet dreams, Pretty Lady."

"Goodnight," she said, closing the door behind her.

FELICIA
21

All I could do right now was call His name…JESUS, help me, please. Stephon had lost his mind. After falling asleep in his tub that day, I could tell he must have drugged me with something. When I snapped out of it and confronted him, he went ballistic. We had a knock-down, drag-me-across-the-floor fight and I wound up cracking him across his head with a heavy vase. He chased after me, but I hollered and screamed so his neighbors could hear me. After they came outside, he let me go. He promised me, though, that he was going to get me and get me good.

Since then, I had nowhere to turn. I'd been hiding out at a few hotels, but I needed to talk to someone about this messed up situation I'd gotten myself in to. By the way Stephon acted, I could tell he was back on drugs. And when I realized what that smell was, it was the smell of smoked crack. Damn, I was so disappointed he'd turned to drugs again. I felt all alone, but I knew I still had one last person who wouldn't turn their back on me. That, of course, was Shane. No matter what, I knew he'd help me out of this situation. He'd been upset with me many times before, but it never stopped him from being my friend. Right now, that's all I needed. I knew I couldn't get through this by myself and maybe he could share his advice on what he thought I should do.

Tonight was my final night at the hotel. I went by Shane's place on Friday, Saturday and Sunday, but he wasn't there. I left a note on his door for him to call me, but he still hadn't called. It wasn't like him not to contact me after so many attempts, but maybe he was out of town on business or something. And just as I was about to speculate some more, my cell phone rang. I looked at the phone and thank God, it was Shane.

"Felicia?"

"Yes, Shane, it's me."

"I got your note. What's up?"

"Can I please, please, please, come by and talk to you about something? This is an emergency and I really need your advice."

"Now?" he griped.

"Yes, please."

"I just got back in town and I have plans with Scorpio tonight. Can't this wait until morning?"

"Shane, this is very important. I promise you that if Scorpio shows up when I'm there, I won't say one word to her."

He hesitated and then spoke. "If you do, I will throw you out of my house so fast...

"You have my word."

He hung up.

I grabbed my purse and left the hotel with the same clothes I had on three days ago when I checked in. I was afraid to go home, and I was even afraid to go shopping. I didn't know if Stephon was following me or not, so every time I left the hotel, I asked security to walk me to my car.

It took me less than thirty minutes to get to Shane's place. I kept watching my back because he and Stephon lived less than ten minutes away from each other. I hurried out of my car, rushing to the door. I banged hard enough so Shane would hurry up and answer. He did, and when he opened the door, it was a sight for sore and tired eyes. His muscular bare chest was tight, and his white and blue pajama pants that tied around his perfect waistline showed his goods. I couldn't help but suck on my bottom lip, even at a horrible time like this.

"Come in," he said in a shitty mood.

I stepped inside and he closed the door behind me. I glanced at his nail gripping ass and I'll be damned if he didn't quickly turn around and bust me.

"Felicia, I hope you didn't come over here thinking...

"No, I didn't. But, looking never hurt anybody."

"Lusting, Felicia," he said, placing his finger on my chin and lifting it up to close my mouth.

"Okay, well, damn. I'm busted, but, uh, can we go sit down and talk?"

Shane cut his eyes at me and strolled off to his kitchen. I followed closely behind and shook my head. His swagga was nothing to play with. I regretted that Scorpio had him for so long, but I decided to save my words to her for later.

Shane pulled back a chair for me to have a seat and I did. He leaned against the counter, folding his arms in front of him. I continued to drop my eyes below his waist.

"Do you mind sitting down?" I suggested. "That lil slit in the front of your pants ain't working for me right about now."

Shane looked down and slid his hand down inside of his pants. He shifted his dick to the side, making sure nothing was poking through his slit.

"Is that better?" he said.

I squinted and nodded. "Much better."

He got serious. "Felicia, you have wasted ten minutes of my time. When Scorpio gets here…

"Okay, look. Since last week, I've had some bad experiences with Stephon. He's back on drugs and I am seriously afraid for my life. We got into a heated argument that caused me to hit him with a heavy vase. He came after me, and he's been after me ever since. I'm scared, Shane. I've never been so afraid of anyone in my entire life and I don't take Stephon's threats lightly. I think he might try to do something to me, and I can't go home, I'm afraid to go to work, and I'm so afraid of being alone."

"So…so what do you want me to do? You knew what you were getting yourself into by fucking with him. I told you so, the last time I saw you. All I know is this might be some stupid game you and Stephon are playing. After y'all messed over Jaylin, I don't trust you, and I for damn sure don't trust Stephon."

"I understand how you feel, Shane, but this is not a game. I wish it were a game, and I wouldn't stoop low like this."

Shane slightly tooted his lips. "For as long as I've known you, Felicia, all you've been about is game playing. Honestly, I'm sorry things haven't worked out for you and Stephon, because the both of you deserve each other. My suggestion to you would be to let things cool down. Try him in a week or two and I bet that all will be forgiven and forgotten. If anybody knows how to work that magic between her legs, it's you. You've done it before, and I don't think it'll be a problem for you to do it again."

I stared at Shane and my eyes couldn't help but to water from his insulting words.

He pointed his finger at me. "Don't come over here and try this crying game on me, Felicia. I'm already hip...

Tears poured down faster on my face and I gritted my teeth. "Do I look like I'm playing a game with you, Shane! If I do, then send me to Hollywood to be an actress! I am afraid of this man, and if anything happens to me, I hope like hell you don't have to live with it! I'm here as a friend in desperate need! I need a place to stay for a few days! Will you help me, please!"

After all the sobbing and disappointment I felt, Shane ignored me. He looked at his watch and sighed.

"Fuck it!" I said, standing up. "I shouldn't have ever come here. I thought...nevermind." In a panic, I left the kitchen and hurried to the front door. Shane grabbed my arm, shoving on his couch.

"Listen," he yelled. "You'd better not be fucking around with me, Felicia! I'm going to go see Stephon tomorrow, and if I find out that you or him are bullshitting me, somebody ass gon' get hurt! Do you understand!"

"I swear to you I wouldn't...

"Bit," he paused. "Did I make myself loud and clear?"

All I could do was nod.

Just then, the doorbell rang. I knew all hell was about to break loose, and when Shane asked me to go into the kitchen, I did as he asked, with the exception of cracking the door a bit so I could see into the living room.

No sooner had he opened the door, Ms. Hood Rat was all over him. Her tongue damn near choked him, and when her hand went down inside of his pants, I could have died. *What a fucking freak*, I thought. She was already half naked in the hipster jeans that almost showed the crack of her ass. The top she had on was useless. She was about to take it off, until Shane stopped her. I couldn't hear much of what he was saying, but I could tell by the look on her face she wasn't happy. Minutes later, he yelled my name and I walked out from the kitchen. I tried to be nice, after all, I wasn't going anywhere.

"Hi, Scorpio," I said, dryly.

She didn't speak, but turned to Shane. "So now what?" she asked.

"So, I'm going to get dressed and we are going out to have a wonderful evening together."

Scorpio's brows arched and she was ready to blow her top. "I don't want to go anywhere. I want to stay right here with you, and I was so delighted you'd made it back from Florida. Felicia needs to go home."

"And she will go home. I just need some time alone to tell you what's been going down with her and Stephon. She came to me for help and...

Her voice rose. "To hell with her and Stephon, Shane! What business of this is yours? You're going to have to work out issues with her and Stephon some other time."

"All I'm saying is...let's go somewhere else, have a good time, stay out all night long, and by tomorrow, all of this will be resolved."

"No," she said sternly and darted her finger at his chest. "You got five motherfuckin' seconds to tell this bitch to leave. If not, I'm leaving. If I leave, Shane, I'm not coming back."

Wowwww. She knew better than to speak to Shane like that, didn't she? He didn't put up with much nonsense, and the look on his face implied that she was about to get it. I bit my tongue the whole time because I promised Shane I wouldn't say anything to Scorpio. But, when he looked at me and opened his mouth...

"Felicia, you heard her *demand*, so I'm asking you to leave."

"And, I'm telling you and your woman that I'm not. By asking me to walk out of your door right now, you're asking me to die. I'm not ready to do that just yet."

Shane looked at Scorpio. Fire was in his eyes. "I did as you demanded, but as you can see, your demands don't mean shit. You refuse to handle things my way, and I don't give a damn if you walk out of this door or not."

I'll be damned if he didn't casually walk off to his bedroom and slam the door. The whole house shook and Scorpio and I stared eye to eye with each other.

"Get out, Felicia," she ordered.

"M-A-K-E me," I spelled it out for her.

She chuckled. "You know what, you ain't even worth it. You want me to show my ass and I will not allow you to get underneath my skin. I can't do it, Felicia. Never ever will I stoop to your level again. Whatever is going on between you and Stephon, I hope he handle his business and give you what you deserve. As a matter of fact, starting tonight, I plan to put my request in prayer."

"First of all, the moment you walked in the door, your ass was already showing. Secondly, if anybody knows how well Stephon can handle his business, I'm sure it's you. Lastly, I'm not worried about him handling it with me because I have Shane to protect me. He's always had my back and that doesn't stop because you came on the scene. Either way, today is not your lucky day. He's upset with you, and unless you want to stay in the same house as me, then goodbye."

Scorpio stood quietly for a moment. She looked towards Shane's bedroom, sucking her teeth. After rolling her eyes at me, she reached for the doorknob.

"Do me a favor. Tell that son of a bitch, Shane, not to call me again. And as for you, Felicia...have mercy on your corrupted ass soul."

I put my hands together. "Ooooo, please say a good prayer for me. You know how bad I need it."

The front door slammed and the whole house shook again. I waited for Shane to exit his room, but he never opened the door to come out.

By morning, I was slumped over on the couch, sleeping better than I had slept in days. I was startled when Shane shook my shoulder to wake me.

"Wake up," he said.

"What time is it?" I asked.

"Almost seven o'clock."

I sat up and yawned. I then looked at Shane fully dressed in a black shirt and stone washed jeans.

"Where are you headed off to so early in the morning?" I asked.

"Stephon's shop opens up at eight o'clock. I plan to be there as soon as he gets there. That way, we can work this out and you can get the hell out of my house. In the meantime, there are some towels and a change of clothes on the bed in my guestroom. I suggest you go get busy."

"Do I look that bad? And, what kind of clothes do you have here for me to wear. You know darn well I ain't putting on nothing that belongs to Scorpio."

He glared at me and didn't respond. He patted his pockets, walked back to his room, and moments later, he left.

I got off the couch and headed back to his guestroom. The towels and clothes were on the bed, and when I picked up the clothes, I saw one of Shane's oversized t-shirts, and a pair of sweat pants. Both were entirely too big, but they looked better than the wrinkled and smelly clothes I had on for days.

I silently thanked Shane for helping me out and hoped that everything went smoothly between him and Stephon.

SHANE
22

My blood was boiling, as I sat at Waffle House by myself and ate breakfast. Now, I knew exactly what Jaylin meant about getting away from all of this bullshit. This was an ongoing thing, and frankly, I was getting tired of it. So many things with Felicia didn't sit right with me. Once upon a time, I dated her, worked with her, and even gave her my love. I knew how scantless she could be. One minute she was cool, and the next minute she wasn't. She was being nice now because she wanted...needed something from me. I was positive that once all of this mess was over, she'd be singing a new tune. And by knowing so, I wasn't sure about what it was about me that wanted to help. My good spirit said, don't turn my back on her, but it was obvious my spirit was tripping. I guess it was my mother's words that told me I had to forgive those who not know better. She taught me to be a forgiving person, and most of the time I tried to live by what she'd taught me.

As for Scorpio, I knew for a fact she was more than livid with me. Thing is, I hated to be talked to like a punk. I hated for a woman to curse at me, and even though I wanted her to stay last night, her tone set me off. I had plans to go see her later, but I wasn't about to apologize for what had happened.

While finishing up breakfast, I reached for my phone to call Jaylin. Just in case anything went down, I wanted him to know the details. I was hesitant about telling him about Felicia, simply because I knew how he felt about her. But, the phone call had to be made, so I made it.

Surprisingly, with it being so early, Jaylin answered the phone.

"You're up rather early," I said. "Got something on your mind?"

"Yeah, some more sleep. Jaylene got a cold and I've been up all night. Her *mother*, Nanny B, cut out on me and fell asleep."

I laughed. "Well give Jaylene a kiss for me. I'm sure she'll feel better after that."

"Only a kiss from her Daddy will make her feel better. Giving her one from you might be a dangerous thing."

"I doubt it, but give her one anyway. I hope she gets better."

"I do to. So, why in the fuck are you calling me this early?"

"Because I was having breakfast, thinking about what you said. I'm on my way to see Stephon this morning. Apparently, he's back on drugs and causing a lot of trouble. Just in case something happens to your cousin, I wanted you to be informed ahead of time."

"Shane, you and I both know that I disowned Stephon a few years ago. After all that he's done to us, I don't know why it is any concern of yours if he's causing trouble. Trouble is his middle name. Always has been and always will be. There is nothing you can say to him that will change him. You're wasting your time."

"I ain't trying to change him. But, I feel compelled to talk to the brotha about bullshitting people around."

"A bull-shitter, will always be a bull-shitter. What in the hell brought all this about anyway?"

"When I got back from out of town, there was a note on my door from Felicia. Last night, she stopped by and told me that he jumped on her and possibly drugged her. Now, I know how you feel about her, but I had a hard time turning my back on her. She's afraid of him and afraid to go home. She asked if she could stay with me last night, or until things cool down."

Jaylin was quiet, and then he spoke up. "What is wrong with you, Shane? Sometimes, I have a hard ass time figuring you out. Felicia and Stephon are bad, bad news. Are you just plain ole stupid or do you pretend to be that way quite often? I...

"A man such as you, Jaylin, wouldn't understand. As for being stupid, I'm far from it. What is stupid is, a man who has just about everything in life he's ever dreamed of, but when the time comes for him to give back a little bit of himself, he falls short. Forgiving people is something that you should've learned by now, but your arrogance won't let you. It has cost you time, money, and almost your wife and kids, but you still don't get it. That, in itself, sounds stupid to me, and the next time you call me stupid, you need to take a look in the mirror at your own self."

"Fuck you, Shane," he said calmly. "I've been giving handouts to broke-back motherfuckas for years. The only thing it's gotten me is a swift kick in my ass. You talk about forgiveness, and I've been forgiving people for their mishaps all my life. I forgave Stephon for lying to me about my child and fucking not one, but two of the women I loved. I forgave Felicia for all the back-stabbing she did and still gave you and her money to start a business. I forgave Scorpio for lying, cheating, and manipulating me throughout our relationship. And just recently," his voice rose. "I forgave you for calling yourself my, slap-happy-ass friend, but putting your tongue inside of my wife's mouth! How much forgiveness do you want from a nigga, Shane? Please! Don't piss me the fuck off this morning! I'm tired and I'm not in the mood! If you want to be a hero, then go ahead and be one! Don't expect me to be one, too!"

The phone went dead. I wanted to call his ass back, but instead, I closed my phone and placed it in my pocket. I tried to look at it from his point of view, but I couldn't. Now, I was even more than ready to confront Stephon, so I finished my breakfast and left.

By the time I made it to Stephon's shop, he was already there. From the outside, I could see him raising the blinds. I parked my car and he saw me coming from a short distance. He pulled the door open to let me in.

"What a pleasure," he said sarcastically. "You trust me to start cutting your hair again?"

I stood by the door with my hands in my pockets. "Stephon, you know I'm not here to get my hair cut. I came here to correct you about what you did to Felicia."

"Correct me? What in the hell are you talking about?"

"I'm talking about you fucking over everybody who's been there for you, man. When does it stop? It's like you intentionally hurt those who want to reach out and help you."

Stephon walked away from the door and sat in one of the styling chairs. He slowly moved from side to side, massaging his chin.

"I'm curious. Exactly what did Felicia tell you happened between us the other night?"

"You already know what happened. She's afraid for her life and you should be ashamed of yourself for putting fear like that in a woman."

"Felicia ain't afraid of nothing. She's playing you, Shane. She got mad because I was with another female earlier that day and left with her. Later that night, Felicia broke into my house. She started swinging on me and shit, and I let the bitch have it. We started fucking and I put a hurting on that ass. When I woke up, she was gone."

"So you're telling me she's lying about you drugging her? And, about you threatening to kill her?"

"I ain't threatened no damn body. And as for drugging her, I don't associate myself with drugs anymore. I've been clean for over a year and I'm trying to get myself back together. I come to work on time to make decent money, and thanks to my pussy driven ass cousin, my second mortgage on the shop is paid for in full."

"Speaking of Jaylin, why you be dissing him after all he's done for you? I don't understand your hatred for him, but I do understand his hatred for you. You were wrong, Stephon. Dead wrong and you really missed out on having a dear friend and cousin for life."

Stephon punched his chest. "You're forgetting one thing...he's the one who turned his back on me. I tried to reach out to the brotha and apologize, but he wasn't hearing it. Now, after all is said and done, you're fucking his ex and he's best friends with you. It doesn't make sense, Shane, and I don't give a damn who's in my corner these days. I have an agenda and I'm not gon' let Jaylin, you, or Felicia's mental illness stand in my way. That bitch is crazy."

Honestly, I didn't know what the hell to believe. Feeling as if I'd wasted my time, I reached for the doorknob and wished Stephon well.

"You be easy too, Shane," he said, getting out of the chair and walking up to the door.

He reached out for my hand, and even though I hesitated, I reached out to shake his. He gripped it tight and we both let go. As soon as I got ready to walk out, he called my name.

"What's up?" I said, turning to face him.

"I thought you were coming in here to correct me? Since you didn't, I think that maybe I should correct you."

Stephon caught me off guard and butted his head with mine. When I tightened my eyes to fight back the pain, I felt his fist slam at the side of my face. Another powerful blow hit me in the mouth, and the punch to my stomach sent me staggering to one knee. Then came the uppercut. I fell back in slow motion and landed on my back. In pain, I squirmed around on the floor and tried with the little strength I had to get up. Stephon stood over me and placed his foot hard on my stomach.

"You don't want to fuck with me, Shane. And don't forget to tell that bitch Felicia I'm coming to get her. My advice for you would be to mind your own fucking business. Unless, you want to die."

He gathered spit in his mouth and spat in my face. As he was getting ready to walk away, I grabbed his ankle. I held on to it tight and wanted so badly to get up and kick his ass. Instead, he swung his other foot around, swinging it into the direction of my face. I blocked it with my other hand and yanked his ass to floor. Because I was so weak, he slipped from my embrace like butter. All I had was one of his tennis shoes in my hand, and he broke out, running to the back of his shop. I wasn't sure where he was headed, but when I heard a car skid off, I knew he had left.

I maneuvered myself from the floor and slowly made my way to my car. I didn't have time to check for scars, but I certainly knew they were there. I opened the door to my car and squatted to reach underneath my seat. I pulled out my gun, placing it down inside my pants. I felt underneath the seat again for my bullets and put a handful of them in my pocket. I limped back into Stephon's shop, loaded my gun and thought hard before pulling the trigger.

"Mama wouldn't like this. But, sometimes, a man's got to do what a man's got to do."

I pulled the trigger and fired up Stephon's barbershop with bullet holes. Once the gun was empty, I reloaded and emptied it again. I could hear the screams from the residents who lived above the shop, but I made sure not to aim the bullets in their direction. Once I walked out, I fired into the huge glass front windows and quickly jetted.

Needing no sympathy at all, when I got back to my place, Felicia was all over me. She saw the blood on my shirt from the small cut underneath my eye and the gash on my chin. She hysterically cried, following me to my room. I ignored her questions.

"Shane, please tell me what happened! Let me take you to the doctor to get some stitches!"

I walked into the bathroom, ripped my shirt from my chest and reached for a towel in the closet. I ran warm water on it and pressed the towel against the cut on my chin. It appeared to be the most damaging one, so I worked on trying to get the bleeding to stop.

"Let me see it," Felicia said pulling on the towel.

I yanked it away from her. "Would you please go some damn where and sit down! Damn!"

"I'm just trying to help," she said. "Can I take you to the emergency room?"

I lowered the bloody towel on the sink and gave her a look that could kill. She got the message and left the bathroom. She sat on the edge of my bed, placed her hands over her eyes, and sobbed.

I wasn't up for hearing it. I cleaned my face as best as I could, made sure my keys were in my pocket, and went into my bedroom.

"I'll be back. Don't answer my phone or my door. And for your own safety, don't leave here until I get back."

She nodded and I put on a clean button down shirt from the closet and left.

Unable to get the cut on my chin to stop bleeding, I drove to the hospital. In less than two hours, I was all stitched up and ready to go. The doctor put a small healing pad on the cut underneath my eye, and it took several stitches to close the gash on my chin. I was glad the bleeding had stopped, but my body was still in so much pain. Before I left, I'd asked the doctor for a few pain pills, until I made it to the pharmacy to fill the prescription he'd given me. He gave me three aspirin and I downed them in the car. Afterwards, I made my way to Jay's to see Scorpio.

As usual, the place was packed. I found a parking spot down the street and tried to wipe off the several drips of blood on my shirt that had dripped on it before I made it to the hospital. I didn't want Scorpio to panic, but the napkin I used hadn't given me any justice.

Normally, whenever I walked into the shop, everyone got real quiet. Today, the same thing happened, but Jamaica stopped me on the way back to Scorpio's office.

"You can't speak?" she said.

"What's up everybody," I said.

"What happened to your face? Did you fall off your bike or something?"

"Nope," I said, irritated by her questions. "Is Scorpio in her office?"

"Uh, I...I don't think so. I haven't seen her for a few hours."

"Then, I'll just wait for her until she comes back."

Jamaica looked at another stylist as if something was going on. I walked back to Scorpio's office and it was obvious. She was sharing lunch and laughter with a young man in a post office uniform. When she saw me, she quickly stood up from the couch and so did he.

"Shane," she said dryly, "this is my new mail man, Wesley. Wesley, this is Shane. Wesley's been delivering my mail for about three weeks and he asked if he could take a break and eat lunch with me today." Once she got her lie together, she looked at my face and then at my shirt. "What happened to you?"

"Wesley, if you don't mind," I said.

"Oh, no," he said. "My bad. I must get going anyway." He smiled. "Scorpio, I'll see you tomorrow. Next time we do lunch, it'll be on me."

"I'll hold you to it, Wesley. Be careful and stay safe."

She watched as the youngster gathered his mail bag and left. Then, her eyes followed me as I walked over to the couch and took a seat.

"You baby sitting now," I asked.

She ignored my question. "Again, what happened to your face? Your girlfriend Felicia jacked you up?"

"I didn't come here to argue with you, Scorpio. My day hasn't been going well and I came here to lean on my woman's shoulder."

Appearing to be stunned by my words, her brows rose. She leaned back on the couch, crossed her legs and folded her arms. "So, now you need a shoulder to lean on? Last night, my shoulder wasn't good enough."

"I never said your shoulder wasn't good enough. Last night was a reminder to you that I will not be ordered around by anybody, Scorpio. All you had to do...

"I can't believe you," she said, standing up. "First you damn near curse me out for calling Jaylin's house to speak to you, and then, you never called back to apologize for your tone. The whole weekend, you kept your cell phone off, and the only time I heard from you was when you came back in town yesterday. You had been home for hours, Shane, and finally called me when you wanted to get your dick wet. To make matters worse, you allowed somebody like Felicia to come before me. There are no words to express how hurt I am and that is something you promised me you'd never do."

"I told you that we don't have to communicate every single day. Sometimes, I require my space. My purpose for going out of town was to relax and clear my head. I do not owe you an apology for anything I've said or done. If I've hurt your feelings in anyway, that's because of your own weakness."

Scorpio shook her head and walked over by the door. She leaned against it. "You know what your problem is, Shane? Your problem is J-A-Y-L-I-N. You believe everything he tells you and you are so afraid I'm going to become the woman that I was when I was with him. But you know what, it takes two to tangle. I gave him, what he gave me. And, that was a bunch of headache between the both of us. Since then, you've provided me with a better relationship. Finally, I know what it means to truly love somebody, but you've been banking on me to fuck up. You haven't given me the chance I deserve because you don't want to. That way, you and your buddy can sit around and talk about what I did or didn't do. Mr. Shane Ricardo Alexander, I've given you all that I can give. I can't give you anymore and I have nothing else to prove to no one. There is a price that you'll have to pay for last night, and for how you've been disrespecting me. So, I'm asking you to get off my couch, get out of my place of business, and stay the hell out of my life."

I sat quietly, shifted my eyes around the room for a moment, and then looked at her.

"Is that what you really want?"

"I don't ask for things I don't want."

I sat for another moment or two, and then stood up. I walked over by the door and stood in front of her. I looked her pretty self up and down, and then leaned into her soft lips for a kiss. She backed up.

"Save it for somebody else."

"I don't want anybody else," I whispered and wrapped my arms around her waist. She tried to pull away, and when my grip got tighter, she reached up and smacked my face. I closed my eyes and loosened my embrace. When I opened them, Scorpio stood with a tear rolling down her cheek. I reached up, attempting to wipe her tear away, but she pushed my hand away.

"Have it your way, baby," I said. "I hope this is what you want."

I walked out and made my way through the shop. One of the stylists, Bernie, stopped to ask me something, but I paid her no attention. I kept on walking, until I reached my car. Scorpio was making a big mistake, but possibly, so was I.

SCORPIO
23

Just who did Shane think he was, coming up in here trying to butter me up? Last night, my feelings were so hurt that I couldn't even sleep. I wanted to wipe that smirk off Felicia's face, but there was no way I was going to let her see how much she'd gotten underneath my skin. I'd thought hard about Shane's major mistreatment, and I had no problem stepping away from him, until he got it together.

After he left, I went up front with the stylist and chilled with them.

"What was wrong with Shane?" Bernie asked. "He jetted so fast, and the only thing he left us with was a whiff of his cologne."

"Girl, for the moment, Shane and me are over. Last night, he played me like a stepchild and allowed his ex to stay the night with him."

Jamaica's eyes nearly popped out of her head. "Stop lying! Are you serious?"

Jamaica was ready to play around and I wasn't in the mood. Ignoring her for the moment, I took a seat in one of the empty chairs. "Jamaica, please don't get started. I'm not feeling too good today, alright?"

"You ain't been feeling good all week. We sholl know how to tell when your little happy home has crumbled down because you be one moody ass person. In a few days, it'll be okay. You and Shane will be screwing again and we'll soon see your happy and bright smile."

"You mean the same smile you used to have when your man knocked you upside your head one day, and was able to sex you only moments later? Is that the kind of smile you're referring to?"

"No, hoochie. It's the smile that I had when Jaylin brought his fine ass in here and allowed me to put my lips on his. I have dreams about that day...I mean night, as he carried me in his arms and caressed my beautiful Black body later that night." She held her throat. "He might have fractured my throat with his big dick, but the memories I have of him will last forever."

I grinned. "So, you gave yourself to him later that night and he hurt your mouth, huh?"

"Yes, honey. I must applaud you for being able to deep throat such a thing, but he damaged me. Afterwards, he left my place shaken up by what I put on him, and when I mentioned your name, he couldn't even remember who the hell you were."

"Damn, you were that good to him? I've never known any woman so good to Jaylin that it caused him to forget about me."

"Well, trust me, he forgot it. You know I wouldn't lie to you, right?"

"Oh, you'll lie to me. And, I know you're a liar Jamaica because Jaylin was at Shane's place that night. So, sorry, but once again, you've been busted out, Miss 'I've fallen on the floor and can't get up.' You should have been ashamed of yourself. And whether you face it or not, Jaylin would never give his dick to a woman like you. You don't have what it takes to get a piece of him."

Jamaica laughed out loudly. "I'm glad you think so. And now, I see why his wife had to step up in here and smack you back in place. She must have smacked you real hard because...

Bernie interrupted and dropped the curling irons by her side. "Must we sit up here and listen to the two of you go back and forth about Jaylin? We all know Jaylin and his...his goodness got it going on, but don't y'all know of some other men who got it going on, too."

"Blair Underwood or 50 cent?" Jamaica yelled.

"No comparison," Bernie said. "You know damn well that Blair is a force that can't be reckoned with."

"Are you crazy?" I yelled. "It's 50 cent all day long. I guess you didn't see his movie, did you?"

"Movie or not, Blair is a man with class and he is well put together. He...

"No, no, no," Jamaica interrupted. "50 is a straight-up thug! A woman needs a man who will beat the pussy, and based on what I saw, 50 will beat your pussy good. I don't know if Blair is capable of all that."

"That's what I'm saying," I said, standing to give Jamaica five. Most of the ladies in Jay's agreed.

"What about Idris Elba?" Jamaica asked.

"Who in the hell is that?" Deidra asked.

I quickly responded. "*Daddy's Little Girls*, baby. That brotha is off the chain, but it's a toss up between him and Shemar Moore."

"Toss up my butt!" Jamaica yelled. "Did you see Shemar in *Diary of a Mad Black Woman*? Girl, them braids made me look at him in a different way. He was thugged out and...

"And it's obvious that you like thugs," Bernie said.

"Love'em. Can't get enough of them and I'd take a thug any day over some wanna be fake Negro who gon' turn into a thug anyway when you get him in the bedroom. That's why I don't care what anybody says, I love me some Flava Flaaaav!"

"Wowwww," Deidra said, sounding just like him. We all laughed and said Flava's name in unison, "Flava Flaaaav!"

"Flava ain't no thug to me, so next!" I said, continuing to laugh. "Anyhow, what about Brad Pitt, Johnny Depp, Richard Gere, or Justin Timberlake?"

"What the fuck!" Jamaica got serious. "Do you see any white women up in here? Now, I dig me some white men, but we on the brothas right now. Stick to the brothas, alright? If you can't, then I got a pair for you." Everybody waited for Jamaica to respond. She slowly let their names fall from her mouth.

"D-E-N-Z-E-L Washington and J-A-Y-L-I-N Rogers?"

Bernie quickly spoke up. "Now, that's a tough one for me because y'all know how I feel about my Denzel. However, after seeing Jaylin again, I just don't know!"

"It's Denzel for me," I said. "Jaylin ain't got nothing on Denzel."

"Of course you would say that, Your Fakeness," Jamaica said. "If Jaylin had dicked you down while he was here, you'd be jumping up and down for Jaylin like they just called your name on *The Price is Right*, telling you to come on down. And since you won't be honest, I will. Denzel the mutha-f'en bomb, but Jaylin done surpassed him."

"I'm gon' have to disagree," Deidra added. "Now, I've seen Jaylin, and he fine, but not like Denzel. Jaylin can't touch Denzel's swagga."

"Deidraaaa," Jamaica whined. "But, you didn't see Jaylin's diiiiiick. It was a pretty sight, wasn't it Bernie?"

Bernie nodded. "Yeah, it was rather interesting. Scorpio, I hate to say it, but how in the heck did you let something that...that delightful get away?"

Everybody laughed and all I could do was shake my head. When Jamaica decided to compare Jaylin to Shane, it was time for me to go.

"Why you leaving?" she asked.

"Because y'all up in my business, that's why."

"For me, it's Shane all the way, baby," Deidra said. "Anytime a man can get down with you like he did in a limo, at a club, and on a motorcycle, he definitely has my vote."

Jamaica added her opinion. "Baby, from what I heard, Jaylin wasn't short stopping. He laid it down at the movies, on the Metro Link, and on a pool table. And any man who can dig into you on a roller coaster has got to get some votes."

"Y'all are so damn silly," I laughed. "Why are y'all making up lies about my relationships?"

"I guess you told us lies, then," Jamaica said. "Truth or consequences...didn't you tell us...

"I'm out of here and the game is O-V-E-R."

Everybody griped as I headed back to my office. I closed the door and walked over to my desk. I wanted to call Shane, but I was tired of the back and forth. I said he'd have to pay for his mistakes and I meant it.

FELICIA
24

I kept waiting and waiting for Shane to come home. I wasn't sure what had gone down between him and Stephon, but I was even more nervous than before. I kept peeking out of the windows, and every time I heard a door slam, I'd run to it. Since Shane had moved to his new place, I didn't think Stephon knew where he lived so I was a bit relieved. All I could do was sit around and watch TV, while biting my nails.

Finally, when I heard the door unlock, I was sitting in Shane's hearth room watching the news. I quickly stood up and he came into the room to join me.

"I see you've been to the hospital," I said.

"Uh-huh," he said, unbuttoning his shirt. He removed it and laid it across the chaise. He then unbuttoned the top button on his jeans and sat down to remove his shoes. Once he got comfortable, he sat back and placed his hands behind his head.

"Anything good on cable," he asked.

"I'm not sure. I've been watching the news."

"Toss me the remote."

I tossed it to him and he caught it. "Are you going to tell me what happened or not? You know I'm dying to know."

He flipped through the channels. "I don't want to talk about it, Felicia. The least you know, the better," he paused and changed the subject. "Did anybody call?"

"How would I know? You told me not to answer your phone."

"That doesn't mean that you didn't look at the Caller ID."

I smiled. "Your mother called, somebody from the Mayor's Group and Bradstone Broadcasting called, Amber Watson, Jaylin Rogers, and three other names I didn't recognize. One a female."

"What time did my moms call?"

"She called early this morning, right after you left."

"Jaylin?"

"He called about an hour ago."

"Thanks."

"You're welcome. Sooo, have you eaten anything? If you haven't, I can go in the kitchen and whip us up a lil somethin-somethin."

"That's fine, whatever."

I stood up. "I know you're tired. But, do you think that you can take me to my house later on so I can get some clothes. This shirt and sweat pants aren't working for me."

"They look alright to me."

"Please," I said, rising up his big shirt. "Do you see this rubber-band I had to tie on the side of these pants to hold them up?"

Shane looked at my bare midriff and tied up pants. He snickered. "I'll take you tomorrow. I'm in for the night. Besides, I have to return some after hour phone calls to my clients."

He went into his office and I headed for the kitchen. I'd already skimmed through his cabinets and fridge earlier to see what he had to eat. It wasn't much, but the thawed chicken had to do. I saw a can of creamy corn and worked my magic.

I spent the next hour or so preparing dinner. Once I was finished, I took Shane's plate into his office where he was. He was working on a design, but when I placed the food on his desk, he stopped. He looked at the seasoned baked chicken, buttered rolls, and creamy corn to go with it.

"It smells good. I appreciate it," he said.

"Do you mind if I join you?" I said.

"I'd rather be alone."

I left out and closed the door behind me.

Leaving him at peace, I ate my dinner in the kitchen. Once I was finished, he still was in his office so I went back to the guestroom and got ready for bed. I took off the oversized sweats and left on the shirt. I laid in bed for about an hour, but tossed and turned. When I heard Shane go into his room, I waited for awhile, and then got out of bed. I grabbed my pillow, and since his door was shut, I knocked.

"What?" he said sharply.

"Can I come in?"

"For what?"

"Be...because I can't sleep. I don't want to be by myself."

He didn't say anything so I opened the door. The room was dark, but soon, he touched the lamp on his nightstand and it came on.

I searched his nearly bare body from head to toe. The only thing that prevented me from seeing what I wanted to see was his navy blue jockey shorts. I noticed his glassy red eyes.

"Were you sleeping or have you been crying?"

"Neither."

"Well, why are your eyes so red?"

He didn't answer. He got off the bed and went over to the small sofa near the window to lie down.

"You can have the bed. Please don't ask me anymore questions and don't forget to turn off the light."

I climbed in his comfortable bed and turned off the light. I lay on my back for a minute, staring at the ceiling. Moments later, I placed a fluffy pillow between my legs and turned to my side.

"Have you talked to Scorpio today?" I asked.

"What did I just tell you?"

"I know what you said, but I'm bored. Besides, it's good to get things off your chest."

He hesitated. "Yes, Felicia. I talked to Scorpio today."

"What did she say?"

"None of your business."

"It is my business, if you're in the dark crying over her."

"I told you I wasn't crying. I was just thinking."

"Thinking doesn't make your eyes water and turn red."

"Yeah, but a lack of sleep does. Now, please be quiet so I can get some sleep."

I waited for about five more minutes, and then spoke again. "Last night, she told me to tell you to go to hell. I forgot to tell you."

"Good. I guess that sums up what she told me today."

I sat up, wanting to celebrate the good news. "Did y'all break up?"

He hesitated again. "If that's what you want to call it, then I guess we did."

"Did she call it off or did you?"

"What damn difference does it make? Listen, if you keep on bugging me, I'm going to leave you in here conversing with yourself. I had a long day and I need to get some rest. Please be quiet."

Because I didn't want to upset Shane anymore, for the rest of the night, I kept quiet. Actually, he was the one who interrupted my sleep. He complained about his body being sore, he got up to take a shower, and then, had the nerve to turn on the TV. I got a little rest, but it was obvious that he didn't get any.

By morning, Shane was up and out. I didn't know where he'd gone, and when I called his cell phone to see where he was, he didn't answer. I took a quick shower and found another pair of sweat pants and shirt in his closet to put on. As I was getting dressed, he came through the door. He had some donuts and coffee in his hand, and handed them over to me.

"Drink up so we can go?" he said. His phone rang. and since I was sitting nearby it, he asked me to look and see who it was.

"It's Jaylin. Do you want me to answer?"

"Nope," he said.

"Why not?"

He ignored me and left his room with the donuts. I followed behind him.

"Can I have one?" I asked.

He tossed the donut bag over his head and I caught it. I opened the bag and took out a glazed round donut. Afterwards, I sat on his couch and crossed my legs yoga style.

"So, where are we on our way to," I said, biting into my donut.

"To your house," he said, sitting across from me.

"And, after that?"

"I need to stop at the pharmacy to get my pain medicine, stop at the grocery store to get my mother a few items, and then get back here so I can do some work."

"I...I hope I'm not a bother. Maybe, by next week I'll feel comfortable going home, but just not right now. Stephon scares the hell out of me. Had I known he was that messed up in the head...

"Well, now you know. You can't stay here forever, Felicia, so you need to go get a restraining order against him. That way, if he comes near you, you can have him arrested."

"Did he say that he was going to hurt me yesterday?"

"If he did this to me, what he will do to you might be more severe."

"I can't understand how you got so banged up like that. You're much bigger and stronger than he is, and don't you have a Black Belt in Karate? I would've put my money on you any day of the week."

Shane looked as if he were in a daze. "He caught me tripping, Felicia. Motherfucka straight up caught me tripping."

He downed his coffee and so did I. I ate one more donut, and we left.

The day was enjoyable. I gathered a weeks worth of clothing from my house and then we stopped by Shane's mother's place. When we dated before, I had the opportunity to meet her then. He didn't take a woman home to meet his mama, unless he really cared for her. That's how I knew how much he loved me, but I was the one who messed up a good thing. All for the power of a bigger dick. If I had known things would've turned out as they had, I sure as hell wouldn't have ever let him go. It wasn't as if he didn't know how to work me, because he always worked me good. And as for the size of his dick, it wasn't no Jaylin's dick, but it was long and thick enough for me to say, a job well done. I was just too excited about getting with a man like Jaylin who could give me multiple orgasms within a short period of time and he had mega money. Stupid me, I guess. And pertaining to Shane, I'd be willing to turn back the hands of time any day.

As we drove off in his Lexus, Shane's mother waved goodbye to us. She was so nice to me and I couldn't help but keep smiling.

"I don't know what you're smiling so much for," Shane said.

"Because your mother likes me, that's why. I know she wishes I would've been her daughter-in-law."

"Shiiiit," he laughed. "My mother does not like you, Felicia. As a matter of fact, she can't stand you. She was just being nice, that's all."

I cocked my head back and snapped. "Are you crazy? That woman offered to make me some cookies, she invited me over anytime, and when we left, she gave me a warm and motherly love embrace."

"And that's the same woman who pulled me back into her room, yelled at me for bringing you over to her house, and told me she'd kill me if I started dating you again."

"Are you serious?"

"Hell, yeah, I'm serious. My mother hasn't forgotten what you did to me in the past. I'm her baby, Felicia, and when you hurt me, you hurt her."

"Why did you tell her what happened between us? You ain't have to tell her everything."

"I told her that my dick wasn't big enough for you. I don't care to repeat what she said about you after that."

"Oooo, you need to stop," I said, lightly punching his arm. "You didn't really tell her that, did you? She must think I'm some kind of whore or something."

"You said it, she didn't."

I rolled my eyes and looked out of the window. We sat quietly for a moment, and then I asked him about Scorpio.

"Since the last time I asked, you hadn't taken Scorpio to meet your mother yet. Has she met her yet?"

"Nope. I was getting around to it, but I never found the right time to do it."

"It's not like your mother lives in Egypt or something. She's only twenty minutes away. Just as we went there today, you could've taken Scorpio to meet her, if you wanted to."

He looked away. "Maybe I didn't want to."

"If you love her like...

He snapped. "I'm not going to spend the day talking about Scorpio. If you want to, I can take you back home."

"Excuuuuse, me," I said, rolling my head in circles.

When we got back to Shane's place, things had calmed down. He was back at work in his office, and I was back in the kitchen cooking. Every time the phone rang, he asked me who it was. After I told him, he never took one call. Not even from Jaylin. I couldn't believe Shane wasn't answering his calls, and something must have gone down between them. Surprisingly, Scorpio hadn't call. I was so sure was missing what was between his legs, but it wasn't easy for her to find someone to fill her void. Yes, her not calling was a bit surprising to me, but I was also surprised by the other females who called Shane's house, too. What in the hell was up with that? I thought his skeeza had him tamed, but evidentially, I was wrong. I wondered what Scorpio said when she was here and his other women called, especially during the middle of the night.

Shane and I stayed up late eating, playing scrabble and talking. Before he called it a night, it was almost midnight. I knew he was tired from all the yawning he'd been doing and I suggested giving his bed back to him so he could rest.

"You were on the couch tonight anyway," he said. "I missed my bed last night. That's why I couldn't sleep."

"Don't lie. You couldn't sleep because you were thinking about Scorpio."

Becoming a habit, he ignored me. I smiled and watched him down three pain pills before heading off to his room for bed.

Getting comfortable in the hearth room, I chilled on the chaise and watched TV for at least another hour. When I was ready to turn in, I slipped into my popping peach silk nightgown. I headed back to Shane's room and could already hear him lightly snoring. I stood in the doorway, watching his muscular chest heave up and down. He was down to his jockey shorts and his hand was right on top of his dick. The light was on, so I quietly made my way over to it, turning it off. I stood for a moment to see if he'd move, but he was out. I moved his hand away from his goods, and his hand limply dropped by his side. Knowing that he was out of it from the aspirin he'd taken, I pulled my nightgown over my head, and naked, I straddled the top of him. He swallowed and moved his head to the other side. Other than showing those movements, nothing else followed. His snores got louder and I was ready to go where I wanted to for a very long time. I wanted to taste him, but I knew time wasn't on my side. First, I had to get him inside of me, and then maybe I'd have a chance to taste him later. With that in mind, I reached down and slowly removed his dick from the slit in his shorts. It was rather limp, but I came prepared. Before I entered the room, I'd squeezed some KY Jelly in my right hand. I placed it on the tip of his head and worked it down to his shaft. As his dick hardened, I got a grip on his pipe, shining it as best as I could. I could still hear his snores, but when they started to space out, I chilled for a moment. He was still on the rise. To moisten me even more, I teased my walls with the tip of his thick head. It was time to put up or shut up, so I dropped down on it and kept myself still. Instantly, his snoring stopped, but even in the dim room, I could see that his eyes were still closed. I was anxious to make another move, but before I did, I waited until his snores were back again. I started riding him in slow motion, but when it got good to me, I put an arch in my back, speeding up the pace. When I felt him starting to pump inside of me, I was on fire! My pussy must have been satisfying to him, because he tightly gripped my hips and made a sizzling sound with his mouth. I sucked in my bottom lip and wanted to cry.

"Oh, Shaaaaaanne," I moaned. "I missed this dick. Whyyy does it feel so delightful to me?"

Not a moment later, his movements stopped, and maybe it was in my best interest to keep quiet. He felt my hips and ass, and when he snatched his hands away, the lights came on. He blinked several times and widened his eyes as if he'd seen a ghost. Then, his entire body tightened up.

"Get the fuck up off me!" he yelled. I didn't move fast enough, so he pushed me over to the side. But...not before his juices caught me between the legs and seeped out on his hand while he held his pipe tight.

"Damn," he shouted. "What in the hell is wrong with you!" His face showed a serious frown and he hurried out of bed. He went into the bathroom and wet a towel to wipe off his dick and shorts. He stood in the bathroom's doorway, looking as if steam was coming from his ears.

"You need to get your things and go," he ordered.

"I don't understand why you're so upset with me. It's not like we haven't had sex before. It was bound to happen again. You can't tell me that you didn't enjoy yourself, after shooting off like that."

He came into the bedroom and grabbed me by my arm. He pulled me from the bed and shoved me towards the door.

"Get out of here before I hurt you, Felicia."

I stood teary-eyed near the door. "I'm confused. What was so wrong with me wanting to have sex with you? I don't want to leave. I don't have anywhere to go. I'm sorry."

He came face to face with me and yelled. "What was so wrong with it? You know what was so wrong with it, Felicia! I didn't want to have sex with you! If I had wanted to, I would have asked! Besides that, I'm in love with somebody, stupid ass! And if she ever finds out what happened here tonight, I swear it's all over with for you!"

He pushed me away from the door and almost knocked me on my ass. Only in his jockey shorts, he left and slammed the front door behind him.

SHANE
25

Fifty cent said it best, "when it rains it pours." All kinds of crazy shit was going on, but I can't say that I had anyone other than myself to blame. I had opened up my home to Felicia, and it was obvious that protection was the last thing on her mind. She wanted to get fucked, and I couldn't believe she came into my bedroom and took what she wanted. I was so tired and out of it, that when I felt myself fucking, I thought I was dreaming. I just knew I was inside of Scorpio, until I heard Felicia's voice and felt her hips and ass. They weren't thick like my baby, so I knew something wasn't right. And by the time reality had kicked in, I could feel the pussy just wasn't right. By then, though, it was too late. I'd busted one, and I knew some of my shit had gone inside of her. I tried like hell to get her off me, because I felt it coming. *Damn!* She gave me that extra stroke, even after I told her to get up. That, in itself, did it for me. It wasn't much sperm that shot in her, but possibly, it was enough. *Fuck!* I thought, while parked in the garage at Davenports. My mind kept on wandering...and then for her to throw that pussy on me without protection? How could she? She'd been fucking Stephon ole crack-whack ass, and ain't no telling who he'd been fucking. I couldn't stop shaking my head, and sat in the car for at least two hours thinking about where in the hell did I go wrong.

By now, it was almost 5:00 a.m. The only reason I'd come to Davenports was because I had some workout attire locked up in a locker room in the basement of the building. I'd planned on putting on those clothes, but I couldn't get out of the car to do nothing. I looked over at my cell phone laid on the seat and picked it up. Scorpio hadn't called me at home or on my cell, so I guess she was pretty upset with me. Normally, we would've made up by now, but she was probably kicking it with the mailman. Who knows? I remember Jay told me when they broke up, she ran off to Denver and fucked the exterminator. She got pregnant and I couldn't remember if the baby was Jay's or not. Then, just months ago, when we had our disagreement, she ran right to Maxwell. She insisted she didn't fuck him, but a part of me knows better. I knew that if we didn't work our problems out, and do it soon, it was a matter of time she'd be in somebody else's arms.

With that in mind, I dialed out and called Jay. He'd been calling the house like crazy, and since our last conversation didn't go so well, I knew it was time for us to talk. As usual, on the first ring, he answered. I heard a few coughs and then he said hello.

"Are you sick, too?" I asked.

"Naw, fool," he said in a scraggly voice. "I'm just pretending to be." He coughed again.

"It sounds like you need a doctor."

"To me, it sounds like you needed to be returning my motherfuckin' phone calls. What you want a nigga to do, kiss your ass or something?"

"I was gon' call yo ole punk ass back. Shit got kind of hectic and I didn't want to hear your mouth."

"Well, why you calling me this early in the morning then?"

"Because I figured your ole non-sleeping punk-ass would be up."

"You damn right I'm up. Been up for quite some time now playing with my dick. Nokea kicked me out of the room cause I'm sick, and now, her and Jaylene healthy selves in there sleep. I doctored Jaylene back to good health and this is how she repaid me."

I laughed. "Poor, Jaylin. I feel so sorry for you. One night without pussy ain't gone kill you."

"Fool, it's been two going on three days. I'm about to throw a tantrum!" He coughed and told me to hold on. I heard him thanking somebody in the background and then he got back on the phone. "Yeah, I'm back. Nanny B just brought me a bowl of chicken noodle soup. I'll be back to good health in no time."

"You should be ashamed of yourself. Got that woman up this early in the morning babying your grown spoiled ass."

"And what does yo mommy do for you when you get sick? She be running over there cooking, cleaning, feeding and babying your butt up like you ten-years-old."

"That's because I'm not married yet."

"Married or not, she still gon' be doing the same shit and you gon' let her."

I laughed because I knew it was true. "Listen," I said. "Maybe some things that came out of my mouth the other day shouldn't have been said..."

"Yeah, yeah, yeah. Same here, but...pat a nigga on the back, let's squash it and we cool. I was out of line, too."

"Very."

"Okay, nigga, then very out of line. Get over it."

"I'm working on it. But, in the meantime, you know I got my ass kicked, right?"

"Man, who done fucked you up?"

"Your playa hating ass cousin, Stephon."

"You mean to tell me you could not kick Stephon's ass? Hell, I could do that. As a matter of fact, I could've come there and done it for you."

"Now, you know if I wasn't tripping like I was, you would've had to come here and bury that fool," I snickered. "He played me, man. I went to go see him and he was calm and collect. Talked about getting himself together and damn near thanked me for being concerned. Then, all of a sudden, as I was leaving, he head butted me, punched me several times and uppercut my ass. I got stitches underneath my chin and everything."

Jaylin's voice sounded serious. "You bullshitting me, right?"

"I wish I was. Man, I was out. That nigga had some power behind them punches, and I tried hard to catch his ass. He bolted like lightning and jetted."

"So, you didn't get in not one punch?"

"Nothing."

"Shane, I'm disappointed. I was hoping you'd fuck that fool up! He needs to be taught a lesson and I can't—"

"There's a time for everything, Jay. I'm just letting the dust settle, and I'm sure that after I shot up his motherfuckin' shop, this ain't over until the fat lady sings."

Jaylin laughed. "Right, right. So, uh, you shot up the place?"

"Sure did?"

"How bad?"

"Real bad. So bad that I emptied the clip and reloaded."

"That's what that cock sucker gets! You know how much he loves that shop, don't you?"

"You damn right I do. That's why I did it. It gave me some kind of satisfaction, especially after what he did to me."

"So...I guess what Felicia said was true about him?"

"Man, don't talk to me about Felicia right now. She done broke up me and Scorpio, and called herself raping my ass earlier. I'm sitting in a parking garage right now because I had to get away from her crazy ass."

"Hell, naw!" Jaylin yelled into the phone. He laughed. "She did what!"

"Man, all I know is, I was fucking the bitch in my sleep. I woke up, turned on the lights, and got the shock of my life. She was riding my dick like a champ."

"Did you bust a nut?"

"What you think?"

"Shit, I don't know. I ain't never had no shit like that happen to me. If I ever wake up and a woman riding me, I'm gon' pretend to take my ass back to sleep and let her finish."

"A married man and all, huh?"

"I ain't speaking from that point of view right now. All I'm saying, it would be very hard to stop in the middle of something like that. If you didn't bust one, I don't know how in the hell you prevented yourself from doing it."

"Well, something came out. And I for damn sure had no control over where it ended up."

"Damn! All I can say is your future is looking pretty dim. Felicia will be claiming she's pregnant, she gon' want to get back with your ass, and by the end of the day today, I bet Scorpio will know what the hell happened. Now would be the perfect time for you to make your move this way. Things are bound to get ugly."

"Fool, I ain't running from nobody. Felicia needs me right now and she ain't about to do nothing that stupid. As for Scorpio, technically, we were broken up anyway."

"Shane, don't fool yourself. Felicia is a snake that's looking for the right time to bite. And Scorpio ain't gon' buy that, 'we were broken up bullshit." She will smooth your ass over, make you think she's forgiven you, and drop those panties for somebody else."

"Thanks, Jay. You really got me feeling real good right now. I've been thinking about this move, but no decisions have been made yet. The way things going, you might be right. Either way, I'll let you know soon."

"Peace, my brotha. And, be sure to keep me posted."

"Fa sho."

"And, Shane."

"What?"

"Go get yourself checked out. That ho Felicia nasty, Dog, she nasty."

"Like I don't know that. Thanks again for the extra worries."

Jaylin's and my conversation ended on that note. I searched for pedestrians in the parking garage, and not seeing any, I got out of my car. My jockey shorts could've easily been some workout shorts, so I jogged over to the elevator and pretended to be working out. When the elevator opened, no one was on it and I was glad. I pushed the down button, but instead, it went up to the lobby. The doors opened and three white women and one Black entered the elevator, glancing at me. I folded my arms and they eyeballed each other with grins. One of the white ladies pushed the 3rd floor and the Black lady pushed the 11th floor. From the corner of their eyes, they all observed me. And when the white ladies stepped off at the 3rd floor, they waved goodbye and giggled. The Black lady shook her head and the elevator closed. She turned to me.

"Is there any reason why you're on this elevator with your underwear on?"

"I've been working out this morning. I was on my way downstairs to the gym, but the elevator went the wrong way."

"Oh," she said, dropping her eyes below my waist. When the doors opened on the 11th floor, she stepped out and held it open. "Keep up the good work," she whispered.

I chuckled. "I will."

She let go of the door and I held the close door button to keep the door closed all the way to the basement. When I got off, I went to my locker, put on my clothes and headed back upstairs to Davenports. I thought I could get a good nap in, but when I walked in and saw how messed up the place was, I picked up the phone to call the police. I quickly changed my mind because I wasn't sure if I had a warrant out for my arrest for damaging Stephon's place. Instead, I started picking up the paper that was scattered on the floor. Most of Felicia's designs had been destroyed and both office windows had been cracked. No doubt, Felicia's office had been damaged the most. Her leather chair was slashed, her desk had been turned over and the pictures on her credenza were cut into pieces. Somebody had too much time on their hands. If Stephon didn't do it himself, he definitely had the money to pay somebody to do it for him. I didn't want anybody to see me hanging around, so I jetted.

When I got back to my place, I wasn't thrilled about seeing Felicia, but it was time for her to take some kind of action against Stephon. Besides that, I wanted her out of my house T-O-D-A-Y. When I got inside, I thought she might have been up. Instead, she was still lying naked in my bed fast asleep. I called her name twice, but she didn't wake up. When I called it loudly again, she jumped as if I startled her. She reached for the sheets to cover herself up.

"I have a headache, and if you came in here to yell at me about what I did, I really don't care to hear it."

I sat on the edge of my bed. "We're going to discuss what you did to me later. For now, I want you to put on some clothes and go to the police station to report what Stephon did to you. Then, you need to go get a restraining order and see if you can get some kind of police protection. Lastly, I have to ask you to leave. You were out of line for doing what you did, and even though I might not appear to be, I'm damn mad about it. I'm just trying to be nice because you have a more serious problem on your hands. Davenports is a mess. I just left there and it looks as if Stephon sent somebody out to get you."

Felicia covered her mouth with her hands. "Is it really that bad, Shane? What about my de...

"It's pretty bad. When you go there, take the police with you. I would go, but I think I might already be in trouble with the police."

Felicia took the covers off her and reached for her nightgown. She slid it over her head, and for the first time, she didn't give me any back talk. Actually, she looked worried, and I left the room so she could get dressed.

Minutes later, Felicia came into my office where I was. She was casually dressed in a pair of black pants and a silver blouse. Her braids were pulled back into a ponytail and she didn't have on any make-up.

"I wish you would go to the police station with me. I really don't want to go through this by myself."

"I'm sorry, but I can't go. Like I said, I did something the other morning that could very well have me in a lot of trouble. Going to the police station will be like turning myself in."

"They don't have to know who you are."

I gave Felicia a stern look, and she knew that I meant what I said.

"After I finish up at the police station, can I come back to your place? I promise you that I won't touch you again."

"No. At this point, I've done all that I can do. I'll be happy to put you up in a hotel room and check on you every day. But, you and I will not be spending anymore nights together."

She rolled her eyes and left the room. I heard my front door close, so I knew she was gone. Her situation was so messed up, and after all she'd done, I said a little prayer for her.

FELICIA
26

Somebody was about to get seriously hurt. I knew Stephon better not had messed up my place. I didn't understand why the fool was so upset with me. It wasn't like I did anything to him but crack him upside his head, only to defend myself.

I was going about ninety miles an hour in my car, just so I could see for myself how much damage had been done to Davenports. Right about now, to hell with the police. I didn't need them to do nothing for me. As a matter of fact, I didn't need nobody. Shane was acting like a bitch, and if he didn't let me back into his house tonight, I had something waiting for him.

By the time I got to Davenports, Shane didn't lie and he for surely didn't exaggerate. If anything, he failed to give me all of the details. Everything inside was ruined. Stephon had damaged all of my office machines, he busted up my computers and even smashed my windows. The new designs I'd been working so hard on were no good. I was crushed. My heart ached and my head was still banging. Having no place to sit because he'd broken my chairs, I sat on the floor by the window for hours. I released my emotions, and instead of feeling sorry for myself, I started to clean up.

It took me a moment to gather myself, and when I did, I reached for my cell phone in my pocket. I called Stephon's house, and was so pleased that he answered.

"Why'd you do this to me?" I asked.

"Who is this?" he asked, as if he didn't know.

"You know damn well who this is!"

"Trick, I'm busy. Stop calling my house."

"Ah, so it's like that now, huh? I'm your trick now, but I wasn't your trick when I gave you all of that money, was I?"

"Yes you were. You were just a stupid trick then. You need to get over it, Felicia. Tricked means, you got played. When are you going to realize that I used you to get what I wanted? I got it, so our business is finished. I'm moving on to bigger and better things now, so stop calling my house and harassing me. If you don't, you know what the consequences will be."

"Do you honestly think I'm letting you off the hook that easily? If you do, you are sadly mistaken. Trust me, you will pay for what you did to me, and for what you did to my place."

"Yeah, I thought you'd like it. That was just a lil payback for sending your boyfriend over to my shop the other day. He fucked up my shit, so I messed up yours. And when you see him, tell him these few words for me: shake, rattle and roll. He'll know what it means and it's time to do this shit."

"I'll be sure to pass on the message. Until then, I got several words for you too...your ass is dead. I'm sure you're going to take my threat lightly, but it's all over for you Stephon. Make sure your life insurance is paid up and your burial arrangements have been made. And, watch your back. You never know when I might creep up on you."

"Ditto, baby girl. Right back at ya."

He hung up and I already knew what I had to do.

Bottom line, I was pissed and the only thing I needed was to get my hands on a gun. I knew I could get one on the streets, but it was getting late and I didn't want to be roaming around at night trying to get a gun. So, all I needed was one more night to hide out at Shane's place, just in case Stephon was out looking for me tonight. I called Shane's house to see if I could get an extra night, and by the third ring, he answered.

"Shane," I spoke softly and sadly. "This is Felicia. I'm still at Davenports. Would you please come and get me?"

"Why are you still at Davenports?"

"Because I've been here cleaning up. I called Stephon and threatened him. We got into a heated argument. I...I don't want to be alone tonight. Tomorrow I will go home, I promise."

"Did you call the police?"

"Yes."

"What did they say?"

"They made a report, but that was pretty much it. I asked for protection, but they told me to get a restraining order. It's too late, so I can't get one tonight."

"What were the officer's names who you spoke with and give me your report number."

"Uh, I...I don't have the paperwork in front of me. Why do you want it?"

"Because you are full of shit, Felicia. I can tell by your tone that you haven't done nothing I told you to do. If anything, you called Stephon and made more trouble for yourself. Now, you calling here so I can feel sorry for you and come get you. Well, this time, I ain't coming. I told you what to do, but you didn't do it. I'm already in enough trouble as it is messing around with you."

"And, you will be in even more trouble if you don't come and get me! Now, I'm asking you nicely if I can stay one more night at your house. I will not bug you...

"And I'm telling you nicely, no, Felicia. You can not stay at my house another night because I need some space and some time alone. Got it!"

"Shane, I am not the one to fool with right about now. I swear, I will call Scorpio and tell her that you and I made passionate love last night. I know for a fact she'd believe me and...

He laughed. "I knew you were going to say that. I knew it! Not only that, but I expected you to use what happened between us against me. But Felicia, I don't give a damn what you do. It is so typical of you to not see the good in what I did for you, and turn around and fuck me. So, go ahead and tell Scorpio. I ain't got a damn thing to lose, however, you do. If you stab me in my back one more time, you will, from that moment on, be one lonely ass woman."

"If you think I need your so called friendship, you are sadly mistaken. And if you think your lil spill about how good you've been to me is going to stop me from telling Scorpio, again, you are dead wrong. Prepare yourself, Shane, because I'm preparing mine. Thanks for nothing."

I hung up and hurried to the bathroom to get myself together. Before I did anything, I had to pay Scorpio a visit and tell her how good her man was to me. I was sure she'd appreciate my honesty, and we'd see just how much Shane doesn't give a damn.

Since it was a late Friday night, I figured Scorpio would most likely still be at Jay's. I drove there first, and when I saw her Thunderbird parked out front, I knew she was inside. I was in such a bad mood, and who better than her to take my frustrations out on. As soon as I got inside, one of the older stylists asked if she could assist me. I looked at her customer's hair and declined.

"I don't think so, especially if you're going out like that."

Another stylists burst into laughter.

"Don't laugh at her Jamaica, she ain't funny. Is there something I can help you with?"

"I'm looking for the owner of this place."

"He lives in Florida," the ghettofied one said. "You rarely will find him here."

"Would his name just happen to be Jaylin?" I asked.

"You might be on to something, sugga."

"I was on him, quite often, when he lived here," I proudly announced.

"Now, she's only on him in her dreams," Scorpio said, walking into the styling area.

A few people covered their mouths and Jamaica cracked up again. The oldest one spoke up again.

"Jamaica, the shit ain't funny. Miss Boss Lady, do you have this situation under control? If not, just let me know."

"Bernie, I'm cool. Felicia ain't nobody I can't handle. Now, why are you here and what is it that you want with me?"

"I got some news for you. Either I can blurt it out right here, or else we can go somewhere private and talk. The choice is yours."

"Since you're not welcome in here, the alley works better for me. If not, right out front might not be a bad idea either."

"Scorpio, go out front so we can see you," another stylists said. "I don't know what's up with these hoochie mama's coming in here like you owe them something. First Eva, then Jay's wife, and now her. You need to check these bitches."

Before going out front, I turned to the stylists who spoke. "You don't know me to call me no bitch. And if your boss is getting visits from other women on the regular, then maybe she need to learn how to keep her legs closed to men who don't belong to her. The next time I come in here, you all need to refer to me as Shane's long time girlfriend. Scorpio's been with him on a temporary basis, and now the real deal is back to handle her business." I turned to Scorpio. "Sex between us has been delicious. I felt obligated to personally come here and thank you for turning him into a more creative, energetic and passionate man. Basically, you made him for me. And now, you have no choice but to release him."

The place was so quiet you could hear a pin drop. Scorpio stared at me without one blink. "Are you finished? Did you say everything that you came here to say?"

"Oh, I almost forgot. From all the juices Shane's been pumping into me," I rubbed my belly. "We might just have ourselves a lil something on the way. If it's a girl, maybe, just maybe, I'll name her after you so he'll have *some* kind of memories."

She snickered. "Well, congratulations. I wish the both of you well, Felicia. Don't forget to tell Shane I said congrats, too."

Saying nothing else to me, she turned and walked away. Before leaving, I gave a few hard stares at the ladies who were whispering about me and left.

It was late, so I checked into a hotel for the night. I wanted to stop by Shane's place to let him know what I'd done, but I was too tired to go at it again with him. Instead, I got my room, laid back on the bed and stared at the ceiling. For whatever reason, I thought I'd feel some type of satisfaction after going to see Scorpio. But, the more time I had to think about it, I felt kind of bad for doing so. Shane was gone kill me, and he didn't lie about me feeling lonely because, at this very moment, I felt so alone.

SHANE
27

Finally, I was able to get some rest last night. I'd thought about if Felicia had actually called Scorpio, but since she wasn't knocking down my door or ringing my phone, I guess Felicia must have changed her mind. It had been over a week since our break-up and I was really starting to miss her. I'd been missing her before, but not like I was today.

I got out of bed and put on some clothes. My first stop was the flower shop. I wanted to have some long stem roses delivered at Jay's today to surprise her. Then, I called Tony's Restaurant and made reservations for tonight. After that, I went to a nearby hotel to check out the fantasy theme room suites. Normally, they were used for couples who were on their honeymoon, but what the hell? We needed if not one, at least two days to make up for so much lost time. Lastly, I stopped by Jared's Jewelry store. For the time being, I skipped over the engagement rings, but after hours of being particular, I found her a diamond necklace, set in platinum with four aqua blue diamond drops circled around a centered white diamond. It had her name written all over it and I was so excited to purchase it and give it to her.

With all the last minute running around I'd been doing...picking up bottles of champagne, buying her something sexy and seductive to slip in to and taking it back to the hotel, time got away from me. It was almost two 2:45 p.m., and since her flowers were supposed to be delivered before noon, I headed over to Jay's. I looked around for Scorpio's car, but I didn't see it. Maybe it was parked on another street, since the place was packed. I went inside and no one said a word to me. Actually, things were a bit quiet. I figured something was up, so I headed back to Scorpio's office.

"She's not in there," Bernie said while working on her customer's hair.

I stopped in my tracks. "Where is she?"

"She's at home, ill. She left about an hour ago."

As she spoke, I noticed a couple of roses by her work station. When I looked around, all of the stylists had roses at their stations, too.

I think I had my answer, but I had to be sure. "Where did everybody get the roses from?"

"From you," Jamaica blurted out. "Thank you, playa playa."

"Girl, shut up," Bernie said. She stopped working on her customer's hair and asked me to follow her. I followed her outside and she pointed her comb in my direction, tearing into me.

"Look, I don't know what the hell is going on, but you need to get your bitches in order. Scorpio has been through enough shit, Shane, and I thought you were exactly what the doctor ordered. Stop playing...

"What are you talking about?" I said. "I don't know what you're talking about."

"I'm talking about Felicia. She came here last night and showed her ass. Scorpio was down right humiliated and I stayed here almost all night to help calm her down. She really loves you and for you to...

"Look, you have no clue what's going on right now. Please don't judge me, unless you have all the facts." I paused in deep thought. "Where did she go? I need to talk to her."

"She went home. But, give her a couple of days...

"No can do, especially since tomorrow is never promised." I turned to make my way to my car. "Thanks Bernie, and seriously, where did everybody get the roses?"

"She gave them to us. Said she didn't want them."

I nodded and abruptly walked to my car.

Scorpio's condo in Lake St. Louis was a lengthy ride away. Since we'd been together, I'd only been to her place twice. One time I dropped her off to get her car, and another, I had to take her to work because her sister needed to use the car. Other than those two times, she never invited me over. She was very protective of Mackenzie and all I could do was respect her wishes. Today, however, I needed to see her face to face. I knew I had some major explaining to do and talking over the phone just wasn't going to cut it.

I was only minutes away from her condo, so I quickly checked myself in the mirror. I straightened my goatee and patted my face with Kenneth Cole aftershave that was in my glove compartment. My Sean John Pique Polo and "PD" jeans were already working for me. I felt good about my appearance, and hopefully, she wouldn't be able to turn me away.

When I saw her car in the driveway, I was a bit nervous. And when I got out the car and knocked, my nervousness for surely didn't go away. She swung the door opened so fast, that a cool breeze hit me from inside.

"What are you doing here?" she asked.

I put my hands in my pockets. "I came to talk to you. I heard you had a visitor and you can't believe everything you hear."

"Well, I got one question for you. Did you have sex with Felicia?"

I answered her question as best as I could. "No and Yes."

She tried to slam the door, but I used my arm to stop her from closing it. I pushed back on it and my strength was too much for her.

"Shane, I'm not going to do this with you. You've made your choice, so just leave and be done with it."

She walked away and I turned to close the door. I slowly walked to where she was in the kitchen. She was sitting in a chair with her arms folded. Some of her long curled hair was clipped in the back and the rest hung on her shoulders. Her flower printed satin flimsy nightgown showed her perky breasts and her light skinned tanned legs. At that moment, I wanted to hurt myself for how I'd played her.

I pulled back a chair at the kitchen's table and sat in it. "I know that saying I'm sorry isn't what you want to hear, but it seems like the right thing to say. I made a mistake allowing Felicia to stay at my place and I never ever should have done it."

Her eyes were watery, but she held back on the tears. "It's a little too late to be sorry, and are you sorry you fucked her?"

"It wasn't done with intentions. I was asleep, Scorpio. I was thinking about you, and when I woke up, she was on top of me."

"And...so she was on top of you. Did you continue having sex or what?"

"No, I stopped her. Actually, I damn near threw her ass off me."

"Do you really expect for me to believe that? Is that what you came all of this way to tell me? You could've come up with a better lie than that one."

She quickly stood up and walked out. I sat for a moment because I knew this would be harder than I thought. The story didn't even sound convincing to me, and even I would've had a hard time believing it.

When I stepped out of the kitchen, I could see Scorpio enter a room at the top of the stairs. I went upstairs and walked into the room where she was. It was her bedroom and had Feng-Shui furniture with ocean blue walls. Fresh silk flowers adorned the vases and tall candles were placed on her nightstands. A round floor mirror stood by the huge picture window and satin white sheets covered the bed. Scorpio had stepped into her closet and came back out in her black bra and panties. My dick was rock solid hard as I watched her step into a pair of blue jeans.

"I know my story doesn't add up, but I swear to you, baby, that it's the truth."

She sucked in her flat stomach and buttoned her jeans. "Did you cum inside of her?"

"No, I didn't."

"Did you come at all?"

"A...a lil bit." I attempted to be extremely cautious with my answers.

"The entire time she was there, how many times did you do it with her? She told me it was an ongoing thing."

"Are you not listening to me? Of course she's going to say that. You know how Felicia is."

Scorpio pointed her finger at me. "You're damn right I do. It's too bad that you claiming you didn't know how she was. To me, you knew she would do something like this, Shane! All she wanted was to get you to screw her and you did. I haven't a clue how many times, and frankly, it really doesn't matter. This relationship has been over with for quite some time anyway."

"Oh really?" I said, stunned by her words. "And, why didn't I know it was over with."

"Because you were too busy doing what the hell you wanted to do. You never consulted with me about anything, Shane. You ran off to Florida and left me behind, and then didn't even call me. For months, the only time I hear from you is if you're horny. And what about the times that I call you, and you say you're busy, but you never call me back. Then, you tell me you love me, but I don't need to see or hear from you everyday. What kind of fucking relationship is that? You putting your dick inside of Felicia was just the last straw."

Scorpio tried to walk away, but I grabbed her waist. "I didn't put my dick inside of her, she did. What do you want from me? I'm sorry. I fucked up and I won't do it again. From now own, I'll call you every day and I will call you back if I'm busy. You never said those things bothered you, so how was I supposed to know?"

"When you love somebody, Shane, you don't have to tell them how to treat you. It comes naturally, and if I have to tell you how to treat the woman you claim to love, then maybe you should rethink your feelings for me."

She attempted to move my arms from around her, but I held her tighter and closer. "So, I'll change some things. Don't just give up on us like this, alright?"

"I gave up the night you allowed Felicia to stay with you and not me."

I took a deep breath and let her go. "You've been seeing someone else, haven't you? I can tell by the way you're acting."

"I'm acting this way because you fucked up, not me," she fired back.

"I don't believe that for one minute. I make a mistake one damn time, and now, it's over. Jaylin fucked you over time and time again, but you kept running back to him."

I must have touched a nerve and I could tell by the way she cut her eyes at me. "You are not Jaylin and you never will be. Back then, I was stupid and made some stupid mistakes. Since, I've grown to know better. I will not continue to allow any man to make a fool out of me. If you think I'm the same woman that I was with him, then you're fooling yourself. And I'm going to show you, right now, how much I've changed." She pointed to the door. "Get your sorry ass out of my house, pronto."

"I'm not going anywhere. I bought you some flowers, I made dinner plans for tonight, I got us a room, and I bought you something real nice. You need to get dressed, so we can go."

She ignored me, went back into her closet and came back with a shirt on. When she headed towards her bedroom door, I rushed up to it and closed it. No doubt, I was getting angry.

"Did you hear what I said?" I asked.

"No, because your words fell on deaf ears. After I told you to leave, I didn't hear anything else you said."

I looked eye to eye with Scorpio and my feelings were extremely hurt. I picked her up, took a few steps forward and tossed her on the bed. I lay on top of her and she didn't move.

"Can I please make love to you?" I softly asked.

"After being inside of Felicia, not a chance in hell," she spat.

"But, it was okay for Jaylin to fuck her, right? You know, I'm not feeling this ill treatment of yours because you're making me pay for somebody else's mistakes, too. So for the last time, are you going to forgive me for *my* mistake or not?"

"If you mention Jaylin's name one more time, I swear I'm going to scream. How many times do I have to tell you that you're not him, Shane! I am so sick...

I ignored Scorpio and ripped down the middle of her shirt. Her buttons popped off, and as I lowered my head to suck her breasts, she fucked me up with a slap to my face. It stung, but I kept being persistent.

"Wha...what you gon' just take what the hell you want?" she said upset, struggling to push me off her.

"Shit, it's mine. You told me...

"I haven't told you nothing but it's over! I don't want you anymore, Shane. I don't want this relationship anymore! " she yelled.

I was hurt. "Damn it, Scorpio! Don't do this shit to me! I know I've been wrong...

Just then, the bedroom door came open. Scorpio's sister, Leslie, I assumed two of her kids, and Mackenzie stood in the doorway. Mackenzie and a little boy rushed into the bedroom.

"Get off my Auntee, punk," he said, trying to push me off her. Mackenzie started crying because she'd seen Scorpio's watered down eyes.

I couldn't believe what was happening, and I quickly got off Scorpio. I sat calmly next to her on the bed. She pulled her shirt together to cover her breasts. Mackenzie jumped into her lap and hugged her.

"Shane, you need to go," Leslie said.

"I didn't mean nobody any disrespect. I just...

"Just go!" Scorpio yelled.

I looked at her in disbelief. By the look in my eyes, she could tell how devastated I was. She knew how much I loved her, but there appeared to be no reconciliation on her part. Without saying another word, I got up and walked out.

I drove like a bat out of hell, trying to get to Felicia. I called her cell phone, and when she answered, I asked where she was. When she told me she was at home, all I did was hang up on her. I swerved in and out of traffic to get to her as fast as I could. How dare her play me like she did. She didn't waste no time stabbing me in my back, and for her to make up more lies to Scorpio, really had my blood boiling. No word in the English dictionary described how I felt. As I thought about what Scorpio said to me, I couldn't stop shaking my head. When I thought about the messed up impression I left with her family, I almost slammed into the back of a slow driving car in front of me. I hit the brakes, and to avoid hitting the car, I had to swerve into another lane. Not giving a damn, I continued on with my reckless driving all the way to Felicia's house.

As soon as I got out of my car, I squatted and reached for the gun underneath my seat. I placed it down inside my pants and hurried to her front door. I banged hard, and as soon as she opened the door, I reached for the back of her hair and stepped inside. I slammed the door shut with my foot and gripped her braids even tighter. She placed her hand over mine.

"What in the hell are you doing?" she yelled. "You're hurting me, Shane."

"That's good to know," I said, shoving her inside the living room, and onto the couch. I pulled the gun from my pants and aimed it at her. "Go and get your motherfuckin' clothes on so you can go with me."

"Go with you where!" she yelled.

"You're going to tell Scorpio the facts, and apologize to her for humiliating her yesterday. Then you gon' take your ass to Jay's and apologize to the ladies in there as well."

"This bitch pussy must be awfully good if it got you tripping out like this! Put the gun down...

I cocked the gun and dared Felicia to say one more word.

"I swear I will unload on your ass and blame it on Stephon—easily! Now, get your ass up and go get dressed! If not, I'll drag you outside in your bra and panties."

Felicia seriously thought I was bullshitting with her. She got up, moving like a turtle. And as for opening her mouth again, she did. She told me to put the gun away. That touched a nerve with me, so I snatched her by her braids again and pushed her towards the door. Her white socks caused her to slip around on the hardwood floors, but I continued pushing her towards the door. Now, she knew I wasn't playing, and had the nerve to start crying. By then it was too late. We tussled outside and she started yelling and screaming like somebody was killing her. I shoved her inside of my car, and intentionally elbowed her in the jaw so she'd shut the hell up.

"I can't believe you're doing this to me," she said, while holding her lip. I slammed the back door to my car and promised her I'd fuck her up again if she opened the door. She seemed to be listening now, so I opened the front door to my car. As soon as I got ready to sit inside, I heard someone call my name. When I looked, there was a black Cadillac with tinted windows parked right in front of Felicia's house. Immediately, I knew what time it was. It was time to shake, rattle and roll. The window lowered and out came a sawed-off double barrel shotgun. I dived into the front seat of the car, but by then, it was too late. I felt the pressure in my side and then in my legs. I heard several more shots and a whole lot of screaming. After a few more seconds, my blurred vision allowed me to look up and see Felicia. Tears streamed down her face and she was trying to pull me out of the front seat. My blood covered her half naked body.

"Shaaaaane!" she yelled. "Don't you....

Her voice faded. After that, there was darkness.

SCORPIO
28

This had truly been one hell of a day. After Shane left, I was miserable. I'd planned on officially introducing him as my boyfriend to Mackenzie and the rest of my family, but so much for that. Mackenzie couldn't stop asking me if I'd been hurt by him, and Lil James kept talking about how he should have punched him in his nuts. I knew Shane wasn't a bad person, but he simply should've left when I told him to. I couldn't believe how upset he was, and the look in his eyes said that he was one hurt man. Honestly, though, he had no one to blame but himself. Damn him for letting Felicia come between us as he did! All of this could've been prevented, if he just learned how to tell that hoochie "no". It was as if he still had feelings for her or something, and if he expected me to believe that mess about her creeping on him while he was asleep, then he was crazy. Actually, I could see her doing something that devious, but I knew that if Shane woke up in the middle of her pumping on him, he continued. There was no way in hell he pulled out of her.

Besides, he made it out to be as if that were their only time together. What kind of fool did he take me for? If Felicia got him to screw her once, she was manipulative enough to get him again and again. Just the thought of it made me want to cry. I seriously thought Shane and I would be together for a very long time. Even though he had his flaws, deep down, I knew he loved me. At times, I knew he was set in his little selfish ways, but I also knew he'd eventually come around. Maybe space for him was required, but being as tight as we were, a phone call a day wasn't going to hurt nobody. I'd been willing to overlook those things, but his disrespecting me in front of Jaylin, and his ongoing relationship with Felicia was my breaking point. I wished like hell things could've worked out, but I'd have to chalk this one up as a loss, just as I'd done with many of my relationships in the past.

It was getting late. Bernie called and said Jay's was getting more crowded, and since I wasn't there, things were getting out of control. Even though I didn't want to, I put on some clothes and headed out. On my drive there, I couldn't stop seeing Shane's face. My heart ached so badly for him, but I knew I couldn't be with him after he'd been with Felicia. Knowing so, I pulled my car over to the side of the road to gather myself. All the disappointment I'd felt from constantly failing in my relationships caused me serious pain. It certainly didn't matter how beautiful I was, how much money I had, or how well my body was in tact. I wasn't exempt from none of the bullshit and shame on me for ever thinking I was.

By the time I reached Jay's, I had to sit in the car for a moment to get myself together again. I didn't want to go inside being unstable as I was, because I knew everybody would question me about being so upset. When I was able to, I got out of the car and went inside. Just by looking at me, Bernie could tell how upset I was. She stopped styling her customer's hair, walked up to me and squeezed my hand.

"Are you going to be okay," she whispered.

I nodded.

"Would you like to go talk about it?"

"Later," I softly said.

Bernie released my hand, and no sooner had she walked back over to her customer, a loud voice came roaring through the door. I quickly turned, only to see Felicia storming through the door, looking a complete mess. Tears were flowing from her eyes, mascara was running down her cheeks and her braids were scattered all over her head. As I looked closer, she appeared to have stains of blood on her clothes. My heart raced, as the thought of Shane doing something to her never crossed my mind. She staggered up to me, falling all over me.

"Shaaaane," she cried. She was heavily breathing, unable to get words to come out of her mouth. "He....he's gone."

I got angry and shoved her off me. "Fool, what are you talking about! Don't come to me with anymore mess about Shane. I'm sick of it!"

She reached her arms around me and held me tight. "He died, Scorpio! He was taken to the hospital and he dieeeed!"

I heard her words, but then again, I didn't. I pushed her back again. "Don't come in here playing with me like this, Felicia! That is nothing to joke about!"

She yelled at me. "Do I look like I'm joking? I wish like hell I was!"

"Don't you yell at me! Shane is not dead!" Just saying those words caused me to start losing it. "I just saw him a few hours ago!"

Bernie and Jamaica walked up and held me. Slow tears fell from both of their eyes. "What happened?" Bernie softly asked Felicia.

She sniffled and gasped before answering. "He…he got shot."

I was in a daze and turned to Bernie. "Do you believe her? Don't believe nothing she says," I cried while moving my head from side to side. Then, I thought about all that had happened. "Felicia, you didn't hurt him did you? Please tell me that you didn't hurt him! You did, didn't you?"

"I didn't. Stephon di…

Before I knew it, I lounged out at her. I tried to break her fucking neck, but Bernie and Jamaica held me back.

"Get out!" I yelled at her and dropped to the floor. "Please…get ouuuuut!"

Felicia turned to walk away.

"What hospital was Shane taken to," Bernie asked.

"Barnes Jewish Hospital on Kingshighway," Felicia sobbed. She slowly turned and then walked out.

I told Bernie and Jamaica that I had to see Shane. They agreed to take me to the hospital, and Deidra said she'd close up Jay's. When we got to the hospital, I rushed through the emergency doors and called for him out loudly. Two nurses came around their desks to calm me and so did Jamaica and Bernie. I felt a serious loss. This couldn't have been happening, not when I'd just seen him a few hours ago.

"Can you tell me the status of Shane Alexander?" Bernie asked the nurse. "I know he was brought in here, but I'm not sure how long ago it was."

"Are you family?"

"Yes, we're his sisters."

"Your mother is back with him now. Once she comes out, she'll be able to speak with you."

I tearfully held my forehead. "I want to see him. I want to see him now."

"Ma'am, sorry, only one person can go back at a time."

I didn't want to cause no scene, so I started to walk to the waiting area. Before I did, I stopped in my tracks. "If you wouldn't mind telling me, what time did he pass away?"

"He didn't. He just got out of surgery about a half an hour ago."

I was in shock and wiped my tears. "What did you say?"

"I said he just got out of surgery. I don't know how it went, but you have to talk to the doctors."

I let out a deep sigh and reached out for Bernie. She held and squeezed me tightly.

"He's alive, Bernie. Did you hear her say he's alive?"

"Yeah, she did," Bernie said. "Now, let's go sit down and wait until his mother comes out. We'll talk to her when she does."

I was happy, but at the same time, furious with Felicia and praying my butt off. My eyes stayed closed and I begged and pleaded for God to let Shane make it through.

Several minutes had gone by and I was anxious to see Shane. His mother was taking forever to come out, but when I saw Felicia coming through the door, it took everything I had not to get up and knock her the hell out for lying.

She slowly dragged herself in, looking dazed. Jamaica jumped up and approached her.

"Why would you lye about something so serious?"

"Get out of my face. For the last time," she yelled. "I wasn't the one who killed Shane!"

"Who told you Shane was dead?" I asked. "He's not dead and the nurse over there confirmed it. I don't know where you got your information, but you were wrong. Dead wrong!"

She snapped. "I followed the ambulance to the hospital. When they took him out, the paramedic said that he wasn't going to make it. I called his mother, and out of respect, I came and told you! So y'all need to cool the hell out!"

As we continued to go back and forth, Shane's mother walked out. I'd never met her before, but he carried many of her features.

She looked worried, and when the nurse told her that her daughters were over there waiting, and pointed to us, I was embarrassed. She walked over to us with a scrunched up look on her face.

"Felicia," she yelled, "Why are you in this hospital carrying on like this? My son is back there fighting for his life and you and these women are out here acting like damn fools. Don't be telling these folks y'all any children of mine, because I raised my kids to be respectful. If you don't know how to act, especially at a time like this, then you all need to get your grown asses out of here. "

"I apologize, Ms. Alexander," Felicia said. "There just seems to have been some kind of mistake, that's all."

"You're darn right there was. I rushed to this hospital, thinking that my son was gone. I was relieved when they told me he was in surgery."

"How's he doing, Ms. Alexander? My name is Scorpio. Scorpio Valentino. Shane and I have been dating...

She cut me off, "Nice to meet you. He's mentioned you before, but I don't know if my baby gon' make it. All we can do is pray and keep the faith that God allows him to stay with us. Instead of out here arguing with each other, why don't y'all go to the chapel and pray. We need for God to hear us, and with all these loud mouths, I know he'll hear us."

I smiled and agreed. But before I went to the chapel, I wanted to see Shane. "Ms. Alexander, do you mind if I go in and see him?" I asked.

She held my hand. "Go right ahead. He's asleep, but you do what you can do to wake him up."

They all left to go to the chapel, and I made my way back to Shane's room in ICU. When I asked the nurse where I could find him, she pointed to a room that wasn't too far from the nurses' station. I saw his name on a clipboard and walked over to it. After I slid the curtain over, I stepped inside. As handsome as my man was, the person in the bed didn't even look like him. He had a tube in his mouth, bandages on his neck, and his body looked as if it had swelled. I walked up to him and kissed his cheek.

"Baby, if you can hear me, I wanted to let you know that I'm here. I'm not going anywhere until you wake up, so hurry it up, please."

I knew he couldn't hear me because he looked as if he were in a deep sleep. His breathing seemed irregular and the beeps on the machine made me nervous. I took his right hand and squeezed it tightly together with mine.

"Hey, sleepy head, I forgot to tell you how much I love you. You already know I do, and...and even though I forgot to tell you earlier, I ho...I hope it's not too late for me to tell you now." I took a hard and hurtful swallow. "Please get better so I can tell you how much you mean to me, okay?"

I stayed with Shane for a few more minutes, and then went back into the waiting area. Before going to the chapel, I pulled out my cell phone to call Jaylin. If I couldn't bring Shane out of it, I knew Jaylin could. I wasn't sure if he'd be willing to come back to St. Louis, but it sure as hell was worth a try.

On my first attempt, the phone went straight to voicemail. When I called back, Jaylin picked up.

"Speak," he said with attitude, as he must have seen my name on the Caller ID.

"Jaylin, this is Scorpio."

"I know who it is and this call better be good."

"I wouldn't call you, unless it was important."

"Well, what's important to you might not be important to me. I knew that if you had my number, you would use it at your leisure."

At a time like this, I was forced to ignore his arrogance. "Jaylin, Shane's in the hospital. He's been shot. I don't know if he's going to make it or not, but I was hoping that you'd," I paused and couldn't get the words to come out.

"I knew some stupid shit was gon' go down! Damn! What hospital is he at?"

"Barnes Jewish Hospital. ICU."

Jaylin hung up, and since I figured he was on his way, I headed for the chapel.

JAYLIN
29

I rubbed my eyes and sat up in bed. Nokea turned on the lights, reached over and touched my back.

"Who was that calling here this late?" she asked.

"Scorpio."

"Scorpio?" her voice got louder. "What is she calling here for?"

"Shane's been shot," I said, standing up.

It didn't take long for her eyes to fill with water. "Oh my God. How serious is it? Is he going to be okay?"

"I don't know, Nokea. All I know is he's been shot. If he was dead, I'm sure Scorpio would have told me."

I walked off to my closet to get some clothes. When I got back, I tossed my black pants and black ribbed silk sweater on the bed.

Nokea looked at my clothes, then at me with her watery eyes. "Where are you going?"

"Where do you think I'm going? I'm going to St. Louis to see what's up with Shane."

She dropped her face into her hands. "I can't believe this. Must we go through this all over again? How do you know Scorpio didn't call here and lie to you?"

"Because she wouldn't lie about nothing like that."

"And, I'm sure you know her so well. The least you can do is call the hospital and make sure he's there. That way you can see how he's doing and save yourself a trip to St. Louis. I'm anxious to know, too, but I want to make sure this isn't an attempt for Scorpio to..."

"Nokea, you're starting to piss me off. Now, I told you that Shane's been shot. I don't give a shit how serious it is. I'm still going to St. Louis. If you want to go, then I suggest you shut your mouth, get out of bed and put on some clothes."

She reached for the phone and placed it on the bed in front of me. "Watch your tone with me. Just call the hospital first, please."

I ignored her and walked back into the closet to get my shoes. By then, she'd picked up the phone herself.

"Do you know what hospital he's at?"

I opened my safe in the closet, then pulled out my gun. Nokea slowly put the phone down.

"Wha...what are you doing with that?"

I slid the clip inside and placed the gun behind my back. "Nothing," I said.

"Like hell, Jaylin." Her voice rose again. "Don't you lie to me! Do you know something that you're not telling me! I demand to know what is going on, right now!" she cried.

"Toughen up, Nokea! I don't have time to explain nothing and all this crying and shit is working my nerves! Either you're going with me, or you're not! In no less than ten minutes, either way, I'm out the door."

My tone caused her to release her emotions even more. I hated to see her so upset, but hell, I had to go! I left out of the room and went to give both of my sleeping babies a kiss. Afterwards, I stopped in and told Nanny B that Shane had been shot and I had to go. She understood and told me to be careful. She told me not to worry about the kids because they were in good hands. I knew that and so did Nokea. That's why I couldn't understand, at a time like this, why she was tripping. I went back into our bedroom and stood in the doorway. She was still sitting in bed, dabbing her eyes with a Kleenex.

"Am I taking this journey alone?" I asked. "I'd like for you to come with me. I have a long drive ahead of me and maybe you can help me drive."

She wouldn't look up at me. "Why won't you just fly? You know it will be much faster, but you can't get on the plane with that...that gun."

"That's why I'm driving. If I don't have to use it, I won't. If I do, I'm sorry."

She pleaded with me. "What about your family, Jaylin? Are you going to put us through this again? I know that if Shane's really been shot, you're going to do something stupid. Haven't you learned from your previous mistakes? Didn't what we just go through mean anything to you? You promised me that you...

"My family needs to learn how to accept me for who I am, and trust me when shit like this happens. I might keep on making mistakes, Nokea, but I can't stay here knowing that my best friend needs me."

"I need you too," she yelled. "What if something happens...?

"I don't have time for what if's. I love you, Nokea. Tell my babies I love them, too, and I'll see you when I get back."

Having no more time for the bullshit, I turned and headed for the garage. Last year, I'd purchased a brand new black Hummer, accessorized with silver chrome and rarely ever drove it. I bought it to get up and down the high and rocky hills, but most of the time, Ebay took us where we had to go. I got inside, put on my dark shades and started the engine. As I backed out into the driveway, Nokea came rushing outside in her housecoat. I lowered the window.

"Baby, I'm sorry, but my time is minimal," I said.

"Wait for me," she said. "Give me at least fifteen minutes at the most."

I smiled. "Five minutes and you got yourself a deal."

She cracked a tiny smile and hurried inside.

Five minutes had gone by and so had ten. Yes, I loudly honked the horn and was getting very impatient. The time we spent arguing could've been time on the road. I was anxious to get to St. Louis, and if Stephon was the one responsible, Lord help us all.

Moments later, Nokea rushed outside with her hair all in tact, her make-up on, and a pair of tight huggable jeans that plumped her ass up even more, showing her tiny gap. Her sleeveless blouse was Papaya and matched her rhinestone studded high heeled shoes. I removed my glasses just to get a look at how fine she looked.

I intended to get out and open the door for her, but she waved me off. She hurried over to the passenger's side and got in.

I backed up. "No wonder it took you so long. You dressed like you going to a club or something. My friend could be dying and you in there putting on make up."

"Shut up talking to me," she said, putting on a bracelet. "I'm upset with you."

"Why? Because you're stuck with who you married?"

"I'm never stuck with you, Jaylin. For the time being, I'm just borrowing you. When I get tired of you, I'm going to throw you away." She smiled.

"I'm going to throw you away, too. Then, when I need some loving, I'll dig you back out, tap that ass and toss you back in."

"Same here," she said. "Besides, sex is all you're good for anyway."

"Is that it?" I smirked.

"I'm afraid so. You're definitely not good at listening to your wife, and she always offers you excellent advice."

"Not all the time. Besides, I've said it before and I'll say it again, my wife was well aware of what kind of man she married. It's too late to have any regrets now. It's a done deal. She's stuck and ain't no getting out of this...unless I say so."

"Don't be so darn sure of yourself. I love you much, but that gun behind your back better not get you in anymore trouble. As a matter of fact, you need to hand it over to me."

"If I hand this gun over to you, it's gon' cost you big, big time!"

"Whatever it is, I'm willing to pay."

"Alright...then take off your clothes."

"What!"

"I said take off your clothes and ride all the way to St. Louis with me naked."

She laughed. "For what? Why would you want me riding in the car with you naked?"

I placed my hand on her thigh. "You know...so I can mess around with you while I'm driving. Keep my mind preoccupied and maybe the drive will go faster. Besides, you know why we've been doing all this loving making lately, don't you?"

"Yes, because you want to see if we can make another baby. I do too, but it amazes me where you get all this freaky stuff from. Why would I get naked, and allow other people on the road to look over and see me?"

"It's dark, there are not too many cars on the highway and this Hummer sits up pretty darn high. Not too many cars can see in here, and besides all of that, who better to get freaky with than your husband?"

"So, all I have to do is take off my clothes, let you tease me, and you'll up the gun?"

"That's it."

She held out her hand. "Give me the gun."

I smiled and reached for the gun behind my back. It swung on the tip of my finger and she took it. She placed it inside of her purse and put it on the back seat of the truck. After that, she sat for awhile, smiling.

"Hey, you better start getting busy, now!" I said. I snapped my finger and put in a CD by Luther Vandross. No matter where I was, his music could always set the mood.

"I thought my outfit was enough to turn you on. The way you looked at me when I got into the truck said it all."

"Yes, I was very aroused while looking at your butt in those tight jeans, but I need something else to perk me up. Clothes off, Mrs. Rogers, we had a deal."

Nokea turned up the music and started with her blouse. She pulled it over her head and I turned my head sideways to look at her. She placed her hand on the side of my face and turned it.

"Keep your eyes on the road, please."

I kept my eyes on the road, but I could see her from the corner of my eye. She snapped the front of her bra, took it off and placed it on my head. After that, she rose up a bit and lowered her panties and jeans at the same time. She bent over to pull them over her shoes. I reached over, rubbed her back and slid my hand down to her ass. I squeezed it in my hand.

"That's right baby, show me what ya working with. I am one lucky man."

"If anybody knows what I'm working with, it's you."

Nokea rose up and tossed her jeans and panties on the back seat. She placed her left leg on my lap and I couldn't help but look over at her.

"Keep your eyes on the road," she said again and removed her bra from my head. She tossed her bra on the back seat as well.

"I am keeping my eyes on the road. I just wanted to take a peek." I rubbed up and down her smooth leg and massaged it. "Turn your back to the door and scoot closer to me."

No questions, Nokea did as I had asked.

While attempting to keep my eyes on the road, I worked my right hand as best as I could. I massaged between her upper thighs and lightly slid my fingers up and down her slit. When I made rotations inside of her, with my index and middle fingers, she slightly backed up.

"Bring it back to me," I suggested, while keeping my fingers inside.

She scooted forward to get back in place, and I let my thumb relax on her clit. I knew that when I started to tease it, she wouldn't be able to maintain her composure for long. I began to work all three fingers and Nokea couldn't keep still. She rolled her lower body with the rhythm of my fingers and lifted her leg to widen up.

"Let me know when it's coming," I said, still trying to keep one eye on the road.

"Ohhhh, my sweet, dear and satisfying husband, it's coming. You'd better get ready be...because it's coming, nowwww!!"

I quickly swerved over to the side of the highway, put the car in park and dropped my face between her legs. I sucked in her juices and closed my eyes as she pulled hard on my curly hair. After she came, she sat still for a few minutes, heavily breathing in and out. I rose up, licked my lips and puckered.

"Wait a minute," she said, leaning back on the door. "I can't move. Give me a moment to regroup."

I sat up, "That was pretty good, wasn't it?"

"Scrumptious," she said. "We must do that more often."

I pulled my shirt over my head and tossed it to Nokea. Then I unbuttoned the top button on my pants and unzipped them. I put the car in drive and drove off.

"I guess I know what that means," she said, wrapping my shirt around her breasts.

"It means it's time to pay for the good services I provided to you."

Nokea sat up and moved over as close as she could to me. She straightened the curls in my hair with the tips of her fingers and told me she loved me.

"I love you, too," I said.

"I hope Shane is going to be okay. Do you think he will?"

"I hope so. No doubt, we'll soon know."

Nokea lowered herself and I tried hard to stop the fluttering of my eyelids so I could see.

FELICIA
30

Being around Scorpio this long was starting to work my nerves. Thing is, she wasn't leaving the hospital and neither was I. Her friends, Thelma and Louise, had already left, so that left Scorpio and me in the waiting room together. We said nothing to each other and when I'd overheard her calling me a liar, I almost went off on her. Simply because I didn't purposely lie about Shane being dead. I knew what the paramedic said to me and if didn't nobody believe me, to hell with them. Maybe I should've waited around a little longer, but the way those bullets went into him, I didn't think he had a chance. Plus after all of the blood he'd lost, how could anyone survive something so traumatic?

It was already 11:00 a.m., and I was tired of drinking coffee to stay awake. I'd only been back one time to see Shane because his mother was back there with him and I didn't want to intrude. Scorpio had been back several times, and all of us were sitting around waiting until he woke up. His mother promised us that the moment he did, she'd let us know. She even suggested that we go home. But, after what happened at my place, and after talking to this guy about handling some business for me, the hospital is where I intended to stay.

As I sat watching the TV in the far corner of the waiting room, I felt my eyes giving up on me. That was until Scorpio came over and sat directly in front of me. I pretended as if I didn't see her, but that encouraged her to call my name.

"Yes," I said with attitude.

"Now that it's just you and me here, would you mind telling me the truth about you and Shane? He told me something totally different about you and him, but I just want to be sure."

"I guess you need to ask yourself if you believe him, or do you believe me. Since I'm such a big liar, why are you relying on me to tell you the truth?"

She clinched her fingers together. "I thought maybe now would be the perfect time for you to come clean. I'm sure you know we broke up because of what you told me, and if you the least bit want to do the right thing, why don't you be honest, Felicia."

"Okay, so I lied about us having sex multiple times. Now what, Scorpio? Is that all you care about? How about asking me how Shane got shot. Or, if I know who did it. You're not asking because you don't care. All you care about is where he puts his dick and who he gives it to. I had several women to call last night and inform them of what happened to Shane. I got the numbers from his Caller ID and they're not here because you're here. So, if you think I'm such a problem for you, then maybe you should think again."

"I didn't ask you all of that. I asked you about you and Shane, and not about the women calling his house. I can't believe how desperate you've gotten these days. You...

I darted my finger at her. "No, you need to thank me for coming to you last night, telling you what happened. I didn't have to do it, Scorpio, especially how I feel about you. I did it for Shane and don't make me regret my decision. For the record, so you can hurry up and get the hell away from me, I forced Shane inside of me. Yes, he was angry, but it didn't stop him from coming inside of me. If you want more details, wait until he wakes up so you can harass him about it. You and I, we have nothing else to say to each other."

I rushed out of my seat, and on my way to the door, I bumped into this man smelling too damn good. When I stepped back, it, was, Jaylin. Motherfucka didn't even say excuse me and he walked right past me. He went up to Scorpio and she jumped up from her seat, throwing her arms around him.

"I'm so glad you came," she said. "Shane is going to be so happy that you're here."

I was so busy watching the two of them that I didn't notice Nokea until she walked past and ignored me, too. Jaylin hadn't put one arm around Scorpio, and when she saw Mrs. Jaylin Jerome Rogers in the flesh, the bitch took two, maybe three steps back. I wanted to crack the hell up. She looked as if she'd seen a ghost and Nokea walked right up beside Jaylin and took his hand. I'd never smoked a day in my life, but I felt as if I needed a cigarette and needed it bad. No doubt, this was going to get interesting. So, to hell with a cigarette, all I needed to do was find the nearest seat.

I stepped over to the soda machine and got a diet coke. Afterwards, I went right back over to my seat near Scorpio. Jaylin and Nokea had taken a seat close by as well, and we all sat together in one big square. Scorpio was filling Jaylin in on how Shane was doing.

"The doctors said they're not sure if or when he's going to come out of it. Basically, all we can do is wait. His mother has been back there with him for hours and they're only allowing one visitor at a time."

Jaylin stood up. "Well, you know me, I don't follow the rules. I'm going back there to see him now."

Nokea grabbed his hand. "Baby, just sit down for a minute. If his mother is back there, maybe she wants to be alone with him. At least, wait until she comes out and talk to her. Then you can go back there."

"Maybe so," he said. "Do you want a soda or something?" he asked Nokea.

"Not a soda, but bottled water would be great. Thanks."

He walked off to get it, and my eyes searched his fine ass from head to toe. I didn't care that Nokea noticed my stares and I took a sip from my soda can, making a slurping sound while drinking out of it. Scorpio knew she was on fire too, and after taking a clearer glance of him, she crossed her legs, placing her hands between them. Jaylin came back, handed Nokea her bottled water and took a seat. He had a can of Pepsi, and as soon as he opened it, it squirted out on his hands. Nokea removed the can from his hands and placed it on the table beside her.

"Let me go to the bathroom and get you a napkin," she said.

She got up and I turned my head. Yeah, I see ya bitch, I thought. I wanted to stick my feet out and trip her, but since I wasn't very well liked around here, I was trying to play it cool. If anything, she just wanted to be seen. I'd already peeped her expensive Dolce & Gabbana bag that matched her shoes. I had something similar to it at home, but only in a different color. And those jeans, I admit, they were cute. But, did she have to wear them so tight? I couldn't help but notice that they gave her butt a bit more cush. It was obvious that Jaylin thought so too because he couldn't keep his eyes off her. When she came back with the napkins, his eyes dropped right between her legs. He was a horny motherfucker and looking at him gaulk at her made me sick.

After Nokea wiped his hands, Jaylin turned to Scorpio. "Does anybody know exactly what happened?"

"I still don't know. I think Felicia knows, but she hasn't been saying much."

I kept my eyes focused on the TV. I knew Jaylin wasn't going to say anything to me, and he surely didn't. A while later, I even got up and got some cupcakes, just to see if he'd follow, but he never did. But when I walked back to my seat, he made eye contact with me. He stared at me until I sat down in my seat. I took another long sip from my soda and bit into my cupcake. Damn, his eyes were gorgeous. I wondered if being this close to me, Scorpio and Nokea had him thinking about his sexual encounters with all of us. He'd definitely fucked and sucked us good, and to have not one, or two, but three women who knew how big his dick was, in one room together, had to make him uncomfortable. I couldn't help but gaze over at the hump between his legs, and just thinking of the times we'd spent together, made my pussy throb. Then again, Jaylin was probably gloating inside. I was sure he was thinking about every position, all the orgasms, hollering and screaming he'd caused each and every one of us. No doubt, I haven't found a brotha yet who could screw me as well as he did, but I guess all good things come to an end. Hopefully, Nokea's time was running out, too.

I took a deep breath in discouragement when Scorpio got her big booty ass up, flaunting it around. Jaylin was sure to get a peek, and anybody in their right mind could see and tell that he missed that ass. One of Scorpio's girlfriends was back, and she brought her some breakfast from McDonalds.

"I didn't know if you had eaten anything," she said. "But here's a little something from McDonalds."

"Thanks, Bernie" Scorpio said, as they both made their way over to some seats. "I'm not hungry, though. I can't eat a thing." She paused and looked at Jaylin. "Bernie, you remember Jaylin, don't you?"

"Of course, how could I forget," Bernie said, waving at him. "It's nice to see you again, but I'm sorry it had to be under these conditions."

Scorpio intentionally forgot to acknowledge Nokea, who was sitting right next to him. Jaylin, however, wouldn't let her forget. "Bernie," he said. "This is my wife, Nokea."

I placed my hand over my mouth and cracked up on the inside. That's what the bitch get for trying to disrespect that man in front of his baby-maker. The fakeness was too much for me and I had to get up and go somewhere else. Just as I did, Shane's mother came through the double wooden doors. All of us rushed up to her.

"He's still not awake," she said, looking frustrated. "The doctors say this is normal after surgery, but I want you all to go home and get some rest."

"Before I go," Scorpio said. "Do you mind if I go sit with him? I've been waiting all morning...

Jaylin interrupted. "Well, I drove a long way and I really would like to see him now." He looked at Scorpio. "I haven't seen him at all so...

I had to add my two cents. "And I've only seen him once and I've been here all night. Ms. Alexander you know how close Shane and I are. We were just at your house the other day, and all I'd like to do is go back there and see him. I was with him when this happened, and I want to let him know that I'm here for him, as well as tell him that I'm fine"

Scorpio rolled her eyes at me and Jaylin walked off. He went straight through the double doors that Shane's mother had exited from and ignored Nokea when she called his name.

"Let him go," Ms. Alexander said to Nokea. "I know he's been Shane's friend for a very long time."

On that note, I left. I knew when I wasn't wanted, so to hell with them all.

SCORPIO
31

Simply put, I was worn out. I'd been at the hospital for almost two days straight and Shane hadn't woken up at all. I was more worried than I'd ever been, and with Felicia constantly being around, it certainly added to my frustrations. Jaylin and Nokea didn't help either, and I got tired of her reaching for his hand, kissing on him, and rubbing his back every time I came around. The shit drove me crazy, and every time I saw him, something inside of me couldn't help but think about what we shared in the past. His presence always brought back memories, and even though Shane was all I needed, Jaylin's spectacular love making could never be forgotten.

When Jaylin stayed with Shane almost half of the night, so nobody else could see him, that was it for me. I left the hospital, came home, showered and hit the bed.

Today was a new day. I got plenty of rest and after I ate breakfast with Leslie and the kids, I went back to the hospital to see Shane. I had Bernie taking care of everything for me at Jay's, and with her in charge, I really wasn't worried. If anything, I hoped and prayed that when I got to the hospital, nobody was there and I'd have some alone time with Shane.

The waiting area was clear, so I moseyed on back to Shane's room. Surprisingly, when I pulled the curtain over to the side, Jaylin was sitting in a chair next to Shane's bed, and the long tube had been removed from his mouth. His eyes were opened and he stared at me. My heart melted.

"Hi," I said, walking up to him. He blinked and nodded. "Does it hurt for you to talk?"

He nodded again.

"Okay," I said, taking his hand. "Then you don't have to talk, but I want you to listen, okay?" He showed no motion. "I am so, so sorry for what happened between us the other day. If there was any way possible for me to take back the things I said, I would do it in a heartbeat. I love you with all of my heart and I'm never going to let anyone come between us...

He slowly lifted his hand, placing a finger on his lips. He then moved his head from side to side, signaling no.

"I know you don't want to hear this, but I don't know of a better time to say it. Do you forgive me for the way I acted? Will you forgive me?"

He nodded and placed his hand on his heart. Tears fell from my eyes and I quickly wiped them. He held his hand up and motioned with his fingers for me to come closer to him. I did and he pulled me down close to his chest. I laid my head on it and he touched the back of my head. He mumbled something, but I couldn't make it out. I lifted my head from his chest.

"What did you say?" I asked.

"He said that he loves you, too," Jaylin said.

Shane pointed to Jaylin and nodded. All I could do was smile.

For the next few days, things started to get better and better for Shane. He'd been moved to a therapy center around the corner, just so he could get his strength back. Who'd ever shot him, intended for him to die. One bullet hit him in his lower side, and two went into his right leg. I still didn't know all of the details about what had happened, but every time I came into his room, he and Jaylin were up to no good. They'd stop talking, and when they did talk, they spoke in codes. I really didn't care to know what the plan was, I was just happy that Shane was well and alive. Maybe it did take for Jaylin to come and be by his side, and I was surprised that he'd hung around this long— him and Nokea both. She was all over Shane as well. One time, I came into his room and she was sitting next to him, while reading a sports magazine to him. Then when I came again, she was massaging his legs. Both times, Jaylin wasn't around, but after last night, Nokea was on her way back home. I had some time alone with Shane, but sharing my time with his mother and Jaylin was, at times, bothersome. I'd redone his twisties, and his mother said she didn't like them. I moistened and massaged his feet, and Jaylin walked into the room. I could barely get a kiss from him, without the two of them hovering over him. The person who I was surprised hadn't shown back up was Felicia. At first, you couldn't pay her to stay away. But, it seemed when Jaylin showed up, she didn't want to be around. I guess it was too hard for her to be around him, after she'd fuck him over and swindled him out of his money. Me, I had no problem being in his presence. The first day I saw him and Nokea together was a bit challenging, but once I knew that my baby was going to be okay, things got better and better for me. I couldn't let anyone steal my joy and I had so much to be thankful for.

As the days passed, I was one busy woman. I'd been running to the hospital, to Jay's, spending time with my family, and spending a lot of time at Shane's place. He'd asked me to make sure everything was cool, so I did. Last night, I was too tired to go home, so I stayed the night by myself. I couldn't get much sleep, so I lay in bed and listened to Shane's phone ring off the hook. This Amber chick was working my nerves. She'd been calling all night long, so I finally reached over and picked up the phone.

"Yes," I said, in a groggy voice.

"Is Shane around?"

"No."

"Is he still in the hospital?"

"Yes, but how did you know he was in the hospital?"

"Felicia called me. I've been speaking to his mother as well, but I didn't want to keep bothering her."

"Well, he's not home yet. Hopefully, he'll be home soon, but I must ask why you are so concerned?"

"Look, I know that you're his woman, but Shane and I go way, way back. I have every right to be concerned about him and I will always be concerned about him."

"That's good to know, Amber. I'm sure he'll appreciate your concern. I'll definitely have him call you when he's able to."

"Thank you," she said, and then hung up.

I didn't mind his booty call lover calling him, but little did she know that those days were over. What bothered me the most, though, was that every other woman seemed to have a relationship with his mother, except for me. I knew it was the wrong time to trip with Shane, but a part of me felt as if something wasn't right.

Before heading to the hospital, I showered and went into the kitchen to whip up a quick breakfast. As my eggs were boiling, I picked up the phone to call Mackenzie. Leslie said she was still asleep because they'd stayed up late. Before I ended the call, Leslie said that Jaylin had called the house, several times, looking for me. I wasn't sure what for, but I told her to tell him to call me at Shane's place.

Once I finished breakfast, as soon as I sat down to eat, the doorbell rang. I had an idea who it was, and sure enough, when I looked out the window, I saw Jaylin's Hummer parked outside. I had on one of Shane's button down Polo shirts and my hair was a mess. I teased it around with my fingers and headed for the door to open it.

"Good morning," Jaylin said, coming inside with a beige sweat suit on and brand new white tennis shoes. I spoke and closed the door behind him. "Damn, it smells good in here. When did you learn to cook?"

I snickered. "Right after you threw me out of your house and I didn't have anywhere to go. I had to learn some things for myself, didn't I?" I headed off to the kitchen and he followed.

"Now, you know you wrong for that. When I threw you out of my house, I always let you come back."

"Yeah, you did," I said, taking a seat at the table. "But the last time you kicked me out, you kicked me out for good."

Jaylin sat in a chair next to me. He looked me in the eyes. "I had to kick you out for good. I realized my love for Nokea and I knew that staying with you would cause both of us much more hurt."

"Trust me when I say that the pain I endured from losing our relationship was nothing simple. There was no easy way out and I'm still sad that our relationship ended the way it did. There's not much we can do about it now and I know you didn't come here to talk about the past."

"No, but I would like to discuss the future."

"What about it?"

"I want...I have some major plans with Shane. I can't go into details, but I believe he's going to make a big mistake if he refuses my offer because of you. I'm not saying the two of you don't have feelings for each other, but I just don't see the relationship lasting much longer."

"And, why not?"

"Because I got a gut feeling that your heart is somewhere else. Shane is filling a major void for you, but it's not enough. Right now, if I told you that I'm ending my marriage to be with you, what would you say?"

"I'd say you were crazy. I truly understand how you can see it that way, and even though I still think deeply about us Jaylin, my heart belongs to another man. So, whatever offer you're talking about, we'll have to deal with it whenever the time comes."

"Well, it's coming. And, the reason that I'm here is because I don't want to see you hurt again. Shane is not as happy as he pretends to be. He wants, deserves so much more out of life and I don't want you to continue to hold him back. You...

I dropped my fork and sighed. "Jaylin, stop. This conversation isn't about Shane's wellbeing. This is about having your way and getting people to do what you want them to do. I guess you'll be offering me some money to get out of his life, and I'm sure that your dealings with him have money written all over it. Let's be honest here, okay? You're jealous. And even though you're living a happy and fulfilled life with Nokea, you can't stand Shane and me being together. Damn-it, admit it!"

Jaylin stared at me and rubbed his goatee. "Yes, you and Shane together tear me apart," he admitted. "Just as it did when you ran to Stephon, Shane is no different. If you moved on with any other man, I don't think it would bother me as much. But, that's my nigga, Scorpio. We like brothers and it's like you kicking it with my brother. I'll admit, for the first time...okay, I'm jealous. I've been very jealous but that's understandable. You say I've hurt you, but you've hurt me, too. I have a difficult time being around you, and to this day, sometimes, I don't trust myself. Having Shane as my friend and you as his woman, simply isn't working for me. My only hope is that we can all stop playing games with each other. And, we do so by you and Shane ending this."

"That's not going to happen."

"Let that man go, Scorpio. I've been honest with you, and you don't even have to be honest with me. Just be honest with yourself."

I sat quietly and Jaylin stood up. He walked over to the cabinet and removed a glass from inside. Getting a drink, he stood in front of the fridge and let the water flow into the glass.

"Are you thinking about what I said," he asked. He walked over to the table and set the glass of water in front of me. He bent down over me and pulled one side of my hair back with his fingers. He then placed his lips on my ear and softly spoke.

"Just for the hell of it, let's go in the bedroom and make love."

I sat quietly and didn't move.

"There's nobody here and no one will ever know but you and me," he said. "It'll be our secret."

I took a deep breath and turned to look at him. "Don't play around with me, Jaylin. I don't have time for games."

He removed his sweat suit jacket and the white-beater underneath. He stood shirtless, but kept on his sweat pants. "Feel me," he said, bending down next to me again. "And then, once you feel how hard I am, you tell me what kind of game I'm playing."

I looked at his bulge and it showed one hell of a print. Sadly, I was nervous, but considered it. "I...I, not right now. Maybe, but give me a minute to think about it. This might not be the right time for me."

"Now is the perfect time. Let's end this. Afterwards, you go your way and I'll continue to go mine."

"I said, let me think about it, okay? Back away from me and let me think about this."

Jaylin picked up the water and handed it to me. I took a few sips, and instead of backing away from me, he got on his knees and held my hands together with his.

"See, you considering sex with me says a lot. Your heart beating fast, your palms sweating and the look in your eyes says it all. You're thinking about having sex with me in the man's house who you claim to love. You need to face the facts, and once you do, you will feel a whole lot better about your decision."

I couldn't deny my feeling, and since Jaylin was honest with me, I came clean. "What do you want me to say? Yes, I still love you and maybe I always will. The thought of having sex with you excites me, and if given the opportunity, maybe I would have sex with you. I'm confused, Jaylin. I know that I can never have you, but I do love Shane. I'm handling this situation as best as I can and I'm not using him to get back at you. He just happened to be the man who made me love him after, all I'd been through with you. In the meantime, it never stopped me from wanting you again. So there, you wanted the truth and now you have it."

Jaylin touched the side of my face. "Give me hug," he said.

I reached out and we embraced each other. No doubt, it felt good being in his arms. A part of me wished I could stay there forever, but we both knew that this day, moment and time, gave us peace with the way we felt about each other.

Jaylin backed up from our embrace. He stood up and placed his hand on the side of my face again. Sincerely looking into my eyes, he lightly rubbed up and down my face. "Soon, I'm heading back home. Do me a favor and think hard about what was just said. More so, rethink your relationship with Shane, alright?"

I moved his hand away from my face. "Only if you rethink your marriage to Nokea. Are you willing to reconsider some things with your marriage to her?"

He paused. "Scorpio, Nokea and I are going to stay together forever. There's nothing to rethink because there's no doubt in my mind that she was and is the right woman for me. I'm more than happy, and all I want is the same for you and for Shane. Just...

"Just as long as we're not happy together, right?"

"You said it, I didn't."

I stood up, and as far as I was concerned, Jaylin's and my conversation was over. He heard everything I'd said, but I don't think he was listening too well. I made my way to the door and he followed behind me. "Jaylin, I wish you all the best. Whatever the result of Shane's and my relationship will be, I'm sure he'll keep you informed. I can't make you any promises about ending my relationship with him, and having continuous feelings for you or not, I intend for my relationship with Shane to work out."

Jaylin nodded and didn't hang around much longer. Once he put his jacket back on, he jetted. I shut the door and tightly closed my eyes. At that moment, I felt even more closure. It was time to move on with the man who loved me how I needed to be loved.

Another week had gone by and Shane was starting to get more of his strength back. He was working hard in therapy, and even when he wasn't. Several times, I'd come into his room and he and Jaylin were lifting small weights, boxing, and doing sit ups. Shane had to exercise by either sitting in bed or sitting in a chair. His legs still weren't strong enough, but he wasn't giving up. The doctor complained about him overdoing it, but his comments fell on deaf ears. Shane was anxious to get out of the therapy center, and even though I was anxious for him to leave too, I had a feeling that his reasons for wanting to get out had nothing to do with me. When I sat next to him on the bed and asked about my concerns, he played me like I was stupid.

"I'm just anxious to get home, baby, that's all."

"Yeah, get home and do what?"

"Shit, hold you in my arms the right way. I can't wait to feel your naked body next to mine and make love to you. Being in here, I can't do nothing. The doctors say it's going to be at least another week or two before they release me."

"Who says you can't do nothing in here? There's a bed, isn't there? And a floor, a chair, a bathroom and a wall. We ain't ever had a hard time being creative before."

Shane smiled and lifted the white sheet that was lying on top of him. He lowered his hand and held his dick. "You might get disappointed. My man here been tripping on me. I can't get him hard for nothing. Normally, all I have to do is look at you and I'd get an instant hard on. Trust me, I know when something's wrong with my buddy."

"That's because you ain't looking at me in the right way. I'll come back late tonight and we'll see what you working with." I winked. "In the meantime, let me see what I can do."

I slid my hand underneath the sheet and touched his hand. Shane removed it from his goods, closed his eyes and smiled. I worked him with my dry hands and it did nothing for him. I knew there was some Vaseline in his drawer, so I stopped and went over to the drawer to get it. I rubbed a bunch of it between my hands, greasing them good. And as soon as I went back over to Shane and continued my business, Jaylin came through the door. I quickly removed my hands, rubbing them together. I don't know if he'd seen me or not, and frankly, I didn't care.

"What's up, brotha?" he said, walking up to Shane. They slammed hands together and appeared to be happy to see each other.

"Ain't nothing going on, man. Just chilling with my lady and watching a lil TV, that's all."

Jaylin looked at me rubbing my hands together. "Hey, Scorpio," he said. "I didn't interrupt nothing, did I?"

"You always do, don't you?" I said.

"Aw, I'm sorry. But, I won't be long. I got a lil business to tend to today." He looked at Shane and he nodded.

"Listen," Jaylin said. "After I take care of that, I'm jettin. You don't need anything before I go, do you?"

"Naw, I'm cool."

"Have you thought more about my offer?"

"Yeah, we'll see. We will definitely see. You know I'll be in touch."

"Alright then, playa. I'm out, love ya like a brother, and I look forward to seeing you soon."

"Thanks for everything, Jay. Without you, I don't know if I would've made it."

"Not a problem." Jaylin looked at me. "Scorpio, you be good and take care of this fool, alright?"

"You know I will," I assured him.

"I'm sure you will," he replied, and gave me a sinister stare. He turned to Shane and leaned in for a hug. After that, he left.

I couldn't wait to question Shane about the, "I'll see you soon, and without you, I don't know if I would've made it." What the hell? I'd been running around for him like a slave, and to hear him give Jaylin so much credit kind of hurt my feelings. When I told him about it, of course, I was just tripping.

"Why do women try to always make something out of nothing? I thanked the brotha for hanging tight with me, and I do plan to visit Florida and see him again. Maybe not soon, but someday I most likely will."

"Shane, normally when women make something out of nothing, there's usually something to be made. You and Jaylin are up to something and you definitely know I'm right."

He held out his hands. "Baby, it's whatever you say."

For playing me off as he did, I picked up a fluffy pillow and lightly punched his face. He smiled and threatened to hurt me later.

When Shane's mother arrived, I allowed them some time alone. Besides, I had to go check on Jay's and spend some time with Mackenzie. I promised her and Leslie's kids that we'd go to the movies, and once the movies were over, we'd have dinner at Outback

Steakhouse. Leslie said she'd stay behind because she had a date. A month ago, she met a handsome older man who treated her rather well. He lived alone, and hopefully things worked out so she could move in with him. She had lived with me for many months, and it was time that Mackenzie and I had our space.

The kids and I had an enjoyable time together. After dinner, I took them home and waited for Leslie to get home so I could go back to the therapy center to see Shane. She didn't get home until 1:20 a.m., but since she'd been spending so much time taking care of Mackenzie, I didn't trip. I asked if she had a good time, and when she said it was great, I kept my fingers crossed and left out the door.

The therapy center had strict rules just as the hospital did. No visitors after 8:00 p.m. I was another person who didn't play by the rules, and when it came to seeing my man, the rules meant nothing to me. Because it was so late, there was minimal staff on duty. Since I purposely wore a white short dress that could have easily been a nurse's uniform, no one paid me much attention. I hurried into Shane's room and closed the door. The room was dark, but I could see him from the outside light that came through the partially opened blinds. I walked closer to him and laid my purse in the empty chair. Hearing his light snores, I unbuttoned my dress all the way down the front and leaned in for a kiss. At first, his lips didn't move, but when I saw his eyes open, he started to tongue me back. We kissed for at least a minute, and then I backed away.

"What are you doing?" he said softly.

"I'm a woman of my words. I told you I'd be back."

I walked around his bed and lowered the side rails. Then I reached for the remote and lifted him to where he sat up. After that, I dismissed the dress, climbed on the bed and straddled his lap. I put my arms on his shoulders and looked him in the eyes.

"Are you comfortable?" I asked.

"Very," he said.

"If this gets too uncomfortable for you, let me know and I'll stop."

"There wouldn't be a chance in hell that I'd ask you to stop. Gon' and do your thang, girl."

I scooted back to get into position, but Shane placed his hands underneath my armpits and pulled me close to him. I kneeled in front of him and my right breast met up with his mouth. He licked around my nipple and sucked it good, while massaging my other breast with his hand. Moments later, he worked both of them and his hands started to wander. He softly rubbed my waistline and then touched the small of my back. Taking his time, he lowered both hands and tightly gripped the cheeks of my ass. The tip of his tongue continued to work my nipples, and while his hands were rotating on my ass, I had moistened up big time between my legs. I held my arms around his head and dropped my head back in pure pleasure.

"Damn, you make me feel so good," I moaned. "Your touch…I've waited a long time for you to touch me like this."

Shane continued to feel my body, and when his hands went between my legs, I straddled him a bit wider. He teased me from front to back with his fingers and I was dying for him to go inside. Giving him a hint, I lowered my hand and rub my inner thighs. Soon, both of our fingers went inside, and when Shane started to handle the business on his own, I pulled out. I placed my fingers in his mouth and he sucked them. After he licked them clean, I leaned in for a juicy, wet, but warm kiss. Cutting me short, Shane backed away from my lips.

"Why you so wet like this?" he whispered, while still feeling my insides.

"I can't help it. I have no control over the way you make me feel."

"Baby, I am turned the fuck on by your wetness. Reach down and feel me."

He didn't have to tell me how turned on he was because I already knew. I not only saw his hard dick lying against his stomach, but I felt it as well. Just so I could feel it like I wanted to, I removed his fingers from inside of me, angled his goodness in the direction of my pussy and eased down on it. So I'd get the full effect of him, I sat on his lap, and let my legs straddle him like a V. I leaned a bit back on my hands and worked my lower body up and down on him. To keep bringing it to him, I worked my legs as if I was swinging on a swing. No doubt, Shane was enjoying every moment of my hard work.

"Damn, baby," he said. "You got skills. Major skills that I didn't even know you had."

"So, you like," I said, continuing my ride.

"Like it…hell naw! I'm loving it."

"Then, maybe you'll like this too."

I turned around and straddled him backwards. My butt was facing him and I put him back inside of me. As I moved, he rubbed my ass and squeezed my hips. Soon, he tightened up and lifted himself. I knew he was about to come and so was I. I started to move faster, but he wanted me to stay still. He forced my hips down tightly on top of him and pumped up inside of me. I tried to back up off him, because his dick was digging deep into my bottom, causing a slight pain. I softly moaned, but the feeling was so satisfying that I didn't want him to stop. Soon, we both let loose and it was one, electrifying and unforgettable moment.

"Whewww, wee," Shane said. "Now, that was some good sex right there."

"Tell me about it," I said, taking deep breaths, while still on top of him. I'd leaned forward on my knees and my face was below his knees. He smacked my ass hard.

"You the motherfuckin' bomb, Scorpio. You know I love ya, don't you?"

I turned my head to the side and looked back at him. "You're the bomb too, baby. And your love don't come close to the love I have for you."

All I felt was a wet kiss on my ass and another smack. I snickered and cuddled myself into Shane's arms for the rest of the night.

JAYLIN
32

Stephon said it, but Kiley Jacoby Abrams in *No Justice No Peace* said it best...it's time to shake, rattle and roll. Shake a nigga up, rattle his brains, and roll the fuck out. That's what I intended to do.

I'd been keeping my eyes on Stephon all week long. He flaunted around the Lou as if he'd done no wrong. Shane said he'd gotten a good look at the person's hands who pulled the trigger, and said they were rather dark. I knew Stephon hadn't done it himself because he was too much of a punk. And even though he was my cousin, I didn't or couldn't claim a relative who had hurt me, and the ones I loved, as much as he had. After seeing how messed up Shane was, I had to do something about it. Nokea kept bugging the hell out of me, especially since I'd gotten the gun back from her. She was upset, and since I didn't need the additional pressure, I asked her to take a flight back home. She made me promise to make it back to her safely, and I gave her my word. I wanted to tell her what was going down, but Shane and me kept shit under-wraps because so many fools got locked up from running their mouths. Yes, I had enough money to pay somebody to do the dirty work for me, but something inside of me wanted to deal with Stephon face to face. That was my intentions, but then, Shane and I discussed Nokea and the kids. We talked about his future and mine. We knew that if I got caught up, I'd certainly go to jail. So, with that in mind, I made my connection. The shit was supposed to go down once I was back at home, but I decided to stop by Stephon's house and give him my last and final goodbyes.

Before going to his house, I made sure I was strapped. I didn't know what to expect, and since I'd seen him smoking crack this week, I knew the brotha was, once again, unstable.

When I arrived, I could already see that his front door was cracked. I didn't know if it was a setup or not, but I stepped inside, quietly closing the door behind me. I reached for my gun and held it close to my side. I tip-toed my way back to Stephon's room, but he wasn't there, so I looked in his bathroom. There was no sign of him, so I checked the other rooms as well. I saw nothing, until I noticed the basement door wide open. I could hear some soft music playing, so I made my way down the steps. His basement was completely trashed. It looked nothing like the basement I'd paid to have remodeled for him years ago and it smelled like liquor and weed. I stepped further into the basement and that's when I noticed the music coming from one of the bedrooms. My heart raced, and when I opened the door, Stephon was on the bed, lying flat on his stomach. I could already see the heroin needles on the floor, and when I turned him over, he had a bullet hole near his upper chest. I placed my fist over my mouth, taking a hard and hurtful swallow. I couldn't bear to look at him, and stumbled backwards. As I backed into the main area of the basement, I couldn't believe that my connection had not followed the rules. I stood in a trance, already have some regrets. Moments later, I heard a noise behind me. I quickly turned and saw this brotha breaking his way over to the steps. He moved quick and had a black duffle bag on his shoulder. I chased after him, and when I pulled on his leg, he reached for his gun. I yanked him down the steps and the gun fell from his hand. I then cocked my gun and aimed it at his head.

"Did you kill my cousin, nigga!"

He held up his hands. "Don't shoot! Please don't shoot! I...I didn't..."

"Who are you and why did you kill my cousin!"

"My name is Pebo. I wa...was paid to do it," he cried. "I'm sorry, man. I'm real sorry."

I held the gun steady and snatched the bag from his shoulder. When I looked inside, the bag contained money.

"Who paid you?"

"Man, look. I swear that I will leave and...and you will never...

I gripped his collar and shook him. "I don't want to hear all of that bullshit! Who paid you!"

"A...a chick name Felicia. She told me her name was Kimberly, but one of my partna's said he'd dated her before. He said her name was Felicia."

I pressed the gun against his temple. "Get your punk ass up and walk slow. We need to take a ride."

Pebo eased off the steps and slowly walked up them. I followed and we made our way outside to my Hummer. I forced him inside, and not saying one word to him, I drove to Felicia's house. When we got there, I laid my cell phone in his lap.

"Do you want to die today, Pebo?"

"Nope," he said, nervously shaking his head.

"Good. Do you want to go to jail?"

"No, I don't want to do that either."

"Okay. Then, I need your cooperation. You can walk away from all of this, as long as you do what I ask."

He nodded.

"I'm going inside to chat with Felicia," I said. "When I call you on my phone, I want you to come inside, got it?"

He nodded again.

"Don't forget. Don't come inside until I call you on the phone and tell you I need you."

"Okay," he said.

I told him to duck and I got out of my truck. I knocked on the door and Felicia answered.

"Can I please come in and talk to you about Shane?" I asked.

Without hesitating, she invited me in. Slut probably thought I was there to fuck her.

"What about Shane?" she asked and closed the door. I looked to make sure she didn't lock it and she didn't.

I took several steps into her living room and sat on the arm of her couch.

"He's still out of it and I have yet to find out what happened. I'm told that you know the details."

She leaned against the living room's doorway and gathered her silk robe in front of her.

"Jaylin, Shane and I were on our way to dinner. By the time we got to his car, somebody drove by and started shooting at us. I don't know who it was, but Shane and Stephon had a big argument about something. Shane wouldn't give me the details and I didn't ask."

"It didn't have anything to do with you, did it? I thought Shane told me Stephon had done something to you?"

"Stephon didn't do nothing to me. We had a minor argument, he told me he wanted to be with somebody else and I told him to go right ahead."

I rubbed my goatee and couldn't believe how she was lying her butt off. "Hmmm, that's interesting. So...I guess you haven't heard that Stephon was murdered then?"

She put on a serious act and placed her hand over her mouth. She walked into the living room to take a seat, as if the news had startled her. "Jaylin, when did this happen?"

"I'm not sure. I went to his place last night and there he was. Somebody shot him and stuck some needles in his arm."

"That's messed up," she said, starting to tear up. "Did you call the police?"

"Of course. I'm just trying to find out who could've done something like that."

"Stephon had a lot of enemies, Jaylin. There's no telling who might have done it, then again, Shane was awfully upset with him that day. Like I said, I don't know what went down between them, but Shane did have some scars on his face."

No she wasn't trying to blame it on Shane. I continued to play her game. "So, you think Shane may have been responsible? Come on, Felicia. He's been in the hospital. He couldn't have done it."

"I guess you're right, but that doesn't mean he hadn't paid somebody to do it."

"I don't know, but I intend to get to the bottom of this. Stephon and I had our differences, but he was still my cousin. If I could just think of somebody...anybody who would have," I paused. "Hey, let me use your phone."

"You can use the one right next to you."

I picked up the cordless phone and dialed out. Pebo answered. "Say, man, I need you right now." He hung up, but I continued to talk. "I'm trying to get some info on any enemies my cousin may have had. If you can make me a list of those enemies you were referring to, I'd appreciate it."

Just then, Felicia's door came open and she rushed up to see who it was. When Pebo came through the door, her eyes widened. I put the phone back down on the table.

"Jaylin, thi...this is a friend of mine, Greg. We're on our way out, so I have to get dressed and go."

"Aw, okay," I said, standing up. I walked over to Pebo and stood in front of him. I reached my hand out to shake his. "Greg...Greg," I said, pretending to be in deep thought. "I swear you look like somebody I know. Ain't, isn't your name Pebo? I just saw you over Stephon's house and you told me your name was Pebo. You also told me that Felicia paid you to kill my cousin, didn't you?"

He nodded and Felicia stood stoned faced, looking like a fool.

"I paid you to do what!" she yelled.

"Bitch, game over!" I said, and punched her hard in her upper chest. She fell back and hit the wall behind her. I squatted down in front of her and rubbed my goatee.

"You listen to me, and you listen to me good. I got a choice to make, and depending on how well you cooperate, that will determine which route I decide to take. Either, I'm going to call the police, have you arrested for murder and have Pebo vouch for me. Or, I'm going to get in my truck, go back home to my lovely wife and beautiful kids, and pretend that this moment, this day, or this time never happened. The only way I will do so, is if you admit, in writing, to having my cousin killed and you give me back every damn dime that you owe me. In addition to that, you agree to stay the fuck out of my life and out of Shane's business. He or I never want to see you again, and a long trip away from here might not be too bad either."

"I don't want to go to jail, Jaylin, but I don't have all of your money. I gave half of it to Stephon, and the rest, I've been splurging on. I can give you some of it."

"All of it, damn it! Nothing more, and nothing less! Remember? Thanks to Pebo, I have some of the money in a bag in the car, and when I let you know how much it is, I'm giving you one week to come up with the rest. If my money isn't sent to me within a week, you'd better get ready to spend some time in jail."

I stood up and pulled out a small note pad and pen from inside of my jacket. I handed it to Felicia and she took it from me.

"Make it good," I said. She started to write and I turned to Pebo.

"Give me your license," I ordered. He reached in his jacket, giving his license to me. "I'm keeping this. I might need it in the future, and if she fucks up, you'd better be damn ready to testify. Don't cross me, Pebo, because I know plenty of important people. You just never know when you'll turn around and wound up like Stephon."

After a few minutes of writing, Felicia reached the paper and pen out to me. "Here," she said in tears. "Now, get out of my house! I will have the rest of your money to you in a week."

I pointed my finger down at her on the floor. "You're in no position to speak to me that way. I hold the key to your future in my hands. The next time you see me, or if you see me, I want some respect. Got it!"

She rolled her eyes, but hesitantly nodded. I read her letter, front and back, where she admitted to having Stephon killed. She signed it and Pebo and me witnessed it. Having no further business here, I walked to the door.

"Well, folks, it's been real. Don't forget about me, Felicia, and I for surely won't forget about you. Make sure you call the police, have Stephon put away for me the right way, and make sure there are some flowers there from me. Pebo," I said, walking over to him. I held my hand out and he reached for mine to shake it. Instead, I pulled my hand back and punched him as hard as I could in his mouth. I heard his teeth crack and he was instantly floored. He slowly sat up, while holding his mouth. "That's for killing my cousin. You didn't think you'd get off that easy, did you?"

I glanced down at my busted hand, opened the door and walked out.

On the drive home, I couldn't help but reminisce about all the good times Stephon and I had growing up. From the fights we had with the kids in the neighborhood, to the girls we'd snuck into the basement. As we got older, we still had a bond that couldn't be broken, but somewhere along the line he'd developed major hatred for me. I never understood it, but I was often told that drugs made you do crazy things. I hated like hell that it had to be this way, but his situation had been out of my control for a very long time. Even so, I couldn't help but shed a few...several tears for the good times we had.

SHANE
33

Finally, I was out of the hospital and attempting to get back on my feet. The therapy was helping, but I still had a long road ahead of me. Best of all, though, I could walk. At times, it was kind of painful, but I was following the doctor's orders so I could get well soon.

From spending so much time with me at the hospital, Scorpio and my moms had gotten pretty close. My mother said that she liked Scorpio, and more than anything, she could see and tell I was in love.

As for Jaylin, we talked almost every single day. He filled me in on how everything had gone down and I was so happy that it turned out as it had. No doubt, doing things our way may have gotten us some time in the pen. For me, it would've been worth it, but I was so pleased that we didn't have to live with possible regrets. I refused to go through life living with regrets, so I knew that my decision about moving to Florida and starting my business with Jaylin had to be made. Scorpio's and my relationship had been progressing well, and ever since my incident, it seemed that our relationship had gotten even stronger. I didn't mind talking to her everyday and shame on me for not wanting to in the past. Thing is, I knew we could handle a long distance relationship. Once I got settled in Florida, I could come back on the weekends to see her. I didn't want her moving to Florida with me because I knew there was no way possible for her and Jaylin to get over what they'd been through in the past. I didn't feel right continuing to put her or him through it, as well as Nokea. She'd be the most uncomfortable and there was basically no other way around it.

My future, my life, and my career were the most important to me. Before I could make anyone else happy, I had to make Shane happy. That's why after thinking, until I couldn't think anymore, I decided to go ahead and move to Florida for at least six months to a year. If things didn't work out, I could always come back. I knew Scorpio wouldn't agree to it, so that's why I waited until the last minute to tell her. She was on her way over to have dinner, so that would be the perfect time to...discuss it. No matter what the outcome, my mind was made up.

The doorbell rang and my heart quickly sank to my stomach. I was right in the middle of taking the meatloaf out of the oven and placing it on the table. When I opened the door, Scorpio had some flowers in her hand for me. She reached out for a hug and handed the flowers to me, along with a stack of my mail.

"That was nice of you," I said, giving her a kiss for the flowers. We smacked lips, and then made our way into the kitchen. The table had been set for two, a bottle of wine was in the middle and so were two raspberry smelling candles. I pulled back the chair so she could take a seat, and immediately served out our food. Feeling as if I'd wasted enough time already by not telling her my decision, I spoke up to tell her my plans.

"Baby, you know I've been thinking a lot about the future of Alexander & Company. Due to my incident, I kind of got behind on some things and now I have to work hard at building it back up. Jaylin agreed to help me out, but only if...if I move to Florida. What do you think?"

She continued to look down at her plate and chew her food. "I think you're out of your mind, that's what I think."

"Why do you say that?"

She laid her fork down next to her plate. "Because moving to Florida would mean losing me."

"No it wouldn't. I'd come here every weekend to spend time with you. We would still be together and talk on the phone everyday. Not much would change."

"Shane, I can't believe you still don't get it. I don't want a long distance relationship with you. I want you here, with me, every single day. What would make you think I want anything differently? Let me guess...Jaylin. This was all his idea, wasn't it?"

"He's been suggesting it for a long time, but after all that's happened, there's no way for me not to agree to it."

She looked hurtfully at me. "You know what, I just want to sit here and cry my eyes out. But, what good will it do me? If moving to Florida is what you want to do, then you go right ahead and do it. Your decision is based on what Jaylin wants, not on what I want. I have no plans on stopping you from furthering your career, but how soon do you plan to go?"

"Tomorrow. But, I was hoping that you'd...

Scorpio wiped her mouth and dropped her napkin on the table. She scooted her chair back, "Good luck to you. I hope everything goes well."

I reached for her hand. "Now, wait a minute. Why can't you be happy for me...for us, as I plan for our future? If you'd just allow me six months to a year...

Her beautiful watery eyes stared me down. "Shane, I don't have six months. I," she paused and let out a deep sigh. Moments later, she reached for her purse and stood up to leave.

"I need to get out of here," she said. "I have some major thinking to do and I'll call you later on tonight."

"I'm not going to force anything on you, and if time is what you need, then I'll allow you that. Please don't make me leave here under these conditions. We can work this out, alright baby?"

Not saying one word, she stepped away from the table and headed for the door. I sat and listened for it to close, and soon after it did.

Feeling bad about the news I had to deliver to Scorpio, I didn't feel like being alone. I packed up the dinner I'd made and took it over to my mother's house. Always, she was glad to see me and when I showed her the meatloaf I'd cooked, she was even happier.

"Did you cook this for me?" she asked, while putting it in the oven.

"Mama, now you know I'm not gon' lie to you, but no I didn't. I made it for Scorpio's and my dinner, but that didn't go too well."

"So, I guess you finally got up enough nerve to tell her about your move to Florida?"

"Yes, I told her. She wasn't too thrilled about it either, but for the time being, I have to do what's best for me."

"What a selfish thing to say, Shane Alexander. After all that woman has done for you, you should have considered her feelings, too."

"I did take her feelings into consideration, Mama. But, this is an opportunity of a lifetime. You want me to continue to be a successful business man, don't you?"

"Yes, I do. And, you're already a successful business man, aren't you?"

"To some extent, but I want more. What's so wrong with me wanting more?"

"Nothing at all," she said. She took the meatloaf out of the oven and I helped her fix our plates. Afterwards, we sat down at the table. She took my hands, holding them with hers. After saying a lengthy prayer, we started to eat.

"This isn't too bad," she said. "I can't believe you made this."

"You're just saying that because you're my mother. You're supposed to say those things."

"Am I supposed to tell you when I think you're making a big mistake by moving to Florida?"

I quickly caught an attitude. "Mama, how am I making a big mistake? I'm a grown man and I have to make my own decisions. People might not like them, but oh well, I can't please everybody."

"No you can't, but I surely thought that once Scorpio told you about her test, you'd see things a bit differently."

"Test? What test?"

My mother covered her mouth. "So, she didn't tell you?"

"What kind of test are you talking about? Is she sick or something?"

"I'd better let her tell you."

"Tell me what!" I yelled. I was getting angry.

"You'd better lower your tone. Grown man or not, I can still spank your butt."

"I...I'm sorry for yelling, Mama, but what kind of test are you talking about? Scorpio didn't tell me anything about no test."

"Who could blame her? After the news you broke to her, I wouldn't have told you either."

The bites into my meatloaf slowed. "Is she pregnant? Did she tell you she was pregnant?"

"While she was over here last week helping me hang my curtains, she told me that she thought she was. We went to the store to get a pregnancy test, and once she took it, it showed positive. I can't tell you who cried the most, her or me. She was so happy about telling you Shane, but I asked her to wait. Right now, I can't even imagine how she's feeling."

"Damn," I said, placing my hand on my forehead. I closed my eyes and then lowered my hand to rub them. Right about now, I was so, so confused.

"Shane?" my mother said.

I could never stand to let her see my emotion, so I quickly stood up. I kissed her on the cheek and told her I had to leave. She knew where I was headed and she refused to stop me.

As soon as I left my mother's house, I used my cell phone to call Scorpio's house. Leslie said she was at Jay's, so I headed there to see what was up. When I pulled up, the place was almost empty, but her car was parked outside. Bernie's car was outside too, and as I looked inside, I could see her doing one of her customer's hair.

Bernie and her customer were the only two upfront, and when I asked where Scorpio was, she told me I could find her in her office. I moseyed my way on back, and when I got there, she was sitting at her desk with her back turned. I cleared my throat and she quickly turned around.

"Why didn't you tell me about the baby?" I asked.

"Would it have made any difference? You seemed to have had your mind all made up. Besides, I didn't want to use my news to keep you here. If you have plans to move to Florida, then go."

I walked further into the room, standing with my hands in my pockets. "How far along are you?"

She shrugged. "I don't know yet. I suspect that I got pregnant when we made love at the therapy center that night."

"Yeah, that was definitely possible," I smiled. Scorpio gazed at me with a look of disgust in her eyes.

"I hope you're not upset with me," I said. I walked around her desk and pulled her up from her seat. I held her in my arms, but she turned away. "Okay, so I deserve the cold treatment. But, I want you to know that this...this changes everything. There's no way in hell I'm leaving at a time like this."

She finally looked at me. "But, if you stay, I won't feel right. We will know what ultimately made you change your mind, and I can't live with that."

"Listen, if I had moved to Florida, we could've easily made things work. There's no way that our relationship couldn't have survived from long distance. Now that we're having a baby, like I said, this changes everything. I have no intentions on not being here for you or for my child. If anything, we're going to do this together. My wanting to move to Florida didn't change my feelings for you. I still love you, and right at this moment, I love you even more. I'm excited for us and for our child. We have a bright future ahead of us, and you've got to stop giving up on us and hang in there with me."

Scorpio bit her bottom lip. "Damn, Shane. Why does it take the baby for you to want to stay? I wanted you here with me, no matter what. I'm going to always wonder if I hadn't gotten pregnant...

"Sweetheart, things in life happen for a reason. All I can say is, thank you God for being on time. Our child is a gift from Him and we had no control over the timing."

"I...I understand, but...

Scorpio gagged and placed her hand over her mouth. I thought she had the hiccups, but when she puked right in my face, it was too late for me to step away.

"I'm sorry," she said while holding her stomach. I wiped as much of her vomit off my face and hurried her to the bathroom. She threw up some more, and afterwards, we cleaned up ourselves in the bathroom. She complained about being tired, so we left Jay's and headed back to my place.

When we got there, we lay in my bed, embracing each other. For a long time, we talked about the baby and about all that we had to look forward to. Scorpio seemed happy and so was I. In such a short period of time, we'd been through a lot and our relationship had definitely encountered its ups and downs. Eventually, I knew it would all work out for the best, and even though she shared with me her feelings for Jaylin, she knew that she'd someday have to put her feelings for him to rest.

Once Scorpio fell asleep, I eased out of bed and gave her a kiss on the forehead. I pulled the sheets over her and smiled. Feeling more than excited, I opened my drawer and pulled out the necklace I was supposed to give her. Now, seemed like the perfect time, but first, I wanted her to get some sleep. I laid the necklace on the dresser, closed the bedroom door and went into the kitchen. Before I made another move, I called my mother and thanked her. She couldn't stop telling me how blessed we were, and deep down in my heart, I truly knew it. I also knew that I'd be an even better man to Scorpio, especially since she'd be the mother of my child. I hadn't been perfect, and allowing Felicia to stay with me, and letting females continue to call my house was wrong. I kept holding back on my relationship with Scorpio, because I expected her to be the woman that she was with Jaylin. I was worried about hurting Jaylin's feelings, while depriving myself and Scorpio the happiness we both deserved. Until now, I hadn't realized that she'd grown into a better woman...one that I knew she could always be.

After I ended the call with my mother, I thumbed through my mail, and decided to call Jaylin. Routinely, he answered the phone and sounded upbeat.

"What you so excited for?" I asked.

"Shit, I just got my money from Felicia! She broke it up in installments, but the final cashier's check just came today."

"So, I guess you're a rich man again, huh?"

"I'm a richer man, Shane. I keep on climbing up the ladder, not down it."

"Well, I'm afraid, through your eyes, I might be climbing down it. I've decided not to make a move to Florida, and Scorpio and me gon' chill right here."

Jaylin was quiet. "So, when did all this come about? I just spoke to you this morning and you were on your way tomorrow. I made arrangements for you to have a nice place, and I found an office for Alexander & Company. What...what's going on, Shane?"

"Man, I don't know any better way to say it, other than I'm in love. I know you have never seen it that way, but I can't just drop everything and leave Scorpio like that. I appreciate your friendship and all that you've done for me. It will never, ever be forgotten. I wish you wouldn't have asked me to choose, but I understand not only your reason, but your purpose as well. My decision is to stay with my woman, and my baby that's on the way. I hope you'll be happy for me, as much as I've always been happy for you and Nokea."

He hesitated and let out a deep sigh. "A baby, huh? Are you sure it's yours?"

"I expected you to ask that, but I'm 100% positive that it's mine. Scorpio gives me what I give to her. That's peace, understanding and respect. It's all she's ever asked for."

"Well, Shane, congrats to you and I do wish you well. I won't lie to you and say that we can all sit around and be one big happy family because you know that's not possible. I'm not happy about your decision, but I'm proud of you for making the right one for you. If any woman makes you feel how Nokea makes me feel, then don't lose out. Who knows, maybe, one day I'll get over my selfishness and be able to cope with the situation. That goes for Nokea too, but for right now, you'll have to give us some time."

"I will," I said, while reading over a mailed letter from Felicia that apologized for her ignorance, but informed me that she'd "missed a few periods." She said that if she was pregnant, the child was most likely Stephon's, but there was a small possibility that it could be mine. She assured me that she'd keep in touch.

"Shane," Jaylin said, responding to my quietness.

"Yeah, I hear you," I said, balling up the letter and tossing it in the trash. "I was just reading a letter from ole girl, informing me of a possible pregnancy."

"Who?"

"Felicia"

"I told you that shit was coming, didn't I? She amazes the fuck out of me, and her bullshit is on going. All I can say, Shane, is welcome to my world. Been there, done that shit before. Handle your business though, Dog. One of my threats to her was to not interfere with you anymore. If you need for me to make her disappear, I will."

"Man, I ain't worried about Felicia. I got too much to be thankful for and I'm looking forward to my baby coming into this world. I hate to bring this up, but are there any changes with Nokea's situation. Since the accident, have the doctors said anything about her being able to conceive another child?"

"They say it's not possible. I, on the other hand, see it another way. As long as I keep *spreading* and *giving* my love to her, anything's possible."

"I agree and please keep the faith. In the meantime, take care of your family and give them plenty of kisses and hugs for me."

"No kisses for my wife," he joked. "Only for the kids and Nanny B. During our down time, you take care of your family, too. I know you'll be a good damn daddy, and be extra good to Mackenzie. She deserves extra special treatment because she still belongs to me."

"I'll do my best."

"I've seen your best. Your best ain't good enough, so do better."

"I bet I be better at fatherhood than you. As a matter of fact, I'm a better man, a better worker, a better lover...."

"Shane, don't get carried away. The proof has been in the pudding and you can't touch nothing I do with a ten-foot pole."

We laughed, and for the next hour or so, we continued to have our disagreements, debates and disputes over the phone. Sometimes, I might have misjudged Jaylin a lot, but the one thing I knew was he needed my friendship and I needed his. Out of respect, I intended to give him all the space he needed, but I was positive that time without our friendship would give him time to heal. I didn't expect for our time away to be long, and I looked forward to the day we all could get along and accept each other for who we were...down to earth, entertaining, and real people with a whole lot of everlasting drama.

LaVergne, TN USA
15 October 2010

200960LV00002B/1/P

9 780978 929244